THE GOLDEN WEB

By

ANTHONY PARTRIDGE

The Golden Web

by Anthony Partridge

Copyright © 2023

ISBN: 978-93-57271-91-2

Published by

DOUBLE 9 BOOKS

2/13-B, Ansari Road, Daryaganj
New Delhi – 110002
info@double9books.com
www.double9books.com
Tel. 011-40042856

ABOUT THE AUTHOR

E. Phillips Oppenheim was born on October 22, 1866, in Tohhenham, London, England, to Henrietta Susannah Temperley Budd and Edward John Oppenheim, a leather retailer. After leaving school at age 17, he helped his father in his leather business and used to write in his extra time. His first novel, Expiration (1886), and subsequent thrillers piqued the interest of a wealthy New York businessman who eventually bought out the leather business and made Oppenheim a high-paid director. He is more focused on dedicating most of his time to writing. The novels, volumes of short stories, and plays that followed, numbering more than 150, were about humans with modern heroes, fearless spies, and stylish noblemen. The Long Arm of Mannister (1910), The Moving Finger (1911), and The Great Impersonation (1920) are three of his most famous essays.

CONTENTS

BOOK ONE

CHAPTER I
A LIFE FOR SALE

The contrast in personal appearance between the two men, having regard to their relative positions, was a significant thing. The caller, who had just been summoned from the waiting-room, and was standing before the other's table, hat in hand, a little shabby, with ill-brushed hair and doubtful collar, bore in his countenance many traces of the wild and irregular life which had reduced him at this moment to the position of suppliant. His complexion was pale almost to ghastliness, and in his deep-set, sunken eyes there was more than a suggestion of recklessness. He was so nervous that his face twitched as he stood there waiting, and the fingers which held his hat trembled. His lips were a little parted, his breathing was scarcely healthy. There was something about his whole appearance indicative of failure. The writing upon his forehead was the writing of despair.

The man before whom he stood was of an altogether different type. His features were strong and regular, his complexion slightly bronzed, as though from exposure to the sun and wind. He had closely-cropped black hair, keen gray eyes, and a determined chin. He sat before a table on which were all the modern appurtenances of a business man in close touch with passing events. A telephone was at his elbow, his secretary was busy at a smaller table in the corner of the room, a typist was waiting respectfully in the background. His confidential clerk was leaning over his chair, notebook in hand, receiving in a few terse sentences instructions for the morrow's operations. Stirling Deane, although he was barely forty years old, was at the head of a great mining corporation. He had been the one man selected for the position when the most important and far-reaching amalgamation of recent days had taken place. And this although he came of a family whose devotion to business had always been blended with a singular aptitude for and preëminence in sports. Deane himself, until the last few years, had played cricket for his county, had hunted two days a week, and had by no means shown that whole-hearted passion for money-making which was rife enough in the circles amid which he moved.

He wound up his instructions, and dismissed his clerk with a few curt and final words. Then he turned round in his chair and faced his visitor.

"I am sorry to have kept you, Rowan," he said. "This is always rather a busy day in the city, and a busy time."

His visitor, who had been waiting for an hour in an ante-room, and was then esteemed fortunate to be accorded an interview, looked around him with a little smile.

"So you've prospered, Deane," he said.

"Naturally," the other answered. "I always meant to. And you, Rowan?"

The visitor shook his head. "I have tried many things," he said; "all failures,—disposition or luck, I suppose. What is it, I wonder, that keeps some men down while others climb?"

Deane shrugged his shoulders. "Disposition," he said, "is only an appendage, and luck doesn't exist. In nine cases out of ten, if a man's will is strong enough, he climbs."

Rowan nodded gloomily. "Perhaps that's it," he assented. "I never had any will, or if I had, it didn't seem worth while to use it."

"Take a seat," said Deane. "You don't look fit to stand. What can I do for you? We shall be interrupted in a few moments."

"I want something to do," Rowan said.

"I can't give it to you," answered Deane, firmly but not unkindly.

"You don't beat about the bush," the other declared, with a hard little laugh.

"Why should I?" Deane asked. "It would only waste our time, and be, after all, a mistaken kindness. There isn't a man about my place who hasn't grown up under my own personal observation. It's an important business this, Rowan. I daren't risk a single weak link. To be frank with you,—and you see I am being frank,—I'd sooner pay your salary than have you here."

"Give me a letter to someone else, then," Rowan begged. "I'm just back from Africa, broken."

"I can't do that," Deane answered. "I know you well. I like you. We have been friends. We have been together in difficulties. More than once you have been in a way useful to me. I have every disposition to serve you. But you were never made for business, or any form of regular work. I would not offer you a place in my own office, and I cannot pass you on to my friends. What else can I do for you?"

Rowan looked into his hat, and laughed a little bitterly. "What the devil else is there anyone can do for me?" he demanded.

"I can lend you some money," Deane said shortly.

"I shall take it," Rowan answered; "but it will be spent pretty soon, and I doubt whether you'll ever get it back. I want a chance to make a fresh start."

Deane shook his head. "I can't help you," he said, — "not in that sort of way, at any rate. If you wanted to settle down in the country, I'd try and find you a place there."

"No good," Rowan answered. "I want to make money, and I want to make it quick."

The telephone bell rang, and Deane was busy for several moments answering questions and giving instructions. Then he turned once more to his visitor.

"Rowan," he said, "you talk like all the others who come down into the city expecting to find it a sort of Eldorado. I can do nothing for you. How much money shall I lend you? Stop!" he said, holding out his hand. "I don't want to seem unkind, but I am a busy man. I don't want to lend you ten pounds to-day, and have you come and borrow another ten pounds next week, and another the week after. You and I went through some rough times together. We've heard the bullets sing. We've known what a licking was like, and we've shouted ourselves hoarse with joy when the good time came. I don't forget these things, man. I don't want you for a moment to believe that I have forgotten them. Ask me for any reasonable sum, and I'll give it you. But afterwards we shake hands and part, at any rate so far as the city is concerned. You understand?"

Rowan leaned forward in his chair. He wetted his dry lips nervously with his tongue. The look of ill-health in his features was almost painfully manifest. The writing which it is not possible to mistake was on his face.

"Look here, Deane," he said hoarsely, "don't think I am ungrateful. You've put the matter straight to me like a man, and, if needs be, I'll ask you for a good round sum and go, and I'll take my oath you'll never see me again. But listen. I am in a bad way. I was in the hospital last week, and they told me a few things."

"I am sorry," said Deane. "You shall go away and recuperate. When you're feeling stronger you can think about some work."

Rowan shook his head. "That isn't it," he said. "I'm a sick man, but I'm not that kind of invalid. I have somewhere about twelve months to live—no more. I want, somehow or other, before I die, to make a little money. I don't want a fortune—nothing of that sort—but I want to make just a little."

"You have a wife?" Deane asked quietly.

Rowan shook his head. "A sister. Poor little girl, she's wearing herself out typing in an office, and I can't bear the thought of leaving her all alone with nothing to fall back upon."

Deane drummed with his fingers upon the table. His manner was not unsympathetic, but betrayed the slight impatience of a man of affairs discussing an unpractical subject with an unpractical person.

"My dear Rowan," he said, "don't you see that your very illness makes it absurd to imagine that you can take a position and save any amount of money worth mentioning in it, in twelve months? The idea is absurd."

"I suppose it sounds so," Rowan admitted. "But listen, Deane. You know I have many weak points, but I am not a coward. I like big risks, and I am always willing to take them. The doctor gives me twelve months—that means, I suppose, about seven months during which I shall be able to get about, and five months of slow torture in a hospital. I mention this again so that you can understand exactly how much I value my life. Isn't there any work you could put me on to where the risk was great—the greater the better—but if I succeeded I could make a reasonable sum of money? Think!"

Deane shook his head. "My dear Rowan," he said, "we are not in Africa now, you know. We are in a civilized city, where life and death have no other than their own intrinsic worth."

"You are sure?" persisted Rowan. "I don't mind what I do," he added, in a lower tone. "I've lived in wild countries, and I've lived a wild life. My conscience is elastic enough. I'd take on anything in the world which meant money. You have great interests under your control. You must have enemies. Sometimes there are enterprises into which a man in your position would enter willingly enough if he could find a partner who would be as silent as the grave, and who would risk everything—I mean that—not only his life, but everything, on the chance of success."

Deane shook his head slowly, and then stopped. A sudden change came into his face. He had the air of a man absorbed with an unexpected thought. A flickering ray of sunshine had come struggling through the dusty window from the court outside. It found its way across Deane's desk, with its piles of papers and documents. It rested for a moment upon his dark, thoughtful face. Rowan watched him eagerly. Was it his fancy, or was there indeed a shadow there greater than the responsibilities of his position might warrant?

CHAPTER II
THE PURCHASE

Deane looked across the room towards his secretary. "Give me five minutes alone, Ellison," he said,—"you and Miss Ansell there. See that I am not interrupted."

The young man got up at once and left the room, followed by the typist. Deane waited until the door was closed. Then he turned once more to his visitor.

"Listen, Rowan," he said. "Do I understand you rightly? Do you mean that you would be willing to undertake a commission which you would certainly find unpleasant, and perhaps dangerous?"

"I do mean that," Rowan declared, beating the palm of one hand with his clenched fist. "I am a desperate man. I have no time for long service, for industry, for perseverance, for any form of success which is to be won by orthodox means. I am like a man who has mortgaged every farthing he has in the world to take a thirty-five to one chance on a number. Don't you understand? I want money, and I can't wait. I haven't time. Give me a chance of something big. Remember what I have told you. Twelve months of suffering life is worth little enough in the balance."

"You misunderstand me a little," Deane said slowly. "What I am going to suggest to you may seem difficult enough, and, under the circumstances, unpleasant, but there is no actual risk—at least," he corrected himself, "there should be none."

Rowan laughed scornfully. "For Heaven's sake, don't pick your words so carefully," he begged. "If the thing is big enough, I am not afraid. If it is dishonest, say so. I am not a pickpocket, but I am past scruples."

Once more Deane was silent for several moments. It was a chance, this,—just a chance. He looked out of the window, and he seemed to see in swift panorama all the splendid details of his rise to power. He saw himself as the central figure of that panorama — respected, honored, envied, wherever he went, east or west. It was a life, his, for a man to be proud of. There was no one who had a word to say against him, — no one who did not envy him his rapid climb up the great ladder. He carried power in both hands, so that when he moved even amongst the great people of the world a place was found for him. He realized in that one moment what it might mean to lose these things, and he drew a little breath. He must fight to the end, make use of any means that came to his hand. It was a chance this, only a chance, but he would take it!

"Listen, Rowan," he said, turning once more to the man who had been watching him so eagerly, "I am taking you at your word. I am believing that you mean exactly what you say."

"God knows I do!" Rowan muttered.

"Very well, then," Deane continued, "I want you to understand this. The company of which I am managing director owns, as you may have heard, the greatest gold-fields in the world. Our chief possession, though, is the Little Anna Gold-Mine, which was once, as you may have heard, my property, and for which the corporation paid me a very large sum of money. Did you ever hear anything of the history of the Little Anna Gold-Mine, Rowan?"

Rowan nodded. "It was a deserted claim which you and some others had a shy at. Dick Murray was one of them. That brute Sinclair put you on to it."

Deane nodded. "You have spoken the truth, Rowan," he said. "It was a deserted claim. Four of us took possession, but the other three never knew what I knew. I bought up their shares one by one. I won't go into the matter of law now. I simply want you to understand this. The mine grew and prospered. What it has become you know. I sold it to this corporation, as I wished to have no outside interests, and the price paid me was close upon a million sterling. Three days ago, in this room, the man whom you have just spoken of — Richard Sinclair — produced documents, and tried to convince me that he was the real owner of the Little Anna Gold-Mine, that it had never been deserted, and that our taking possession of it was nothing more nor less than an illegal jump."

Rowan was plainly amazed. "But it was Sinclair," he exclaimed, "who gave you the tip."

Deane nodded. "That," he said, "may have been part of his scheme. He hadn't the money or the patience to work it himself, and it may have occurred to him that if he could get someone else to do all the work, believing that they had acquired the mine, it might be worth his claiming afterwards. I have weighed it all up," Deane continued. "I have been to some mining lawyers, and I have spent a small fortune in cabling to the Cape. The conclusion I have come to is this. If Sinclair prosecutes his claim — and he means business — and goes to law, there is just a reasonable chance that he might win."

"A reasonable chance," Rowan repeated.

"It isn't only that, though," continued Deane. "There are other things to be taken into consideration. We don't want a lawsuit. Several of our smaller mines are doing rather badly just now, and we have been spending an immense amount of money upon developments. Any suspicion as to the validity of our title to the Little Anna Mine would be simply disastrous at the present moment. Our shares would have a tremendous drop, just at the time when we are least prepared for it."

"Where do I come in?" Rowan asked quietly.

"Sinclair," Deane said, "has only been in the country three days. He has no friends, he drinks most of the day, and he is staying at the Universal Hotel, where I imagine that he spends most of his time at the American bar. Now I can't treat with the fellow, Rowan. That's the trouble. If I were to show the least sign of weakness, the game would be up. My only chance was bluff. I laughed in his face and turned him out of the office. But bluff doesn't alter facts. You and he are old acquaintances. I know very well that you never hit it off together, although I never knew what was the cause of your quarrel. However, there's nothing to prevent your going to see him. He's in that sort of maudlin state when he'd welcome anybody who'd drink with him and let him talk. That is where you come in, Rowan. You can drink with him, and listen. Find out whether this is a put-up thing or whether he believes in it."

Rowan nodded. "Anything else?" he asked in a low tone.

"There is no reason," Deane continued, "why you should not, if he gets confidential, open up negotiations on your own account."

"He has some documents, I suppose?" Rowan asked.

"His claim to our mine," Deane answered, "is contained in a single paper, which he told me never left his person. You were a lawyer once, Rowan. You know how to argue, to handle facts, to make a bargain. The return of that document to me would be worth ten thousand pounds."

Rowan's breathing seemed suddenly to have become worse. His lips were parted, there was a strange glitter in his eyes. "Ten thousand pounds!" he muttered.

"It is a great deal of money, I know," Deane said, "but understand this, Rowan, once and for all. If this enterprise appeals to you, you must undertake it absolutely and entirely at your own risk. Above all things, it is important that neither Sinclair nor anyone else in the world should ever dream that I had been behind any offer you might make, or any course of action which you might pursue. All that I say to you is that I am willing to give ten thousand pounds for that document."

"Ten thousand pounds!" Rowan muttered. "It would be enough — more than enough."

"If you fail," continued Deane, "and find yourself in trouble, I know nothing of you. I shall not raise a finger to help you. I demand from you your word of honor that you do not mention my name, that you deal with Sinclair simply as a speculative financier disposed to be his friend. Remember that the slightest association of my name with yours would give him the clue to the whole thing, and would mean ruin here. On the other hand, before you go, if you tell me that you are going heart and soul into this enterprise, I shall give you five hundred pounds. Some of this you will need for clothes, to make a presentable appearance, and to be able to entertain Sinclair, and play your part as a capitalist. If you fail, you can keep the balance as a loan or a gift, whichever you like. Now you can take your choice. I am placing a good deal of confidence in you, but I think that I know my man."

Rowan struck the end of the table with his hand. "Yes, you do, Deane!" he declared, looking at him with kindling eyes. "You do know him, indeed. If I were to die to-morrow, Dick Sinclair is the one man in the world I should die hating. He served me a shabby trick once, and I've never forgotten it. Perhaps," Rowan added, — "perhaps I may now turn the tables upon him."

"No mention of my name, mind," Deane repeated emphatically.

Rowan held out his hand. "I take my chance, Deane," he said, "and on my honor I'll play the game."

CHAPTER III
A FAMILY AFFAIR

A few hours later, Stirling Deane sat at a small round dining-table, side by side with the father of the girl to whom he had been engaged for exactly three days. His hostess, the Countess of Nunneley, and her daughter, Lady Olive, had only just left them. It had been a dinner absolutely en famille.

"Draw up your chair, Deane, and try some of this port," Lord Nunneley said.

"Thank you," replied Deane, "I'll finish my champagne, if I may."

"Just as you like," his host answered. "I notice you are very careful never to mix, Deane. Perhaps you are right. There's nothing like being absolutely fit, and you fellows in the city must have a tremendous lot on your minds sometimes. I suppose, however prosperous you are, you never have a day without a certain amount of anxiety?"

"Never," Deane assented quietly.

Lord Nunneley, who had a great reputation as a peer of marked sporting proclivities, crossed his legs, and, leaning back in his chair, lit a cigarette.

"I never thought," he continued, "that I should be glad to give Olive to anyone—to anyone—you won't mind if I say it—outside our own immediate circle. Of course, I know your people were all right. I've ridden to hounds with your father many a time, but when a family drifts into the city, one naturally loses sight of them. You will find me a model father-in-law, though, Deane. I never borrow money, I wouldn't be a director of a public company for anything in the world, and I haven't a single relation for whom I want a berth."

Deane smiled. His manner was natural enough, but only he knew how difficult he found it to continue this sort of conversation—to keep his attention fixed upon the somewhat garrulous utterances of his prospective father-in-law.

"You are very wise to steer clear of all that sort of thing, sir," he said. "The city is no place for men who have not been brought up to it, and the days of guinea-pig directors are over."

Lord Nunneley nodded. "My lawyers have been making inquiries about you to-day, Deane," he said. "You insisted on my doing so, so I let them, although it was more for your satisfaction than mine. According to their report, you seem to have rather underestimated your position. They tell me that yours is one of the richest corporations in the mining world, and that you yourself are very wealthy."

Deane inclined his head slowly. He leaned across the table, and helped himself to a cigarette. A few nights ago he could have listened to such a speech with a feeling of genuine satisfaction. Now, everything seemed changed. The rock upon which he had stood seemed to have become a shifting quicksand. Dick Sinclair was a blackmailer and a thief, he told himself, with a fierce desire to escape from the shadow which seemed somehow to have settled upon him. The document he had brandished was not worth the paper it was written on! His attack, even if he ventured to make it, could prove no more venomous than the sting of an insect. Yet the shadow remained. Deane, for the first time, possibly, in his life, felt that his nerve had temporarily gone. It was all that he could do to sit still and listen to his companion's easy talk.

"Of course, I am glad enough for Olive to marry a rich man, especially as her tastes seem to run that way," Lord Nunneley continued; "but I tell you frankly that I shouldn't have fancied a marriage for money pure and simple. I am not a wealthy man, but I can keep my places going pretty comfortably, and I don't know the meaning of a mortgage. Olive will have her thousand a year settled upon her for life when she marries, and something more when I die. In a sense, it's nothing, of course, but it will help pay for her frocks."

"I am sure you are very generous," Deane murmured. "I had not even considered the question of dowry so far as Olive was concerned."

Lord Nunneley nodded. "As I remarked just now," he went on, "I should have hated the idea of a marriage for money pure and simple. I have seen you ride to hounds, Deane, as well as any man I know, and there's no one I'd sooner trust to bring down his birds at an awkward corner than you. That sort of thing counts, you know. I always meant to have a sportsman for a son-in-law, and I am thankful that your city life hasn't spoiled you for the other things. By the way, how old are you, Deane?"

"I shall be forty my next birthday," Deane answered.

His host nodded. "Well," he said, "you won't want to go wearing yourself out making more millions, surely? Why don't you retire, and buy an estate?"

"I have thought of it," Deane answered. "I mean to take things easier, at any rate, after my marriage."

Lord Nunneley sipped his wine reflectively. "I have never done a stroke of work all my life," he remarked, "beyond looking after my agent's accounts, which I have never been able to understand, and trying a little scientific farming, by which I have invariably lost money. I do respect a man, though, who has been through the mill and held his own, and against whom no one has a word to say. At the same time, Deane," he added, "don't stick at it too long. If you'll forgive my mentioning it, you don't look quite the man you did even two or three years ago."

"I am a little run down," Deane said. "I am going to take a holiday in a few weeks."

"You are coming to us in Scotland, of course," said Lord Nunneley. "But holiday or no holiday, take my advice, and even if you have to sacrifice a bit, don't stay in harness too long. The money you can't spend isn't worth a snap of the fingers. You and Olive could live on the interest of what you have, and there's scarcely a thing you need deny yourselves."

Deane hesitated for a moment. "That is true enough," he said, "but it is never quite so easy, when one is involved in things as I am, to escape from them. The Devil Spider spins a golden web to catch us mortals, and it's hard work to get out of it. I am afraid that my shareholders would consider themselves very much aggrieved if I sent in my resignation without at least a year's warning."

"A year," Lord Nunneley remarked reflectively. "Well, I should feel quite satisfied if I thought that you were going to chuck it then. Don't misunderstand me, Deane," he went on. "Please don't for a moment believe that I am such an arrant snob as to mind having a son-in-law who's engaged in business. I look upon yours as a jolly fine position, and I can assure you that I have a sincere respect for a man who has attained to it at your age. It is simply that I fancy you are carrying a much heavier burden than you sometimes realize — simply for your own sake and Olive's that I would like to hear of your taking things more easily."

"I understand," Deane said, — "I quite understand. You are really very kind, Lord Nunneley! Even if it is impossible for me to escape just for the moment, I can assure you that I shall take the first opportunity of doing so."

The butler, with an apologetic bow, came softly across the room and delivered a message. Lady Olive was going to a party, and would be glad if Mr. Deane could come into the drawing-room at once.

CHAPTER IV
A MURDER

Deane, with the air of one who was an habitué to the house, found his way to the drawing-room, where Lady Olive was seated before the piano, playing softly. She rose as he entered, and came to meet him.

"I have barely a quarter of an hour, Stirling," she said. "It was too absurd of you to be sitting there talking to father all the time. Come and say nice things to me. Mother has gone upstairs to put on her tiara."

He held her at arm's length for a moment, looking at her. She was not very tall, but she was graceful, and she carried herself as the women of her family had done since the days of Elizabeth. Her face was a little cold, except when she smiled, and her eyes were large and brilliant. There was about her toilette and her features a sort of trim perfection, which left no room for criticism. She was considered, amongst those whom she called her friends, handsome rather than beautiful, and ambitious rather than affectionate. Nevertheless, she blushed most becomingly when Deane stooped to kiss her, and her face certainly seemed to lose for the time its somewhat cold expression.

"You are going to the Waldrons', I suppose?" he remarked. "You look charming, dear."

She made a little grimace. "It's too bad that you won't be there. However, in a few days that will be all right. Now that our engagement is announced, everyone will send you cards, of course, for everywhere I go."

He smiled a little doubtfully. "You won't expect too much of me in that way, will you?" he asked. "My afternoons, for instance, are nearly always occupied."

"You will not find me exacting," she said, with a reassuring nod. "I don't expect you to play the part of social butterfly at all, and although we must be seen together sometimes, of course, I haven't the least desire to keep you dangling at my heels. Tell me, what has father been talking to you about?"

"He has been urging me to leave the city," Deane said, "and buy an estate."

Lady Olive looked thoughtful. "That is very interesting," she said.

"What have you to say about it?" he asked.

"It depends," she answered, "very much upon circumstances. I am not sure that I approve of a man having nothing whatever to do. Besides, I have no idea how rich you are, Stirling. I think I ought to warn you that I am very extravagant."

"I am delighted to hear it," he assured her. "I should dislike a wife who wouldn't spend my money."

They were sitting side by side upon a sofa, and she toyed with her fan for several moments. Then she held out her right hand to him, and allowed it to remain in his grasp. For Lady Olive, this was distinctly a lover-like proceeding. She was not at all sure in her own mind whether such a liberty was judicious, having been brought up always to consider any display of affection as utterly bourgeois.

"It seems a curious question to ask," she said thoughtfully; "but, after all, it would be only affectation to pretend that I was not interested. Tell me what your income is — about, Stirling?"

"In round figures," he answered, "it is to-day, I should think, a trifle over twenty-five thousand a year."

She nodded approvingly, and yet without a great deal of enthusiasm. "We ought to be able to make that do," she said. "Do you mean that it would be as much as that if you gave up business? Perhaps you could give it up partially, and keep a few directorships, or something of that sort?"

"I could not give up my work at all," he told her, "for two years. I get a very large income from my company, and I have an agreement with them. Besides, my own interests are so woven up with theirs that I could not run the risk of having anyone at the head of affairs in whom I had not complete confidence."

She nodded. "That is quite reasonable," she admitted. "You get holidays, of course?"

"Naturally," he answered.

There was a short silence. Lady Olive was half inclined to wonder why, having possessed himself of her hand, he made none of the other overtures which she had always understood were usual. Deane, however, was in no humor for love-making. She had represented to him, only a few days ago, a part of his future life which was altogether inevitable, and which he could easily come to find pleasant enough, but just now there seemed to be a barrier between them. Notwithstanding Lord Nunneley's kindness, and his wife's approval, he knew very well that it was not only Stirling Deane who had been accepted as a suitor. It was the millionaire, the man of great affairs, the man of untarnished reputation. Dick Sinclair's threats were still ringing in his ears. He somehow felt that he was not even playing the game to be sitting there, holding the hand of this most exclusive young lady.

"You are a little quiet to-night," she remarked.

"Perhaps," he answered, smiling, "I am a little shy."

She was inclined to take his words seriously. There had been moments before their engagement when he had certainly looked at her in a very different manner, when she had realized that if she really did say "yes" to him, she might find herself in danger of having to submit to something a little more vigorous than the ordinary love-making she knew anything of. She had even made up her mind, with a faint blush, to submit to it,—had grown to expect it. Somehow, although she would have found the admission distinctly humiliating, she was a trifle disappointed.

"I wonder," she whispered, looking down upon the carpet, "if you need—if you really need encouragement."

She felt a sudden thrill as his arm touched her, a sudden sense of his enveloping presence. Then the door opened, and she withdrew herself quickly. The Countess came into the room, a curious replica of her daughter, except that her hair was gray, and the light in her eyes a little steelier.

"So sorry you are not going with us," she remarked to Deane. "Inquire if the brougham is waiting," she continued, turning to her maid. "No, don't bother, Stirling," she added, as he moved toward the door. "We are really in plenty of time."

Lord Nunneley came in, with the evening paper in his hand.

"Is there any news, George?" his wife asked.

He shook his head. "There never is," he answered. "The evening papers aren't worth looking at now. Shocking murder, by the bye, at one of the big hotels."

Deane turned slowly round. "A murder?" he repeated.

His host nodded as he lit a cigarette. "Fellow just arrived in the country," he remarked, — "supposed to have had a lot of money in his pocket. Found dead in his room at about seven o'clock to-night."

"Do you remember the name of the hotel?" asked Deane.

Lord Nunneley glanced at the paper which he still held in his hand. "The Universal," he answered, — "that huge new place, you know, near the Strand."

"Was the murderer caught?" Deane asked.

"Arrested just as he was leaving the hotel," Lord Nunneley answered, — "at least they arrested the man they thought had done it. Here's the paper, if you have a taste for horrors."

Deane stood perfectly still for several minutes. Lady Olive was buttoning her gloves, and did not notice him. Her mother was standing at the further end of the room, helping herself to coffee. Lord Nunneley alone was conscious of the change in his guest's expression.

"Nothing wrong, I hope, Deane?" he asked. "You didn't know the fellow, by any chance, did you?"

Deane shook his head. He spoke very quietly and very distinctly. Except that he was unusually pale, his manner showed no signs of emotion. And yet, all the time he felt that he was being stifled! In his ears was the singing of tragedy!

"No!" he said. "I never heard of him in my life."

He crossed the room to help Lady Olive with her cloak.

"Stay and have a smoke with me," Lord Nunneley suggested. "I am going round to the club in about an hour's time, and then I am going to pick these people up at a ball somewhere."

"You are very kind," Deane answered. "To tell you the truth, I have just remembered a very important letter which I ought to have written. If you will excuse me, I am going to hurry away at once. I should like to catch my secretary before he leaves."

Lord Nunneley nodded. "You will have to get him to give it up," he said to his daughter. "Fancy having to write a business letter at ten o'clock at night! Perfect slavery!"

"Shall I see you to-morrow, Stirling?" Lady Olive asked, walking with him into the hall.

"We'll lunch, if you like," he said. "Or shall I come to tea? I shall not be busy much after noon."

"I am not quite sure what I have to do to-morrow," she answered, "but I think that I would rather that you came here. We'll meet sometime, anyhow. Good-bye!"

He raised her fingers to his lips. "Enjoy yourself," he said.

She shrugged her shoulders. "Absolutely a duty dance," she murmured, waving her hand. "I know that I shall be bored to death! By the bye, Stirling, don't forget that in about three weeks' time I want you to give a luncheon party at the Carlton to Julia and her husband, and some of the others."

"As soon as you like," Deane answered.

"Julia won't be back till then," Lady Olive said. "Au revoir!"

CHAPTER V
A DEBT INCURRED

A little stream of people came suddenly out from the dark, forbidding-looking building into the sun-lit street. The tragedy was over, and one by one they took their several ways, and were swallowed up in the restless life of the great city. Yet there was not one of them who did not carry in his face some trace of those hours of gloomy excitement, some reminiscent shadow of the tragedy which had spread itself out into passionate life before their eyes. The most callous was conscious of a few minutes' unusual gravity. Some of the more impressionable carried with them the memory of that hot, crowded room, the air of tense excitement, the slowly spoken, solemn words, throughout that day and many days to come.

"And may the Lord have mercy upon your soul!"

There was one man who issued from the building and made his way into the street, who seemed altogether dazed. His lips were drawn tightly together, his eyes were set in an unseeing stare. It was not until he had walked fifty yards or so that he seemed even to realize where he was. Then he came to a sudden standstill, and retraced his steps. Standing outside the building which he had just quitted was a small electric brougham, in front of which he stopped. He glanced at his watch. It was a few minutes past one o'clock. All around was the great stream of city men and clerks, hurrying to their mid-day meal. Once more, as he stood with the handle in his hand, he looked back down the dark passage, guarded by a single policeman, through which he had come a moment or two before. The scene in the little courthouse spread itself out with almost hideous precision before his reluctant eyes. He saw once more what is certainly the greatest tragedy which the mechanical side of our every-day life can offer to the seeker after sensations. He saw a man stand up and listen to the words pronounced which are to deprive him of life, — "And may the Lord have mercy upon your soul!"

Deane turned to his chauffeur. "The Carlton!" he said, and stepped inside.

The brougham glided away, swung in and out of the traffic, and ran smoothly along the Embankment, westward. Deane let down both the windows, took off his hat and placed it on the seat opposite him. Then he drew a small fine cambric handkerchief from his pocket, and wiped his forehead.

"God in Heaven!" he muttered to himself. "Twelve men, and not one of them could see the truth. Twelve men, all fools!"

He took a cigarette from a small gold case, and lit it with trembling fingers. Then he leaned out of the carriage window. "Stop at the Métropole, Richards," he ordered.

The man was just swinging into Northumberland Avenue, and he pulled up in front of the hotel. Deane went in hurriedly, and made his way to the smoking-room, exchanging abrupt greetings with one or two acquaintances. There he ordered and drank quickly a large brandy-and-soda. When he retraced his steps, he felt more composed.

"To the Carlton now," he ordered. "Hurry, please. I fancy that I am a little late."

In the foyer of the restaurant, Lady Olive came slowly forward to meet him. She was beautifully dressed, and she wore her clothes with the air of one who has been accustomed to be clad in silk and laces from the days of her cradle. She had been a beauty for so long that no one questioned her looks. It seemed even incredible that she was twenty-nine years old. One realized that she was of the order of women who refuse to grow old, — women without nerves, unruffled by emotions, women who come smiling through the years, unconscious devotees of the essential philosophy. To Deane she had never seemed more desirable than when she greeted him with a slight uplifting of her eyebrows, and turned to present him to another man and woman who were standing by.

"Mr. Deane is going to make the usual excuses, I know," she declared. "Let us anticipate him, and say nothing about our wait. We won't even ask whether it was a directors' meeting, or a message from the governor of the Bank of England. Stirling, this is my cousin, Mary Elstree, and her husband, Major Elstree—Mr. Deane! The others are somewhere about. What a tiresome person Julia is! She has drifted away over there with a lot of people whom I don't know. That is the worst of taking Julia anywhere. I think that she would discover acquaintances in an A B C shop. Do find her, Stirling. No, don't bother! Here she comes."

A tall, dark woman detached herself from a neighboring crowd, and came up to Deane with outstretched hands. "My dear man!" she exclaimed. "How dare you look so cool and nonchalant! Do you realize that we are all starving? We have been waiting here for you for more than half an hour."

"I am sorry," answered Deane. "You see, you people here have taken to lunching so early nowadays. You make it hard for a man to get through any work at all in the city."

"Early lunches have come in with the simpler life," Julia Raynham declared. "One has so many more hours to look forward to dinner, and so much more appetite when it comes. I suppose we must forgive you," she went on. "At any rate, you are better than my husband, who won't come out to lunch at all. He says that all restaurant food is poisonous, and I can't drag him away from the club. Why a man should put his digestion before our society, I can't imagine. I hope you will never be so ungallant, Mr. Deane. Shall we go in, Olive?"

"If you will excuse me for one moment," Deane said, passing on ahead, "I will just see that the table is all right. I telephoned to Gustave, but even a maître d'hôtel forgets sometimes."

He looked into the room, and nodded to the presiding genius who came hurrying up. The table was there, duly reserved, and covered with the dark red roses which he had ordered. He turned to Mrs. Elstree and the others who were following her.

"I think we can go in," he said. "I hope you people have not lost all your appetites waiting for me."

Lady Olive looked at him a little curiously as she took the seat at his left, hers by unspoken consent as his fiancée. "My dear Stirling," she whispered, "have you had a very trying morning? You look somehow as though you had been worried."

He hesitated. "Well," he answered, "scarcely that, perhaps. I had rather a bad hour or so. Things don't go always our way, you know, in the city, even when one is most prosperous."

"You are foolish to worry," she said calmly. "Half the people in the world spoil their lives by giving way to that sort of thing. I should have thought that your temperament would have saved you from that."

Deane smiled. "Remember," he said, "that I have been in other places when I might have been with you, and excuse me."

"You are much too gallant," she said, with a little laugh, "to argue with seriously."

"By the bye," Major Elstree asked, "has anyone seen a special edition? I wonder if the Rowan case is finished."

Deane set down the wineglass which he had just raised to his lips. "The verdict was given just as I left the city," he answered. "Rowan was found guilty!"

CHAPTER VI
AN IMPERIOUS DEMAND

There was a little murmur of interest. On the whole, although the result of the trial had seemed fairly certain, everyone was surprised.

"Guilty of murder or manslaughter?" Major Elstree asked.

"Of murder," answered Deane. "There was not even a recommendation to mercy."

Lady Olive looked reproachfully at him. "My dear Stirling, you really shouldn't have told us at luncheon time. If I hadn't been so very hungry, I am sure it would have taken my appetite away. He was such a good-looking fellow, and he has been so brave all through the trial."

"Brave or callous, do you think?" Major Elstree asked.

"Brave, I think," Julia Raynham declared, leaning forward in her place. "I went to the trial the first day. He followed every question that was asked, and he was always making suggestions to his solicitor. I think when one understands like that, when one's intellect is working all the time, that you cannot call it callousness."

"I agree with you," Lady Olive declared. "I was there myself, and except that he looked so ill, he seemed quite indifferent, and absolutely free from nervousness. Yet I am quite sure that he realized his position. My dear Stirling, how thoughtful of you to remember the Homard Americaine. I adore hot lobster, don't you, Julia?"

"Delicious!" Julia murmured.

"I wonder," Major Elstree said reflectively, "what must be the state of mind of a man who has gone through a trial lasting four or five days, and suddenly realizes that it is over and finished, and that he has lost. This poor fellow, for instance. When he woke up this morning, he perhaps hoped to be free to-night,—things went altogether his way yesterday. And instead of being free, he has been taken back to his cell, and knows — even at this minute he is realizing — that he will never leave it again until he leaves it to die. Personally," he continued, "I think that the period of time between the pronouncement of a sentence and its execution ought to be swept away. I cannot imagine anything more horrible, especially to a man who has to spend the long nights alone with that one thought racking his brain!"

Lady Olive laid down her fork. "My dear Harry," she declared, "do be a little more considerate. How are we to enjoy our luncheon if we think of that poor man?"

Major Elstree bowed across the table. "I forgot," he said. "Let us enjoy our luncheon, by all means. At the same time, I am going to drink my first glass of wine to a reprieve. We won't discuss the question of whether he deserves it or not. We will talk instead, if you like, of directoire gowns, and Flying Star's chance for the gold cup. But — I drink my toast."

"You are very quiet, Stirling," Lady Olive murmured to the man who sat by her side.

Deane smiled at her. "I am afraid that sometimes when I come away from a maze of figures, my brain, or at any rate my tongue, is not so nimble as it should be. I'll keep pace with you all presently."

A frock-coated, white-waistcoated maître d'hôtel came smiling up and addressed him confidentially. "Mr. Deane," he said, "you are wanted for a moment upon the telephone."

"You are sure that it is I who am wanted?" Deane asked, a little doubtfully.

"Quite sure, sir," the man replied. "The inquiry was for Mr. Stirling Deane."

Deane rose to his feet. "You will excuse me?" he begged, turning to his guests. "I suppose they have found out at the office that I am here, and they have probably something to say to me."

Nevertheless, as he left the room and crossed the hall Deane was conscious of feeling more than a little puzzled. He was quite certain that he had not told a soul at the office of the Incorporated Gold-Mines Association, over which he presided, that he was lunching at the Carlton. He was equally certain that he had not told anyone else. He took up the receiver of the instrument with some curiosity.

"Who is it?" he asked.

"Who are you?" was the reply.

"I am Stirling Deane," Deane said. "Who are you, and what do you want with me? Is it the office?"

"No!" was the reply, in a voice wholly unfamiliar to him. "It is not the office, Mr. Deane. It is someone with news for you."

"News?" Deane repeated. "I should like to know who you are first, and to hear your news afterwards."

"Who I am is of no consequence," was the reply. "My news is that Basil Rowan has been found guilty, and has been sentenced to be hanged. The verdict has just been pronounced."

The receiver nearly fell from Deane's fingers. He restrained himself, however, with an effort. "Well," he said, "what is that to you or to me?"

"That is a matter which we will not discuss over the telephone," was the calm reply. "I rang you up to tell you this because I thought it was well that you should know quickly. I ask you now what you are going to do."

Deane's was the face of a strong man—a man who scarcely knew the meaning of the word "nerves." Yet he felt himself struggling with a sudden sense of being stifled. Something seemed to be hammering at his brain. His breath was coming in little sobs. He answered this mysterious voice almost incoherently.

"What do you mean? How can it concern me? Tell me who you are at once," he said.

"It does not matter who I am," was the reply. "You have no time to think about that. What you want to realize is that Basil Rowan has been found guilty, and that he will be hanged within a fortnight, unless—"

"Unless what?" Deane gasped.

"Unless someone intervenes," was the quiet answer.

"Who could intervene?" he demanded hoarsely. "How can anyone intervene?"

"You know," was the quiet answer.

Deane staggered out of the telephone box with those last words ringing in his ears. He felt dazed, scarcely master of himself. The healthy color seemed to have been drawn from his cheeks, as he turned mechanically back toward the restaurant. Half-way there, however, he paused. For the moment, he felt it impossible to face his guests. He turned into the little smoking-room and sat down. The place was empty. Even the little bar was deserted. He sat in one of the green leather chairs, his hands clutching the cushioned arms, his eyes fixed steadily upon the wall. Slowly it seemed to fall away — to crumble into nothingness — before his rigid gaze. Again he saw the sombre-looking courthouse, the judge upon the bench, his sphinx-like face set in an attitude of cold attention. He saw the barristers, with their wigs and gowns, the few distinguished strangers upon the bench, the crowd of sightseers behind the barriers. And in the centre of it all — Basil Rowan, his pale face and drawn features standing out vividly against the gloomy background. It was no ordinary trial, this. The subtle, dramatic excitement, which only a question of life or death seems to generate, was throbbing through the dreary court. It was only, comparatively speaking, a few days ago that the man who stood there now waiting to hear his doom had found his way down into the city, and sat in his office, and made his passionate appeal. Deane's hands gripped the sides of the chair, and his lips moved. He told himself, as he had told himself a hundred times before, that this act was none of his doing, that not a single word of his had suggested or approved of it. He had spoken of arguments, of influence. Was it any responsibility of his that the man who had listened had gone further — had chosen to gamble instead with life and death? Deane went back through that conversation, word by word. No, he was guiltless! He had not suggested violence! He even told himself that he would not have approved of it. And yet the weight upon his heart was not lightened. The little picture was still there, reproduced with almost photographic exactness. Was it his fancy, or had the trembling man's eyes really turned towards him — had his white lips really framed that passionate, unspoken appeal which seemed to ring in his ears?

Deane rose to his feet with a little stifled cry. He seemed to understand now how men who were left alone with their thoughts might find madness.

CHAPTER VII
LOVE OR INTEREST?

Deane found his little party drinking their coffee in the palm lounge. Lady Olive greeted him with upraised eyebrows.

"My dear Stirling!" she exclaimed. "Have you been telephoning to the other end of the world?"

"I am so sorry," he answered, taking the vacant chair by her side. "I came away from the office feeling that I had forgotten something, and it took me quite a long time to straighten things out. Tell me, what are you all going to do this afternoon?"

"We are going down to Ranelagh," said Lady Olive. "There is some tennis, and Dicky is playing polo in the regimental finals. Don't you think that you could take an hour or so off, and come down with us? You really look as though you needed some fresh air."

Deane shook his head. "Nothing in the world," he declared, "is more impossible. I have an appointment in the city at half-past three, and another at four. After that I have at least a hundred letters to dictate."

"I am beginning to discover," Lady Olive remarked, with an air of resignation, "that there are disadvantages in being engaged to a city man."

Deane smiled. "Let us hope," said he, "that after you are married you will still regard the situation in the same light. Your friend Julia, for instance, declares that she would never have married anyone who was not kept away from home at regular intervals."

Lady Olive leaned a little towards him. After all, he had been very nice. The Elstrees had found him delightful, and there was no man in the lounge half so good-looking. She decided to say something charming.

"Julia," she whispered, "was never in love with her husband, even before she married him."

"And you?" Deane murmured.

She laughed at him and looked away, but he was suddenly insistent, taking her hand, and forcing her to turn again towards him.

"Tell me," he said quietly, "do you really care for me, Olive? Oh! I know you care enough to justify you in marrying me, but I mean something different. I mean do you really care in the great fashion, you know, like the people one reads of, — like Iseult, and Amy Robsart, and those others?"

She looked at him as though he were speaking some foreign language. The earnestness in his face was unmistakable. She answered him with a perplexed little frown upon her forehead. "Ah, I wonder!" she murmured. "What a very strange question to ask me, Stirling, just now! Frankly, I don't know. I can only tell you that there is no other man. You are quite alone."

The others were all discussing some subject of kindred interest. Deane felt curiously prompted to continue his questioning. His engagement had been such a very matter-of-fact affair. To a certain extent it was understood that he was marrying for position, and she for wealth. And yet in all their conversations they had discreetly concealed the fact. They had told each other that they cared, if not with passion, at least in the most approved manner. There had been no suggestion in their many tête-à-têtes that they were about to embark upon a mariage de convenance.

"Tell me," Deane persisted, "if things should go wrong with me, or if you had met me simply as a struggler, with my feet upon the early rungs of the ladder, — tell me, could you have cared then, do you think?"

She looked at him curiously. There was something in his face which compelled the truth. "I do not know," she said. "Let me think."

"Think, by all means," he continued. "Remember that I was introduced to you, even, as one of the youngest millionaires. Forgive me if I seem egotistical, but I have a fancy to put things plainly. There is a glamour about wealth. I came to you with that glamour about my name. I am rich, of course, and wealth means power. How much of your affection, Olive, came out to the man, and how much to the millionaire?"

"You want me to give you a perfectly honest answer?" she asked.

"Absolutely," he assured her. "Don't be afraid of hurting my vanity. I want nothing but the truth."

"At first, then," she told him, "nothing to the man, and everything to the millionaire. This afternoon," she continued, "I rather fancy that the man has the larger share. You are quite a fascinating person, Stirling, when you choose to make yourself agreeable."

"You can't accuse me," he remarked, "of making any special efforts in that direction to-day."

"No!" she answered. "You were rather quiet, but still you were yourself. Personally, I am beginning to find something very attractive about a silent man. You speak quite often enough, and what you say is to the point. It seems always to be the pronouncement of the man who knows. You have what Julia calls an air of reserved strength about you, which I fancy that my sex finds a little attractive. Tell me, why all this questioning?"

Deane looked away—through the cluster of palms into the little smoking-room from which he had issued a few minutes before.

"Even the houses," he said, "which according to the injunctions of Scripture are built upon a rock, are liable to destruction by earthquakes. So, even, the strongest of us in the city have always the hundredth chance working in the world against us. The most amazing collapses have taken place. I was really wondering what would happen—how greatly it would affect you—if my riches were to vanish into thin air."

"What an unpractical person you are this afternoon!" she murmured, looking at him curiously. "Supposing I were to sit here and worry about the fit of the dress which Madame Oliver is sending me home this afternoon for the ball to-night. I could make myself miserable in five minutes without the shadow of a reason."

"Madame Oliver," he declared, "would deserve bankruptcy if she failed to fit a figure like yours."

Lady Olive laughed. "Really," she said, "you are becoming quite a courtier."

"Dear people," Julia Raynham murmured, leaning over, "if we may bring you back to the mundane world, everybody else is dying to start for Ranelagh."

Lady Olive made a little grimace, and rose to her feet at once. "Stirling and I have only been boring one another because you all seemed so occupied," she declared. "Ranelagh, by all means. It is quite time we made a move."

They made their way toward the Pall Mall entrance of the restaurant. Lady Olive fell back once more with Deane.

"It's such a nuisance about this wretched dinner to-night," she said. "I think it was very bad taste indeed of the Duchess to ask us without you. You won't forget to come in and see me for half-an-hour before we go on to the ball? I shall be in my room at eleven o'clock punctually, and I will arrange so that I can take you on to Amberley House."

He bowed. "I shall be with you."

"Where are you dining?" she asked.

"At the club, most likely. I never dine out on Wednesdays, if I can help it. We are always so busy. I shall have a quiet, comfortable evening."

"Au revoir, then!" she said, stepping into one of the two automobiles which were waiting.

Deane made his adieux to the rest of the party and watched them drive off. Then he called a hansom.

"Messrs. Hardaway and Sons, Bedford Row," he told the man. "Drive as quickly as you can."

CHAPTER VIII
AN AWFUL RESPONSIBILITY

John Hardaway, although he was a solicitor in a very busy practice, did not keep his friend waiting for a moment. "Come in, Deane, old chap," he said. "Is this business or friendship?"

"Mostly business," declared Deane.

Hardaway glanced at the clock. "Twelve minutes, precisely," he said. "Fire away, there's a good fellow. You are not going to give me the affairs of the Incorporated Gold-Mines Association to look after, I suppose?"

"Not I," Deane answered. "They need a more subtle brain than yours, I am afraid. I have come to see you about the other affair."

The lawyer nodded. "You heard the result?" he asked. "We did what we could."

"Perhaps," Deane answered. "The only thing is that you did not do enough. I am perfectly convinced, Hardaway, that that man did not go there with the intention of murdering Sinclair."

"The evidence," Hardaway remarked, "was exceedingly awkward."

"Do you think," Deane asked, "that there is any chance of a reprieve?"

"As things stand at present," said Hardaway, "I am afraid not."

Deane for the first time sat down. With frowning face, he seemed to be engaged in a deliberate study of the pattern of the carpet. "Hardaway," he said finally, "I want to ask you a question in criminal law."

The lawyer laughed dryly. "Not on your own account, I hope?"

"You can call it curiosity, or whatever you like," Deane answered. "The only point is that I want you to answer me a question, and forget that I have ever asked it you. Your lawyer is like your confesscr, isn't he — your lawyer and your doctor?"

"He should be," Hardaway answered gravely.

"Then here goes," Deane said. "I put a case to you. I mention no names. You can imagine, if you like, that I am writing a novel. A man is tried for murder, and he is sentenced to be hanged. All the time there has been watching this case, listening to every word of the evidence, a person who knows quite as much of it as the prisoner himself, — someone who, if it had been possible, could have gone into the witness box and could very likely have induced the jury to have reduced the charge from murder to manslaughter. Never mind the reasons which made that man hold his tongue. Consider only the fact that he did hold his peace, believing in his heart that it was not possible, on the evidence which was submitted, for the man to be sentenced. As it happened, the case for the prosecution was worked up with almost diabolical cleverness, and the prisoner was found guilty — guilty of murder. He was sentenced to be hanged. What can this person do to save his life? The trial is closed. It is too late for him to offer himself as a witness."

Hardaway nodded. "I understand," he said. "The procedure is very simple. He should go to the solicitors for the defence, and they will communicate with the Home Secretary."

"The case cannot be reopened?" Deane asked.

"No!" answered Hardaway, with a shake of the head. "Our criminal law has many anomalies. The only thing that could happen in the prisoner's favor would be that if this favorable evidence were convincing enough, the prisoner might be granted a free pardon, and the facts made known through the Press. Anything more I can tell you?"

"Nothing," Deane answered, rising. "Many thanks, old fellow. You have told me just what I want to know."

"Six-and-eightpence, please," Hardaway remarked, holding out his hand.

Deane laughed, and shook his head. "I sha'n't pay," he declared. "You can run it in with the other account, or I'll stand you a dinner when and where you please, — a dinner and a box at the Alhambra, if you like."

Hardaway smiled. "We can't run our office on such clients as you," he remarked, pressing the bell.

"You should never try to fleece your friends," Deane said.

"Referring for one moment to the other affair —" began Hardaway.

"Well?"

"The only real chance of a reprieve that I can see," Hardaway continued, "is on account of the fellow's health. I believe he is really very much worse than he appears, and I fancy that if we had a medical examination it would give us at least a chance. The trouble is that he really seems quite indifferent. Are you thinking of trying to see him, Deane?"

Deane shook his head. "No!" he said. "I am afraid I must not do that. There are reasons why I dare not let my name be associated in any way with this affair. They may come out later on, but just at present I would rather not tell even you what they are. By the bye, has anyone representing the dead man turned up at all — I mean has anyone claimed his effects?"

"No one," the lawyer answered. "From what I can learn they are very insignificant."

Deane nodded. "Can I rely upon you," he asked, "to let me know at once if anyone should come forward to claim them?"

"By all means," Hardaway answered.

Deane went out into the street, and stood there for a few moments a little aimlessly. Then he called a cab and was driven to his offices, a great block of buildings like a bank, situated in a small court off Throgmorton Street. He passed through the outer offices slowly, asking several questions, and shaking hands with one or two acquaintances. When at last he reached the inner room, his own sanctum, he turned out his secretary ruthlessly, and locked the door. He sat in his leather chair in front of the open table, covered with letters and books of reference. It was before this table that he had built up the fortunes of the great corporation at whose head he was. He sat there now, erect in his chair, with his hands stretched out on the table before him, and his eyes looking through the frosted panes of glass opposite. Was there any compromise, he asked himself,—any possible compromise? Again he was looking into the gloomy court. Again he saw the white face of the man who so short a time ago had sat in this very room, only a few feet away, and had begged so hard for his chance! The whole scene came flashing back to Deane as he sat there. How much of blame, after all, was his? He had not suggested violence. He refused even to admit that it had entered into his head. Yet he had known what manner of men these two were! He had known, and their meeting had been all his making! Never in this world would he be able to escape from the responsibility of it,—never in this world would he be able to hear those awful words without a sense of real and personal guilt,—"And may the Lord have mercy upon your soul!"

CHAPTER IX
WINIFRED ROWAN

The clerk who brought in the little slip of paper was both timid and apologetic. He felt himself between two fires. The young lady outside had been a little more than insistent. The man into whose presence he had come was one who never forgave a mistake.

"You will pardon me, sir," he said. "I hope that I have not done wrong. The young lady outside positively declined to go away until she had seen you. I thought that I had better at least bring you in her name. I remembered that a few weeks ago you saw a gentleman of the same name, although it was one of your busiest mornings."

Deane held out his hand, frowning. "A young lady," he remarked shortly. "Well?"

He took the little slip of paper into his hands, and read — Winifred Rowan. He looked up into the clerk's impassive face, and back again at the slip of paper. "The young lady is waiting outside?" he asked.

"She is outside, sir," the clerk answered. "I explained to her that you were not in the habit of seeing any callers except by appointment, and I begged her to write and fix a time, if she really had business with you. She declared, however, that the matter was an urgent one. Mr. Sawday and I both heard what she had to say, sir, and we thought it best that I should bring you in her name."

Deane nodded slowly. "I daresay you were right, Gray," he said. "Since the young lady is so persistent, you had better show her in. See that I am not disturbed again this afternoon, however. I have a good deal to do."

The clerk departed with a great weight off his mind. It was obvious that he had done the right thing. He left the door ajar, and Deane sat with his hands clenching the sides of his luxuriously padded writing chair. Winifred Rowan! It was a relative, then, — most likely the sister of whom he had spoken. What was he to say or do? How much was he to·admit? Perhaps she had brought him a message. Perhaps she could tell him the one thing which he was on fire to know. Winifred Rowan! Half unconsciously he uttered the name aloud. What sort of a woman would she be, or girl, or child? He had no knowledge of Rowan save as a fellow adventurer, a seeker after fortune in a strange land, a brave man, willing always to take his life into his hands if the goal were worthy. Perhaps it might be that she had been with him. Perhaps she was bringing a message.

He heard the murmur of voices outside. The door was pushed open. The clerk stood on one side.

"This is the young lady, sir," he announced, — "Miss Winifred Rowan."

Deane rose for a moment to his feet. The clerk, with a little deferential movement, closed the door and departed. They were alone in the room together. Deane, whose self-control was one of the personal characteristics which had counted for something in his rapid access to prosperity, felt a nerveless exclamation break from his lips. The girl who came so slowly into the room seemed so perfectly to represent what Rowan himself might have become. She was an idealized likeness of the man by whose side he had fought and suffered and rejoiced, the man who only a few weeks ago had stood in her place and made his desperate appeal, — an idealized likeness, perhaps, in more ways than one. She was younger, and the stress of life had only lately set its mark upon her. She was fair, as he was fair, with gray-blue eyes, brown hair, and quivering lips, a figure slim and yet pliant, a manner, even in silence, appealing, — enticing. Deane felt himself curiously moved at the sight of her. Then he remembered suddenly how great was his need of self-control. She was the sister of this man who lay under sentence of death. Perhaps she had come to plead for his help. He must be careful. All the time he must be careful!

"You wish to see me?" he asked, a little brusquely. "I am Stirling Deane. Will you take a chair, and tell me in as few words as you can what you want?"

She ignored his gesture of invitation. She came on until she had reached the table before which he was seated. Then she leaned across, and the light of her eyes, the very insistence of her presence, seemed like things from which no escape was possible.

"Mr. Deane," she said, "I am Basil Rowan's sister. I have come from the Old Bailey prison. I have come," she added, with faltering voice, and a sudden new terror in her face, "from the condemned cell."

Deane had a reserve stock of courage to draw upon, and he drew upon it freely. He looked at her with upraised eyebrows. "You have come to me," he repeated. "Why?"

"First of all, then," she answered, "I will tell you why."

"I think," he interrupted, "that you had better take a seat."

She seemed, indeed, in need of some support. She sank into the chair which he had indicated. It was close to his side, and yet placed so that the light which fell upon her face left him in the shadow.

"You have come from your brother," he said. "Do I understand that he sent you—that he knew you were coming to me?"

"Yes!" she answered. "He told me to be very careful, to be sure that no one else knew, and never to mention your name, but I have come at his bidding."

"Very well," Deane said, "I shall be glad to hear your message."

"He gave me no explanation," she said. "He allowed me to ask for none. He told me to come to you and say this. There is no one," she asked, in a lower tone, looking nervously around, "who could possibly overhear us?"

"Not a soul."

"He told me to say," she continued, leaning forward, and with her eyes suddenly a little distended, "that he had no difficulty in finding the man of whom you two had spoken—the man whom you used to call Bully Sinclair. He spent the evening with him, drank with him, went back to his hotel by invitation. Then he tried very carefully to open up negotiations. Sinclair became at once suspicious. He was very violent, and declined to discuss the matter at all. He swore all the time that he had been robbed, and that he was going to have his revenge. My brother tried to reason with him, and in the end they quarrelled. It was Sinclair who struck Basil. My brother only returned the blow. And then he told me to say that before he could search him, before he could search the room, he found that the man was dead."

"Anything else?" Deane asked.

"He told me to say that any papers which the man Sinclair might have had must be in the room among his effects, which have all been put together, and are still there, locked up, waiting for someone to come and claim them. He told me to say that he had done his best, and that whatever the consequences might be he was ready to face them. If you cared to run risks, the number of the room at the Universal Hotel is 27. It is locked and guarded, but there might be ways. That is what he said."

Deane leaned a little forward across the table. "But of himself?" he demanded. "Did he say nothing of himself?"

She shook her head. "It is wonderful," she said, "but he never thinks of himself. He is more composed, more cheerful, than when I bade him good-night at Southampton, the day he left home. He made me promise that I would tell you these things first, before I uttered a word on my own account. I have kept my promise. You understand what I have told you?"

"Perfectly," Deane answered.

"Then I am going to speak to you now on my own account," she said, raising her eyes to his. "Mr. Deane, I do not pretend to be a clever person, but one thing is perfectly clear to me. Basil entered into this adventure for your sake. Your name was never mentioned in the trial, and they all seem to have believed that it was to rob Sinclair, and for nothing else, that Basil went there that night. Mr. Deane, I don't believe it. His quarrel with Sinclair, and its awful termination, was an accident. You must come forward and say that he went there to serve you, and not for purposes of robbery. It is for you to save his life. You can do it, and he is my only brother."

Deane's eyebrows came a little closer together. The girl who looked at him wondered no more at the hopeless way in which her brother had spoken of this man. His face was as though it were carved out of a stone.

"Miss Rowan," he said, "if there is anything which I can do for your brother, I will do it, for the sake of the days when we lived together, and when we were so near the very heart of life and death. But I tell you frankly that I see very little chance of successful intervention on my part. It takes a good deal in this country to stay the arm of the law, and your brother has grievously offended against it."

She struck the table before which he sat, with the palm of her hand. "If he did," she cried, "it was for your sake! I am sure of it! He went to do your bidding, and you must save him!"

"May I ask," said Deane, "why you are so sure that he went to do my bidding?"

"Yes! Ask, if you will, and I will answer you. I know it because this was the real point of all his message to you. This was what I had to say. This is really why I have come. The document—the document, mind,—he said no more, but he told me to make this very clear to you—the document is in a worn leather case, sewn inside the breast pocket of the coat Sinclair was wearing when he died."

Deane drew a little breath. "Young lady," he said, "it seems to me that you have been unnecessarily prolix. Your brother sent you here to tell me this?"

"Yes!"

"He did not send you here," Deane continued, "to beg for help—to waste my time in purposeless recriminations?"

"No!" she answered faintly.

"He knew very well," Deane continued, "that no mortal man can help him. The trial is over and the case is lost. The only thing to work for now is a reprieve."

"But that is not what I want," she interrupted. "He must be pardoned!"

"That," answered Deane, "is impossible. Neither I nor anyone breathing can work miracles."

She leaned towards him with accusing eyes. "But it was you," she declared,—"it was you for whom he undertook this enterprise!"

Deane shrugged his shoulders. "My dear young lady," he said, "you are mistaken. I cannot explain to you yet the full significance of those various messages which you have brought me from your brother, but believe me, what he did, he did knowing well the risks he undertook, and without any thought or hope of aid from me if he should fail. I will be quite honest with you, if you like. I will tell you the exact truth. Your brother and Sinclair were once friends. Sinclair and I were always enemies. There was a little matter of business open between us, and I thought that your brother might very well arrange it. I had no idea of his quarrelling with Sinclair. I did not encourage him to do so in any way."

"You sent him there," she persisted doggedly.

"I send messengers to every part of the world," Deane answered, "but I do not incite them to enter into murderous quarrels with the people whom they go to see. I will do what I can for your brother, but it must be in my own way."

"You will be able at least to save him from—from—"

Deane held out his hand. "Of course," he answered. "You need not think about that. His health alone would be sufficient to put that out of the question. What I can do for him, I will. I promise you that."

The girl rose up, and held out her hands a little piteously. "Remember," she begged, "I have no one else to go to, no other hope but in you. If I lose Basil, I shall be alone in the world!"

The tears were in her eyes. Every line of her face, every feature, seemed to be pleading with him. Deane led her to the door himself. His tone was unusually kind.

"I will do my best," he promised once more.

CHAPTER X
AT THE THEATRE

The door had barely closed upon his visitor when Deane was back once more in the throes of business, answering questions, giving quotations, receiving offers. The telephone was reconnected, and rang out its impatient summons every few seconds. He signed half-a-dozen drafts, deputed an understudy to receive some of his visitors who were weary of waiting, and dictated several important letters. When once more the pressure had abated, and the telephone had ceased to ring, he leaned back in his chair with a little exclamation of relief. The visit of Rowan's sister, and her passionate appeal, had unnerved him for a moment. He found himself trying to recall her last words, even at the moment when he realized that she was still in the room, sitting at a distant corner.

"Miss Rowan!" he exclaimed. "Why, I thought that you had left!"

"I went as far as the outer office," she said apologetically, "and then I slipped back again. You were so busy that I did not like to interrupt."

Deane rose to his feet, — he was a little cramped from long sitting. He lowered the blind and turned on the electric light, walking around the room, and casually touching the door to see that it was closely shut. Then he came back to his place, and leaned over once more toward the girl. "Why have you come back?" he asked.

"To ask you a question," she answered.

"Well?"

"Basil went on your behalf to see this man, Sinclair," she said. "He had a commission from you, had he not, and he failed?"

"Yes!" Deane said. "He failed!"

"It was to make an offer for some document, was it not?"

Deane nodded. "Yes!" he said. "It was."

"You are doing your best for Basil," she said, her voice trembling a little. "You paid for his defence, I know. You have promised that you will do all that you can, even now. I thought, perhaps, I might be able to do something in return. Why couldn't I get this paper for you?"

He looked at her steadily for several moments. "You could," he answered, "if you had the pluck."

"Tell me how?" she asked.

"You are his sister," he said. "Presumably you are interested in his defence. The details of the struggle between those two are, of course, important. It makes all the difference between manslaughter and murder if a weight, for instance, be held in the hand or thrown. You know the lawyers who defended him?"

"Of course," she answered. "Go on."

"If they apply to the proper authorities," he continued, "they can obtain an order to re-examine the apartments in the Universal Hotel in which the struggle took place. No doubt you also could find your way there. Supposing I tell you the truth. Supposing I admit that your brother did take upon himself a desperate enterprise, and that that enterprise was to recover from this man Sinclair, by purchase or guile, or any means which suggested themselves to him, the pocket-book of which you have brought me news. Remember I commit myself to nothing. I make no definite statement. I simply tell you that it may have been so."

"It was," she said firmly. "You and I know that. Well?"

"You are his sister," Deane said, "and you have exceptional facilities. If you could gain possession of that pocket-book, you would be doing me a service which I should find it hard indeed to repay."

She rose to her feet. "Very well," she said, "it shall be done. I promise you that it shall be done."

For the first time, when he saw her standing up, and realized how frail a creature she really was, a wave of pity swept away his own predominant sense of self-interest.

"But you are not strong enough for such work as this," he declared. "Better let things drift. I can take care of myself."

She shook her head. "I have made up my mind," she said. "I am going to make my effort, whatever happens."

"You will remember," he said, "that my name must never pass your lips. No, don't look at me like that!" he added quickly. "Don't think of me as a coward, or an utterly selfish person! I am here for what I represent. Welfare in this concern or business undertaking—call it what you like—doesn't mean only ruin or wealth for me. There are hundreds of us, hundreds who are dependent upon the reins I hold. It isn't for myself so much that I care. Try and believe that, will you?"

She looked into his eyes. "I will," she murmured. "I will believe everything, but you must save Basil."

"Whether you bring me the pocket-book or not," he answered, "I shall assuredly do all that a man can do for him."

For the rest of the day, Stirling Deane was his normal self. He transacted business with his usual acumen. He received his callers, and went through the ordinary routine of his position, with no indication of any mental disturbance. He had, indeed, little time to spare for thought. At half-past six he was whirled away westward in his electric brougham, changed his clothes, dined hurriedly in his room, and at a quarter to nine was in the stalls of the St. James' Theatre, sitting between Lady Olive and her mother. The mechanical part of the day's arrangements he had found it easy enough to carry out, but to keep his thoughts engrossed upon his surroundings was a sheer impossibility. He was not even conscious when the curtain went down, until he found Lady Olive's eyes fixed curiously upon him.

"Stirling," she said, "I don't think I like you when you have been at the office all day. Tell me, what can there be about this money-making so engrossing that you carry it about with you after you have finished your work, like a shadow?"

He was at once duly apologetic. "My dear Olive," he said, "if I was distrait for a moment, please forgive me. Consider. It is not my occupation alone which is engrossing. Supposing, for instance, that I were a politician. Don't you think that I should be better employed in thinking over an impending crisis than in listening to an exceedingly dull play?"

"Perhaps," she admitted, "but crises do not occur in political affairs every day. I might even be vain enough to suggest another and a simpler means of escape from your boredom."

"I am very justly rebuked," he admitted, holding her fingers for a moment, "only you must remember that it is new for me to have so delightful a means of escape ready by my side. Give me a little time to realize my good fortune."

"So long as it doesn't become a habit," she murmured. "I am sure I am not exacting, but I should hate to feel that you were always so engrossed in your thoughts that you did not even realize whom you were sitting next."

He touched her fingers once more, and his pressure was gently returned. Then, as if conscious that she had been a little more than ordinarily complacent, she withdrew her hand, and leaning over began to talk with her mother about some people whom Deane knew nothing of. A man from behind touched him on the shoulder. He looked up quickly and recognized Hardaway.

"Come and have a cigarette," the lawyer said. "It is a quarter of an hour's interval, and I should like to have a word with you."

Deane excused himself to his companions, and joined his friend in the foyer. "Well?" he asked tersely.

Hardaway toyed with a cigarette case, and glanced quietly around. He was tall and thin, clean-shaven, with hard, pronounced features and sunken eyes, gray hair parted in the middle, and a single eyeglass suspended around his neck by a narrow black ribbon. He looked exactly what he was—a criminal lawyer.

"I wanted to have a word with you, Deane," he said, "about this Rowan case."

Deane nodded. "Is there anything fresh?" he asked.

"Nothing particular," the lawyer answered. "Come upstairs for a moment."

They found a corner of the refreshment room where no one else was within hearing. Deane lit his cigarette with perfectly steady fingers. There was nothing in his face to indicate the fierce anxiety which was consuming him.

"With reference to that case," his companion commenced, "the facts were all so simple that there was no need for the prosecution to consider any other motive than the obvious one of attempted robbery. Therefore, no very searching investigation has been made into the dead man's papers. Yesterday afternoon, it occurred to me to look them through once more, in case anything had been overlooked. I came across a clumsy sort of document purporting to be the deeds of a gold-mine. I should not have taken any particular notice of it but for the title of the mine."

"Well?"

"It was the Little Anna Gold-Mine," Hardaway continued. "These deeds stated that Sinclair himself was the sole owner."

"A very extraordinary document," Deane remarked. "I suppose you couldn't manage things so that I could have a look at it?"

"It would be quite impossible," the lawyer answered. "Mine was, of course, a privileged inspection, and I am going beyond my duty in mentioning this affair to you. It certainly did seem very singular."

"Especially," Deane remarked, with a faint, hard smile, "since you are in a position to know that I have paid for the defence of the prisoner."

"It is not my business to connect such facts," the lawyer remarked.

"Someone will appear upon the scene sooner or later, of course," Deane said, "and claim this man's effects."

"Naturally," Hardaway answered, "although, except for this rather remarkable document, they do not seem to have been very valuable."

"If you should hear of anyone," said Deane, "I should be glad if you would let me know without a second's delay."

"I will do so," the lawyer promised.

The bell tinkled. The men at the bar finished their drinks, threw away their cigarettes, and hurried off. Deane and his companion rose to their feet.

"Hardaway," Deane said, "some of the papers are talking about a reprieve for this man Rowan. Will it come to anything, do you think?"

"I do not know," the lawyer answered cautiously.

They moved along the passage leading down to the stalls. Deane held his companion back until the little throng of hurrying men had passed by.

"Listen, Hardaway," he said, "I speak to you as one speaks to the dead, because you know the secrets of your profession, and because I trust you. Is there any way in which a man of great wealth, who had the command of money say up to fifty thousand pounds, — is there any way in which such a man could help towards obtaining a reprieve?"

Hardaway hesitated for a moment. "Of course," he admitted, "influence is always a useful thing. Those who have the ruling of these matters are sometimes hesitating between two minds. A very straw might turn the balance."

Deane nodded his head. He looked for a moment behind. His hand rested upon the curtain which led into the stalls. There was not a soul in sight. The play had recommenced.

"Hardaway," he said, "I will give fifty thousand pounds, if necessary, to have that man reprieved. The verdict should have been one of manslaughter. I am convinced of that. I was in court. I heard the sentence. I saw Rowan's face. I saw the judge put on the black cap, and I heard those hateful words. Up to fifty thousand pounds, mind, Hardaway, and I sha'n't have your bill of costs taxed...."

Lady Olive was almost petulant. "What a time you have been, Stirling!" she said.

"Do forgive me," he begged. "I met a man outside who kept me gossiping about trifles. Tell me, do you think that we can persuade your mother to come out to supper?"

"We've nowhere else to go," Lady Olive answered. "Do see if you can talk her into it. It would be very pleasant."

"I'll try," he promised.

CHAPTER XI
AN APPEAL

A morning paper, apparently in lack of a new sensation, suddenly took up the cause of Basil Rowan. An evening paper, conducted under the same auspices, promptly followed suit. This was a case, they both declared, of obvious manslaughter. The evidence clearly pointed to a quarrel between the two men. A prominent criminal lawyer allowed his name to be associated with what rapidly grew to be an agitation. Petitions began to appear. The Home Secretary was bombarded with documents. Everywhere people were saying that the man should never have been put on his trial for murder. The jury had been confused by their instructions. It was a case of manslaughter, pure and simple.

Three days after her first visit, Winifred Rowan sat once more in Deane's office. There were lines underneath her eyes. She seemed to have become thinner and more fragile. Deane himself, save that he was a trifle paler, was unchanged,—carefully dressed as usual, and with unruffled demeanor. He sat in his accustomed place, and guided the destinies of those great affairs which lay under his control. For the moment he had relaxed. He was doing his best to console the girl who had come to him in a sudden whirl of terror.

"My dear Miss Rowan," he said, "I have certain intelligence from my friends. I have gone to great lengths in this matter, and I can assure you that there is not the slightest doubt about a reprieve being forthcoming."

She glanced at the calendar. "But think," she said, "already for three days he has lain there, sentenced to death. Think of what he must be suffering. Oh, it is horrible! It isn't only death," she cried.

"Think of the manner of it,—the hideous disgrace, the cruel, cold ugliness of it! Oh, if it should come—"

He held out his hand. She was on the verge of hysteria. "It shall not come," he declared firmly. "I have promised you that."

"If they are going to reprieve him," she continued, "why do they let him suffer these agonies? Why do they not tell him so at once? I saw him this morning. He says nothing. He is as brave as a man can be, but his eyes are awful, and when he tries to speak his voice dies away. Oh! Mr. Deane, do something! Oh! do something!"

She laid her hands suddenly upon his shoulders. He took them gently in his.

"My dear Miss Rowan, I am doing everything that man can do. Believe me that I am. I only wish that your brother had done as he threatened, and walked into the river, before he came to me."

She went away at last. Deane lay back in his chair, feeling absolutely unfit for work. Twice he laid his hand upon the telephone, and twice he withdrew it. Then he turned to his secretary, who had just entered the room.

"Get Mr. Hardaway upon the telephone," he directed. "I want to speak to him."

In a few moments the bell of the instrument by his side tinkled. He put the receiver to his ear.

"Is that Hardaway?" he asked.

"Yes!" was the answer.

"This is Stirling Deane. You remember the subject of our conversation the other night at the theatre? I am referring now to the matter of documents of which you spoke."

"I remember," Hardaway answered.

"In whose possession are those documents at the present moment?" Deane asked.

"In whose possession," Hardaway repeated. "Do you mean—"

"I mean have they been sent to Scotland Yard, or are they still in that locked-up room at the Universal Hotel?"

There was a moment's pause. Then Hardaway answered. "To the best of my belief," he said, "they are still in the room at the hotel. They may be removed to Scotland Yard at any time, though."

"No one has yet claimed Sinclair's effects, then?" asked Deane.

"No one," was the answer.

Deane was on the point of ringing off, but Hardaway suddenly put a question to him. "Shall you be in your office for ten minutes, Mr. Deane?"

"For longer than that," Deane answered.

"I am coming around," the lawyer said. "I hope you can spare me a moment."

Deane set down the telephone with a frown. Perhaps his question had been a clumsy one, or was Hardaway already suspicious? He welcomed the lawyer, when he arrived, a little coldly.

"Five minutes, please," he said. "I have a large mail to go through, and an early dinner-party to-night."

The lawyer nodded. "I don't want to detain you, Deane," he said. "Send your secretary away for a moment, there's a good fellow. What I have to say can be said in half-a-dozen words if we are alone."

Deane pointed to the door. "One moment, if you please, Ellison," he said. "Get everything ready for me that you can."

The two men were alone. Hardaway, who had not taken a seat, deliberately drew off his glove, and tapped the table with his fingertips.

"Deane," he said, "have you any idea of paying a visit to the Universal Hotel?"

Deane met him on his own ground, coolly, and with perfect self-possession. "I have not made up my mind," he said. "It might be worth it."

"It wouldn't," the lawyer said. "There's nothing haphazard about the way these things are conducted. There's a detective watching Number 27, day and night."

"It occurred to me," Deane remarked, "that as there is no mystery about this affair, Scotland Yard would not have thought that necessary."

"It is as I have told you," said Hardaway. "At any time after to-morrow, the man's clothing and documents, and everything belonging to him, will be removed, unless they are claimed. Until they are claimed they are watched. It wouldn't do, Deane, for a man in your position to be seen in this place, especially when one of those papers bears the name of your mine, and Sinclair has just been murdered by a man for whose defence you have paid."

"That's plain speaking," Deane remarked.

"It's what I came to say," Hardaway answered. "Don't do it, Deane. We are not in Africa, you know. Your methods were splendid there. They might spell ruin here. Good-night!"

"The reprieve?" Deane asked.

"A certainty," Hardaway answered, looking back from the door. "It may be a week before it is issued, but it is a certainty all the same."

Deane sat in his chair, looking through the dusty window out into the court, — a dull vista enough, and uninspiring. Of the lawyer's words he took little enough notice. The reprieve would come, of that he was certain, but nevertheless he was beginning to feel the severity of the strain. He was a man who would have been kind-hearted but for the continual pressure of business obligations. He was a great schemer, a man of imagination, and a brilliant financier. There had been little room in his life for the gentler side of his nature to develop. Yet it had been a genuine horror which he had felt, which he had carried about with him since the day he had visited the court and looked into Rowan's white face, and heard those awful words of condemnation amid a silence intense, unnatural, hideous. It was a memory from which he could not easily rid himself, a memory which had penetrated even that splendid armor of indifference in which the man of toil and thought gradually encases himself. The girl's white face, too, and her plaintive eyes, had touched his heart. He felt that this period of suspense was growing almost unendurable!

His secretary entered the room quietly. "Did you wish me to make any arrangements, sir," he asked, "for the journey to Scotland?"

Deane looked at him for a moment as a man without understanding. Then he suddenly remembered that to-morrow was the day on which he was to leave London to join the Nunneley's house-party.

"I am not sure, Ellison," he said doubtfully. "I will let you know in a few minutes."

Once more he was alone. More impossible, even, than the grim monotony of the days in town seemed the thought of that prim country house, with its well-ordered days, its fashionable, easy-going crowd of people. He suddenly lost heart as he thought of Lady Olive and the prosecution of his well-ordered courtship. These things for the moment he felt were impossible. He wrote out a telegram and sent for a Bradshaw. The next day he disappeared from London.

CHAPTER XII
RUBY SINCLAIR

Twenty-four hours later, Deane walked upon a wilderness of marshy sands, glittering here and there with the stain of the sea, blue in places with the delicate flush of sea lavender. In the background, a village of red-tiled roofs. Before him, an empty sea. Behind and around, nothing but this stretch of bare, flat country, empty even of the sea until the tide should come and thrust its long arms of glittering silver up into the heart of the land. A few wandering gulls screamed overhead. From inland, a great silence. Here, too, the sea, flowing in upon the level sands, was quiet and noiseless. Deane felt every nerve of his body at rest. He realized to the full the marvelous joy of solitude. All the strain of those last few days seemed to have fallen away. He looked back upon that passionate chapter of his life as a stranger might look back upon recorded happenings. The tragedy of Basil Rowan, condemned to death amid the awful silence of that spell-bound court, sitting now in his cell with his head turned toward the door, passing through long hours of torture waiting for the reprieve which might never come, appealed to him now only as it might appeal to a million others who read the newspapers. He was almost able to forget that it was he in a measure who was responsible for that episode. He was able, even, to forget the tragical side of Winifred Rowan's visits,—to remember only her gentle, appealing ways, her passionate pleading, her gratitude, tempered still with anxiety, which had triumphed at their last interview over the repugnance which she had at first plainly shown towards him. All these doings and happenings were of another world. Here, trouble and anxiety were like the noxious playthings of a race of children. The sea that rippled in so softly on to the firm sands remained untroubled. The seagulls wheeling above his head in lazy content filled the air with their soothing cries. Everywhere the sunshine lay about the sea-stained places. The green marshes sparkled like emeralds. The wet seaweed, lying about in little heaps, seemed struggling to express new subtleties of color. Down one of the reaches came a brown-sailed fishing-boat, steered by a man who lay at full length upon the deck, his head upon a coil of rope, one hand only grasping the tiller. A few cows were standing about in the drier part of the marshes, swinging their tails, and moving slowly from one to another of the little plots of herbage. The very smoke from those red-tiled cottages went straight to Heaven, unruffled by even the faintest of breezes. To Deane it seemed that he had found an idyll of still life, and with a strong instinct of relief, he felt the desire for sleep, so long denied him, creeping over his hot eyes. The drowsiness of the place numbed his senses. The pain ceased. He was content to forget. He threw himself upon the sands, with his back to a sandy knoll covered with weedy green grass, and with the murmur of the sea in his ears, he slept.

Deane was awakened by a light touch upon his arm. He sat up, and was aware of a girl bending over him.

"I am sorry to disturb you," she said, "but if you sit there for another five minutes, you will be very wet."

The tide was already within a few feet of them. Deane realized the position and struggled to his feet. "It was very kind of you to wake me," he said. "I have come down here for a rest, and I suppose I was entering into the programme a little too thoroughly. After London, the sea air is just a little strong."

She looked at him with interest, and he returned the gaze. She was tall—almost as tall as he was himself—slim, with dark eyes, heavy eyebrows, and complexion burnt brown by exposure to all sorts of weathers. She wore plain tweed clothes, in the cut of which his critical eye quickly detected the village tailor. Yet there was something about her appearance which seemed to remove her definitely from behind the pale of rusticity. Her eyes were long, and a little narrow, her eyelids heavy, her mouth had a discontented turn at the corners, her whole expression was a trifle sullen. He was not in the least prepared for the change in her face when her forehead suddenly relaxed, the corners of her mouth softened, and her lips parted in a dazzling smile.

"You are a Londoner?" she asked simply.

"Very much so, I am afraid."

"Afraid?" she repeated incredulously.

"Why not?" he asked. "I am one of the slaves of the world, a man who sits in his office and toils, year in and year out. We're caught in the Golden Web, you see. The time comes," he continued, "when we find our way into a little corner of the earth like this, and one realizes the gigantic folly of it."

"Your point of view is interesting but unconvincing," she said.

"Why unconvincing?"

"Have you ever thought of the matter from the other point of view?" she asked, — "thought about those poor people, for instance, who have to live in a corner of the world like this, always? All these things, which rest and soothe you here, are beautiful by sheer force of contrast. For a few days—a week or so, perhaps—the contemplation of them would be restful. You would lie about on the sands and in the sunshine and believe that you had found Paradise. And then I think that you would begin to get just a little discontented. The sun doesn't always shine here, you know, and when the sun doesn't shine, all the land is colorless. The sea is gray and ugly, the marshes are flat and dreary, the wind, even in the summer time, is cold."

He looked at her with interest. She had turned inland, walking very slowly, and he somehow or other found himself by her side, her self-invited companion.

"That is rather a pathetic picture," he said. "Anyhow, the solitude remains, and when one has lived with the roar in one's brain, year in and year out, the solitude itself is marvelous."

"And when one has lived," she said, "with the solitude always on one's nerves, lying about one's senses, as though one were the only live thing in a dead and forgotten world, don't you think that one may long for the roar, even as you have come here longing for the solitude?"

"We apparently represent the opposite poles," he remarked lightly. "Tell me, do you live here? I presume, from the feeling with which you speak, that you are a native."

"I have lived here for nine years," she answered. "I live in a small house, which you can see just behind the village there. It is very tiny, but very pretty to look at. I have lived there with an aunt who was a farmer's daughter, and is very domestic, and an uncle who was invalided early in life from the Indian Civil Service, and who has done nothing but play golf and fish and study his constitution for the last fifteen years."

"You don't travel much, then?"

"I have not been out of this county," she answered, "since I first set foot in it, nine years ago. I had almost given up all hope of ever leaving it, until," she added, with a little sigh of content, "a few weeks ago."

He nodded sympathetically. "You are going to travel at last, then?" he asked.

"I hope so," she said. "I have an uncle come home from abroad, who, I believe, is very rich. He wrote to me the day he landed, saying that he was going to send for me to pay him a visit. I am expecting to hear from him now any day."

"He is in London?"

"In London!" with a little sigh. "Fancy," she went on, turning towards him, "I have never been in London! Just say that to yourself, and imagine what it means. The biggest town I have ever seen is King's Lynn. Have you ever been to King's Lynn?"

He shook his head. "I am afraid not."

"Then you can't understand," she said, —"I couldn't make you understand—what it means to me to think that very soon I shall have a glimpse, at any rate, into the world. If I had met you three weeks ago, probably I shouldn't have dreamed of waking you up. I should have let you get wet and then laughed at you. If you had ventured to speak to me, I should probably have stuck my nose in the air and walked away. You see how mellowing an influence even the possibility of escape is."

"What a disagreeable young person you must have been!" he remarked.

She nodded. They were walking side by side now on the top of a tall dyke. On their left-hand side was the creek which flowed into the village from the sea.

"That is precisely my reputation," she declared. "My aunt detests me. My uncle is always irritable because I can beat him at golf. He is out playing over there now," she remarked, with a wave of her hand toward the furthest stretch of the marshes. "Do you play golf?"

Deane admitted that he did not.

"You came here, then, only to rest?" she said.

"Only to rest," he answered.

"Where are you staying?"

He turned around and pointed to the square stone tower which stood on the edge of the sea. "I am stopping there," he answered,— "the old Coastguard's Tower they call it, I believe. It is the queerest habitation I have ever been in."

"You wonderful person!" she declared. "How ever did you get old Pegg and his wife to clear out?"

"I paid them well," he answered. "At least I didn't do it myself. My servant comes from these parts, and he told me about the place and arranged everything. I am hoping to be able to buy it."

There was, as he had remarked from the first, not the slightest reticence about her. She had almost the frankness of a child.

"You have a servant?" she asked, looking at him with renewed interest. "Do you mean that he is there with you now?"

Deane nodded. "I could scarcely be expected to cook for myself, could I?" he inquired. "He completes my establishment."

"I suppose," she said, "you are a rich man."

Deane shrugged his shoulders. "Wealth," he remarked, "is a relative thing."

"Oh! I don't understand those fine sayings!" she declared, a little impetuously. "I only know that to have money is grand, is wonderful. I would give anything in the world to be rich, to have money to spend as I wanted to spend it, and clothes, and jewels, and all the delightful little things of life, to go where I wanted, live as I wished, buy the things I wanted to buy. There's something hideous about being a pauper."

He looked at her curiously. She was certainly, for all her frankness, a new type. Her frankness was more the frankness of a child than the outspokenness of gaucherie.

"Some day," he said, "you may probably have your wish. There is your uncle, for instance."

She nodded. "It is my one hope," she said, "my one hope. I go to meet the postman every morning. It is three weeks since he wrote and said that he was going to send for me. You don't think that he would change his mind?" she asked, turning suddenly towards him with almost tragic intensity.

"Very unlikely, I should say," he answered. "Has he any other relatives?"

"None," she answered. "Even my uncle and aunt with whom I live here are not relatives of his. You see, he was my father's brother. Mr. Sarsby was my mother's brother."

"It is Mr. and Mrs. Sarsby with whom you live?" he remarked.

She nodded. "Yes! And my name is Sinclair," she said, — "Ruby Sinclair."

He stopped short for a minute in the middle of the dyke path. She was walking a little ahead, and missing him in a few moments, turned around. He was standing like a man turned to stone.

"What is the matter?" she asked. "Are you tired, or aren't you well?"

He recovered himself with a little effort. "It is all right," he said. "You know I told you I'd come down here to recoup a little. I get nervous attacks. I was suddenly giddy then."

She came back. Her face was once more softened in its expression of kindly concern. "Would you like to take my arm?" she asked, a little timidly. "We are close to the cottage now. Perhaps you would like to come in and sit down. My aunt would be glad to see you."

"No!" he said. "Let us rest here for a moment."

They sat down on the edge of the high, grassy bank. He tortured himself, gazing into her face, trying to find some likeness between her and the murdered man. There was none, he told himself, — none. The name was a common one — one of the commonest. It was ridiculous to connect this girl in any way with the tragedy under whose shadow he had passed. Yet he felt his fingers nervously clutching the bank upon which they were sitting. The seagulls still wheeled their way across his head. The tide was flowing softly up into the creek below them. A fishing-boat came gliding by. A lark rose almost from their feet, and was singing just above their heads. Everywhere around was peace and quiet. It was the same land in which he had found content only a few hours ago, yet it seemed to him that already the shadow had come.

It was she who rose first. She shook out her skirts a little reluctantly, and turned toward the village, saying: "I am sorry, but I must go. Meals at our house are the one thing more certain than the rising of the sun. We lunch at one, and it is ten minutes to. Do you feel well enough to get back, or will you come on with me?"

"I will go back," he said. "I wonder," he continued, "what are you going to do this afternoon?"

She shrugged her shoulders. "There is nothing," she answered. "Come out here, I suppose, and pray that I may have a letter to-morrow morning."

"Be unconventional," he begged. "Take pity upon an invalid, and come and have tea with me."

"I'd love to," she answered, "if I can get away. About half-past four?"

"Yes," said he. "I shall be waiting for you."

"Don't come to meet me," she begged,—"not that it matters, of course, only if uncle knew that you were staying there, and that you came from London, and that I had talked to you, he would want to come and call. He is one of those fussy people who like to hear themselves talk, and to make acquaintances. It's all very well for you to shiver," she added, with a little smile, "but I have to live with him."

With a laugh he said: "I'll hide, until I see you actually before the door. You will come, though?"

"I'll come," she promised, turning away with a little wave of the hand.

CHAPTER XIII
AN INFORMAL TEA-PARTY

After all, the element of unconventionality was absent from Deane's tea-party. About four o'clock, looking landwards from a little sandy knoll just in front of his strange abode, he saw two figures coming along the dyke path. A few minutes later, Ruby Sinclair and her companion came across the last little strip of shingle, and approached the spot where Deane was waiting for them.

"My uncle would like to make your acquaintance, Mr. Deane," she said.

Deane held out his hand and welcomed his visitor—a small, fussy-looking little man with a gray moustache, and a somewhat awkward air of being at his ease. He wore a tweed knickerbocker suit,—very old-fashioned, and of local make,—a flannel collar, and an ill-chosen tie. He shook hands with his host in a perfunctory sort of manner.

"Thought I must just look you up," he explained, "living out here. Such a lonely spot, too! You are going to play golf, of course?"

Deane shook his head. "I never play," he answered. "I have come here to rest."

To rest! The word seemed a strange one to the fussy little man, who was already taking stock of his surroundings. Photographs in silver frames, a pile of books—all new, a gun and fishing-rod, and other such belongings—all, naturally, the best of their sort!

"Well, but you must do something!" Mr. Sarsby remarked. "You cannot sit here all day and look at the sea,—like the fishermen," he continued, with a little laugh. "A very lazy lot—our fishermen," he went on. "Never go out if there's a ripple on the sea."

Deane nodded. "The tides," he remarked, "are rather treacherous, I should think."

The servant brought in tea and a great dish of strawberries, at which Mr. Sarsby gazed in amazement.

"Strawberries!" he exclaimed. "Why, we don't begin to think about them for another six weeks!"

"Is that so?" answered Deane, carelessly. "I never know anything about seasons, and my man is doing the catering. Miss Sinclair, you must make the tea for us. I am afraid our methods are a little crude, but you see we are trying to get along without any women-servants."

Mr. Sarsby was a little abashed. He had seldom sat down to a table covered by a cloth of such fine linen, and he had certainly never been waited upon, of late years, by a man-servant. His little eyes roved inquisitively around. "You come from London, sir, my niece tells me," he remarked.

"From London," Deane replied.

"A wonderful place!" Mr. Sarsby said, with a sigh. "Since I retired, unfortunately, I have had to drop out of life altogether."

"Your health?" Deane suggested politely.

"My health, and my ridiculously small pension," Mr. Sarsby answered. "I can't make out what the country is coming to. Years ago, pensions were altogether on a different scale. To-day, it seems to me that every government is always trying to shirk its obligations to those who go out and help to build up the empire."

This was Mr. Sarsby's favorite little speech, which he made regularly several times a week in the village, and once a year at a club dinner. Deane received it in sympathetic silence.

"Tell me how you spend your time, Miss Sinclair?" he asked. "You play golf, I think you told me."

"Oh! I do all the obvious things one has to do, living in such a place," she said. "I swim and I fish, I play golf and tennis when I can get any, and I sail a boat when I can borrow one. Those things are all sport to you, I suppose. When they become not a part of your life, but the whole of it, they are a dreary sort of pursuits."

"My niece is seldom satisfied," Mr. Sarsby said sharply.

"Why should I be?" she asked. "You, at least, have had your day. You have seen something of life, in however small a circle. I haven't! I dare say, after twenty years away, I might be content with these things. Life for you is simply a satisfactory thing or not according to whether you have beaten Colonel Forsitt or whether he has beaten you, whether you are heeling your mashie shots or laying them dead, holing your putts or leaving them short. You see, I haven't quite come to the stage when I find these things sufficient."

"At any rate," Mr. Sarsby remarked, with what he imagined was a dignified air, "there is no need to take a stranger into your confidence. Mr. Deane is scarcely interested."

"On the contrary," Deane answered, with a little bow. "But I thought you told me, Miss Sinclair, that you were probably leaving us before long."

"Oh, I hope so!" she replied. "My uncle was not a man to break his promise, and he did promise. I am expecting to hear now every day."

After tea, they wandered out on to the little stretch of sandy shingle which alone separated the cottage from the sea. The girl had walked on a little ahead, and Deane laid his hand for a moment upon her uncle's shoulder.

"Mr. Sarsby," he said, "did I understand that the name of your niece's uncle was Sinclair—the same as her own?"

Mr. Sarsby nodded. "Yes, sir!" he said,—"Richard Sinclair. He was her father's brother, you see,—a queer, wandering sort of fish. However, he certainly did write the girl, a few weeks ago, saying that he was back in England, and hoped to realize a large sum of money on some of his investments, and promised to send for her to come up to town. Since then, we have heard nothing from him."

"Do you read the papers, Mr. Sarsby?" Deane asked.

"I read the Times for an hour every afternoon between five and six," Mr. Sarsby admitted. "I have a special arrangement with Mr. Foulds—the vicar—which enables me to do this,—a special arrangement!" he concluded, with a little gurgle of satisfaction. "Our vicar, by the bye, Mr. Deane, is a highly intelligent man. He will doubtless be coming across to see you."

"I am here for so short a time," Deane said. "It is very kind of people, but really it is scarcely worth their while to trouble to come to see me. I am going on to Scotland in a few days. It is only that I was a little run down, and scarcely felt up to a large house-party, that I came here first."

"You are one of those fortunate people, I see," Mr. Sarsby remarked, a little enviously, "who mix in the world."

Deane shrugged his shoulders. "More or less, I suppose," he admitted. "But I was asking you whether you read the papers. I did so for an object. I wonder whether you have noticed the details of a very sordid murder that was committed in a London hotel a short time ago?"

"I never read of such things, sir!" Mr. Sarsby declared. "They do not interest me. I read the political news and the foreign intelligence. Anything that pertains to India, also, naturally claims my attention. I have always contended," he continued, "that a golf column in the Times, say twice a week, would be much appreciated. We who study the game from the scientific point of view would like to see the attitude the Times would take on certain matters. For instance, I myself—"

"Pardon my interrupting you, Mr. Sarsby," Deane said, with his eyes upon the returning figure of the girl, "but I was speaking about this murder. Curiously enough, the unfortunate man was named Sinclair, and he had just returned from abroad."

Mr. Sarsby slowly opened his mouth. Looking up at his companion blankly, "You don't for a moment imagine," he began, "that there could be any connection between this person and Ruby's uncle?"

"I haven't any idea," Deane answered, "but when she mentioned his name, and told me that he had just come back from Africa, and that she had been waiting for a letter which did not come, it certainly occurred to me to be rather in the nature of a coincidence!"

"Have you a paper?" Mr. Sarsby asked hurriedly.

Deane shook his head. "No!" he said. "But there must be a village library, or some place where the London papers are preserved."

"There is," Mr. Sarsby declared. "I will hurry back. I will go and read about it at once. Does it say whether the unfortunate man," he continued, "was possessed of any means?"

"I do not remember," Deane said. "The object of the murder was supposed to be robbery, but the hotel he was staying at scarcely seemed to be one likely to attract a man of wealth."

"I shall hurry back at once," Mr. Sarsby declared. "If there is anything in this, I must come and ask your advice."

"If the thing seems in any way possible," Deane remarked, "you will have to run up to town and make inquiries."

Mr. Sarsby opened his mouth. "My dear sir!" he exclaimed. "Go to London? But there, there!" he added. "I forgot! If there is anything in it, the estate would, of course, pay my railway fare. Such a busy week, too, as I have next week," he added, taking out his memorandum book and glancing at it for a moment. "I have seven golf matches,— three foursomes and four singles. I scarcely see how I could get away. Ruby," he called, "come along, my dear. We must be getting back."

The girl stifled a yawn. She was beginning to be a bit curious as to why their host had devoted all his attention to her uncle. "Very well," she answered laconically. "I am quite ready. Good-bye, Mr. Deane!"

"If I may," he said, "I will walk a little way with you."

They crossed the strip of shingly beach together. Afterwards, by necessity, the party became detached. Mr. Sarsby walked on ahead. Deane and the girl followed him, a few yards behind.

"You seem to have found plenty to say to my uncle," she remarked curiously.

"If you will spoil an interesting tea-party," he murmured, "by bringing in an elderly male relative,—"

"It wasn't my fault," she interrupted. "He would come—insisted upon it—as soon as he knew that I had spoken to you. Your man has been making purchases and sending telegrams in the village, which has made every one curious. People who live in small places are always such snobs."

He laughed. "Well, I had to talk to your uncle, anyhow," he said.

She nodded. "You know now what I have to put up with," she said. "He is a dull, ignorant, pompous little bore. You have probably found that out for yourself by now."

"You dismiss your relatives a little summarily," he remarked.

"I try to speak the truth," she answered. "I believe in being just to people. If I knew of any good quality that he possessed, I would tell it to you, — but I don't!"

She believed in being just! He looked at her as she walked by his side, stepping along with the delightful freedom of healthy youth, her limbs clearly defined beneath her thin skirt, — for they were facing a land breeze which played havoc, also, with her hair. She walked well, her head a little thrown back. Deane recognized the graceful lines of her neck and throat, the carriage of her chin. There was something particularly rhythmic about her movements. She was a believer in justice! Well, she looked like that. The mouth, in repose, was a little hard, — the jaw determined. He found himself wondering, with a nervous sort of morbid curiosity, exactly what she would say and do if she had known with whom she was walking, and if Dick Sinclair had indeed been her uncle! Supposing she knew the whole truth, — knew of that heated interview, knew of Rowan's enterprise, knew of the paper which was still sewn into the dead man's coat! She would scarcely be an easy person to deal with, he thought.

Her uncle had turned round. They had reached the end of the dyke. A little grass-grown footpath led them now to the side of the harbor, beyond which lay the village.

"Mr. Deane," he said, — "Mr. Deane, I should like to show you the village schoolroom."

Deane nodded. "I should be very glad," he said.

Mr. Sarsby turned to his niece. "Ruby," he said, "go home and tell your aunt where we are. I shall be home in half-an-hour, — perhaps five-and-twenty minutes. If there is any message for me from the golf club, the boy can wait till I return. This way, Mr. Deane, — this way."

The girl turned away with a little grimace, and waved her hand to Deane as she disappeared. The two men climbed the village street side by side.

CHAPTER XIV
AN UNEXPECTED VISITOR

Mr. Sarsby, like most men of his stamp, when brought in touch with larger things than his world knew of, was nervous and helpless. He seemed to throw the whole weight of further action upon this stranger at whose instigation he had commenced the search.

The reading-room was empty except for these two men. Deane was sitting in the little bow window, looking down with apparent interest into the narrow, tortuous street. Sarsby, with a pile of torn and crumpled newspapers in front of him, was still standing, leaning over the long table in the centre of the room. His search was finished. He had no doubt whatever in his mind. The murdered man was indeed Ruby's uncle!

"Mr. Deane!" he exclaimed hoarsely.

Deane turned his head. "Well?"

"There's no doubt at all about it," declared Mr. Sarsby, striking the little pile of papers with the back of his hand. "It's the man—it's Ruby's uncle! The date of his arrival corresponds, and the hotel is the one from which he wrote to Ruby."

Deane nodded. "I fancied that it must be the same," he said.

"It is the same," Mr. Sarsby declared. "What are we to do? Something must be done at once!"

"Exactly," Deane remarked. "Your niece, of course, must claim her inheritance—that is, if the man was really worth anything."

"Of course!—Of course!" Mr. Sarsby said. "Dear me, what an unfortunate business this all is! I suppose I must go to London with her, and London always upsets me horribly."

"I am afraid that you must make up your mind to that," Deane remarked. "As I said before, if there is anything I can do to help you, I shall be delighted."

"But you won't be there," Mr. Sarsby said. "You are going from here to Scotland."

Deane hesitated. "I might," he said,—"in fact I think that I certainly should,—go to Scotland by way of London."

"But we must leave at once!" Mr. Sarsby declared. "At least I suppose so."

Deane rose to his feet. He had not much sympathy for the frightened little man, whose eyes were continually seeking his as though for help and advice.

"Well," he said, "I scarcely see how you can keep away, under the circumstances. You must talk it over with your niece, and let me know what you decide."

They left the place together. As they stepped out on to the pavement, Mr. Sarsby coughed apologetically. "I suppose," said he, "you would consider it necessary for me to tell my niece about this? It will be a shock to her, of course. She had hoped so much from the coming of this uncle, and I am afraid that she is not particularly contented here."

"I scarcely see," Deane answered, "how you can keep it from her."

"There is no mention of any property," Mr. Sarsby remarked,—"none at all. In fact, the papers say that his effects were so small that it seemed difficult to believe that robbery was the motive of the crime. Still, I suppose she must be told."

Deane walked down the narrow street, his hands behind his back, his eyes fixed upon the arm of the river below, dotted now with brown-sailed fishing-boats. Here, after all, was a simple way out of the difficulty! The murdered man had no other relatives. In all probability, no one would ever tell the girl. No one would ever claim the possessions of the dead man, whatsoever they might be. Then common sense reasserted itself in his brain, and he stifled the instinct which he had so nearly yielded to.

"She must be told, Mr. Sarsby," he said. "If you would rather not tell her yourself, I will do so."

Mr. Sarsby shook his head. "It isn't that," he said. "I don't mind telling her. But it's the journey to London, and the excitement, and all that. I hate worry of any sort. It's bad for my health, anyhow."

They stood upon the little quay, and Deane hesitated. "If there is anything further which I can do," he said, "come out and look me up. In any case, let me see you before you start for London."

Mr. Sarsby wrung his hand. "It is very good of you," he declared. "I shall certainly come out before we start,—most certainly! I can't imagine what Ruby will say. Poor girl! Poor girl!"

Deane retraced his steps along the high dyke bank to the marshes which surrounded his tower. Once or twice he looked behind, looked toward the low white front of the cottage which the girl had pointed out as her abode. Once he fancied that he saw something moving in the garden, and he stood on the top of the dyke, gazing with a curious interest at the slowly moving speck passing in and out amongst the trees. Then it vanished. He turned and made his way homeward....

Towards sunset, the heat of the day seemed suddenly to increase. A curiously hot wind sprang up from the land, black clouds gathered in the sky, and unusual darkness hung over the land. The air seemed charged with electricity. Every moment it seemed as though the clouds must break and the storm come. The tide came rolling in, no longer with a faint, insistent ripple, but with great powerful waves, throwing their spray far and wide. Deane left his dinner more than once to stand outside on the little knoll and watch. Every moment he expected to see the banks of black clouds riven with lightning, to hear the far-off muttering across the sea grow nearer and nearer. The whole world seemed to be in a state of suspended animation. The seagulls had ceased their screaming, and had taken shelter in some hidden haunt. A little fleet of fishing-boats had furled their sails. Not a soul was to be seen upon the marshes.

Deane finished his dinner and sat by the wide-open window, leaning upon his folded arms, looking out at the foam-flecked sea,— foam which seemed to glitter with a clear, white phosphorescence in the failing light. There were books by his side, but he felt no inclination to read;—cigarettes and cigars at his elbow, but he lacked the enterprise to smoke. There was something almost theatrical, something breathless, in this pause before the storm! He himself was in an emotional frame of mind. Another page of this tragic chapter had opened before him. The coming of this girl was in itself a catastrophe. She would take possession of the papers belonging to the murdered man,—would show them, probably, to a lawyer. After that, only the worst could happen!

Then, as he sat there, the profound silence was suddenly broken. He heard the crunch of the gravel beneath flying footsteps, the rustle of a skirt, a little half-subdued cry! He looked up in amazement. It was Winifred Rowan who was coming towards him, her hair disordered, her eyes lit with fear,—a strange, half-terrified figure, flying from the storm!

"Miss Rowan!" he exclaimed breathlessly.

Even as he spoke, the clouds were parted at last with a dazzling blaze of forked lightning. The girl gave a little cry and held out her hands. He leaned over, and, as the thunder shook the building, took her into his arms, lifting her over the narrow window-sill into the room.

CHAPTER XV
THE EFFECT OF A STORM

Deane was never quite sure how it had happened. The sudden crash of the storm, the vivid play of the lightning in the darkened room, the curious exultation which any outburst of nature seems to kindle in the forgotten places, had somehow generated a curious excitement—something electrical, incomprehensible, yet felt by both of them. His hands were still about her for a moment after she was in the room. It was perhaps a harmless instinct enough which caused her to draw a little nearer still to him with fear, as the thunder crashed overhead and the ground beneath their feet rocked. Then there happened what he was never able to explain. She was in his arms, her panting breath fell hot upon his cheek, his lips were pressed to hers, before he even realized what was happening. Her head fell a little back, her lips seemed to meet his freely, unresistingly. It was one of those moments of madness which seem to be born and die away, without reason, almost without volition. Deane himself was no Lothario. In his office he had talked kindly with this girl, and it had never occurred to him for a single second even to hold her hand in his. Her comings and goings, except for their association, had left him unmoved. Afterwards, when he tried to think of it, his senses were simply benumbed. Yet the fact remained that she had come into his arms as though she had heard the call of his heart for her, that their lips had met with all the effortless certainty of fate.

The thunder ceased. She disengaged herself from his arms with a little cry. Her bosom was still heaving, her cheeks were white almost to ghastliness, with one little patch of brilliant color where his lips had rested for a moment. She tried to speak, but the words seemed stifled in her throat. He led her to a chair, arranged cushions for her back, and stood over her.

"Is there news?" he asked.

"None!" she faltered.

He shook his head. He was completely bewildered. "How did you find me out?" he asked. "What brings you here at this hour?"

"It is because there is no news," she cried, speaking with difficulty. "I cannot rest or sleep. Every moment that passes tears at my heartstrings. Life has become nothing but a living nightmare. Don't be angry with me that I came. I was obliged to do something or I should have gone mad."

"I am not angry," he said. "I am only amazed, I cannot understand —"

"Oh, I found out where you were!" she said. "I did everything that was mean. I bribed someone to tell me. This morning I saw Basil. I think I came to him at a weak moment. The horror was in his eyes. I shrieked when I saw him. Even now when I think I must shriek. Mr. Deane, I have come to pray, to beg you to go back. You are very rich. There must be ways of saving him. You have influence with people. Go back and use it. What can you do here in the wilderness? It seems almost as though you had left him to die."

He stooped down and took her hands once more in his. "My dear little friend," he said, "remember what I told you in my office. Believe me, I should not have left London if the slightest doubt had remained as to your brother's safety. Never mind how I managed it. You had better not ask; you had better not know. But your brother will be reprieved. It is a certain thing."

She drew a long breath. Once more her face was at any rate human. The lightning filled the room with a sudden glare. She caught at him with a scream. "Oh! I am afraid, I am afraid!" she moaned.

He passed his arm around her reassuringly. "You are overwrought," he said. "You are almost at the end of your strength."

He poured out some brandy and water, and made her drink it. Her hand shook so that he had to guide the glass to her lips.

"Listen," he said, "you must keep calm or you will be ill, and you will not be able to help your brother. Tell me, have you eaten anything to-day?"

"I don't remember," she gasped.

Deane rang the bell. "Something to eat," he ordered, "for one, as quickly as you can. And some wine — anything will do."

It was to the man's credit that he received his orders without comment or surprise. Once more they two were alone.

"If you have any faith in me," Deane said, "or any belief, remember what I have told you. Your brother is safe. To-morrow or the next day the reprieve will be signed."

"Say it again!" she gasped, clinging to his hand.

"To-morrow or the next day," he repeated firmly, "the reprieve will be signed. There can be no mistake. There will be none."

"Ah!" she murmured, half closing her eyes. "It was to hear you talk like this that I came. I could not have borne it alone for another second. Something in my head seemed to be giving way."

"The storm, too, is terrifying," he said. "You were fortunate not to be ten minutes later. Look!"

He led her to the window. Across the marsh was a darkness that was less of the atmosphere than of the falling torrents of rain, — rain that fell in sheets, flung up again from the hard paths of the marshes in a white, fringe-like foam. Seaward, the waves had become breakers. The one white line had become a dozen.

"You would have been drowned," he said, leading her back to her chair.

"It is good of you," she said, "not to be angry. I ought not to have come. I know that. Only I was afraid. In London I should have gone mad."

The servant entered with a tray. Deane stood over her while she ate, walking up and down the room, talking in a disconnected manner of many things. Outside, the storm was passing away. Through the wide-open windows fresh salt air came stealing into the room. Deane stood looking out for a few minutes, and then turned towards his visitor with an air of perplexity. She met his gaze, and her eyes suddenly filled with tears.

"Oh! I know I have been foolish," she said. "I am here and you don't know what to do with me. Isn't that what you were thinking? I have been very foolish," she added, with a sudden flood of color streaming into her cheeks. "But remember, when I came I was mad. You will remember that?"

"Yes!" he answered reassuringly. "I will remember that."

There was an awkward silence. Deane felt that it would have been torture to her if he had alluded to that moment of madness, and yet it was hard altogether to avoid it.

"I am afraid," he said, "that you will have to put up with bachelor quarters to-night. You can have my room here. I have another which will do, but you would find it a little rough."

She looked at him timidly. "Couldn't I — get back to the village?"

He led her outside and pointed. The storm, coming with the full tide, had wrought a strange change in the face of the land. Up to the very top of the dykes was a turbulent waste of waters. The tower had been left as though upon an island. Nowhere in sight was any land to be seen.

"You see," Deane said to the girl, "it would not be safe to try and get to the village. The water is up to within a few inches of the dyke, and in the half darkness one might easily make a false step. From here one cannot quite see, but I should imagine that the flood is over the village street."

She turned back toward the little gray stone building. "If you will let me sleep in your sitting-room, then," she said timidly. "I will not turn you out of your room."

He laughed. "My dear young lady," he said, "if anyone in the world ever needed sleep to-night, it is you. I am going to send you up to lie down at once. You must promise me, promise faithfully, that you will remember what I have said, that you will say this to yourself: 'The reprieve will come!' It is the truth, mind. Say that to yourself and sleep."

Then he touched the bell and spoke to his servant. "Grant, please make my room as habitable as possible for this young lady. We are on an island, and no one will be able to leave to-night. Put out anything of mine you think may be useful to her."

She turned towards him impulsively. "You are very good to me," she said.

"My dear Miss Rowan, I only wish that it were in my power—"

Then he stopped short. After all, it was not wise to tell her too much. He raised her fingers to his lips, and avoided, with a sudden twinge of self-reproach, the soft invitation of her timidly raised eyes.

"You must sleep well," he said, as he pointed the way up the stairs. "Remember, you can take what I have told you as a promise."

CHAPTER XVI
A REPRIEVE

Morning dawned upon a land still as though from exhaustion. The long waves, sole remnant of the storm, came gliding in with a slow, lazy motion, and broke noiselessly upon the firm sands. The sky was blue. Of wind there was none at all. Inland, the flood-tide was still high. Only the tops of the dykes were visible. Everywhere the sea had found its way into unexpected places. Little patches of the marsh from which it had just receded shone with a new glory—a green glitter like the sparkle of emeralds. Deane, who was out early, for his bed had been no more than a sofa, gave a little start of surprise as he opened the door and found Winifred Rowan standing on a little knoll by the side of the flagstaff, looking seaward.

She turned towards him at once with the sound of the opening door. He realized then, more completely than in the dusk of the evening, how great the strain of these last few days had been,—the strain which had driven her into this strange journey. The black rings under her eyes seemed as though traced with a pencil, her cheeks were thinner, there was something pathetic about the quick, startled look which flashed into her eyes at the sound of Deane's approaching footsteps.

"I am afraid," he said gravely, "that you have not slept."

"As much as usual," she answered. "Tell me, what time do your letters come?"

He looked inland. "Generally about eight. They may be a little later to-day."

She nodded. "I must go back," she said vacantly. "When is there a train?"

It was impossible to ask her to stop, and yet he felt all the pathos of sending her back to face alone the shadow of her terrible anxiety.

"There is no hurry," he said. "We will look out the trains after breakfast."

"Are you — going to stay here?" she asked anxiously.

"If I thought," he answered, "that there was the slightest thing I could do in London which I have not already done, I would go back by the first train this morning, but, indeed, you must remember what I told you last night. The matter is practically settled. In a few days he will know."

"It is those few days," she said softly, "which are so terrible."

It was hard to try and make use of any conventional phrase of reassurance. Deane, remembering how intense, how real and startling a thing this tragedy really was, found it hard, impossible, indeed.

"Tell me," he asked, "do you live absolutely alone?"

"Yes!" she told him. "There was a cousin who was with me for some time, but she got a situation the other side of London, and had to move. I was in a boarding-house," she continued, after a moment's hesitation, "until — this happened. Then all the people — well, they meant to be kind," she broke off, "but the woman who kept it thought I had better leave, and I suppose she was right."

"We will go in to breakfast," he said, a little abruptly.

Every moment he seemed to realize more completely the pathos of her position. They turned towards the house. Suddenly her fingers fell upon his arm. "Who is that?" she asked, pointing landwards.

Deane followed her outstretched finger. Riding along the top of one of the dykes, as though unconscious of the sea flowing on either side, came a boy on a bicycle. The bicycle was painted red, and the boy had on a cap whose high peak gave it a semi-official look.

"He is coming here," said Deane. "It may be my letters. Or I think —"

He stopped short. He knew very well that it was a telegram the boy was bringing, but he almost feared to say anything which would bring hope into her face.

"It isn't — it couldn't be a telegram?" she asked, a little wistfully.

"It might be," he admitted. "I get a good many, of course."

He told the lie unblushingly. All the time he watched, with an anxiety which seemed incredible, for the coming of the messenger.

"You must remember," he said, "that even if this should be a telegram, I really do not expect any news yet."

She said nothing. She stood with parted lips by his side, and they watched the boy drive his bicycle along the sea-stained bank. Once he skidded, and she gave a little scream. Deane laughed at her, surprised to discover something unnatural in the sound.

"Well," he said, "we will meet the boy here. I am afraid you will find a few stock exchange quotations inside the envelope, even if he should be—"

"It is a telegraph boy," she interrupted. "I can see the wallet."

She clung to his arm. Deane found himself patting her fragile hand with his strong fingers. He drew her arm through his, and led her a few steps further forward. The boy jumped off his bicycle and opened his wallet, as he approached, with a familiar movement. Deane took the telegram into his fingers and tore it open. His arm suddenly went round her waist.

"Miss Rowan," he said, "be brave and I will tell you some good news. See, you can read it for yourself. The reprieve is signed."

She suddenly fell a dead weight upon his arm, and almost as quickly she recovered herself. Her closed eyes were opened, she clung to him passionately. "It is true?" she cried out.

He held the telegram in front of her face. "Read," he said. "'Reprieve signed last night. Will be communicated to Rowan this morning. Hardaway.'—That is the name of my solicitor, so there is no possible doubt about it. The matter is ended."

He turned to the boy, who stood looking on with wooden face. Then he drew a coin from his pocket. "My young friend," he said, "you are in luck. Take that and go home to your breakfast."

The boy looked at the sovereign and up at Deane. So far as his features were capable of expression at all, they spoke of stupefaction. Then, as though afraid that Deane might change his mind, he mounted his bicycle and rode rapidly away.

"It is a relief to you, of course," Deane said, trying to speak in as matter-of-fact a tone as possible; "but this thing was a certainty all the time. I have always tried to make you believe that. Come in now, and let us have some breakfast. You ought to have an appetite."

She followed him without a word. She seemed, indeed, like a person dreaming, not wholly able to realize the things happening around her, even the moments that passed. Deane waited upon her at breakfast, and talked in a matter-of-fact way, accepting her monosyllabic answers as natural things, — carrying on a conversation, too, with the man who waited at the sideboard. By degrees, a more natural expression came into her face. When at last the meal was over and the servant had left the room, she burst suddenly into tears. Deane took her outside and placed her in a chair, sitting by her side on the sands.

"Now," he said, "that is all over."

"When can I go back?" she asked suddenly. "They will let me see Basil. I must go and tell him."

"He knows, of course," Deane replied, "but naturally he will want to see you. You can leave here in about an hour. I am not sure — perhaps I may come with you."

She sat there quietly, absolutely content to lie still and gaze out at the sea. Presently Grant came out with a note, which Deane silently opened. It was dated from The Cottage, Rakney.

Dear Mr. Deane,

My niece knows, and she insists upon going to London at once. We are all very much disturbed. If it is not troubling you too much when you are passing this way, we should be so grateful if you would call in for a minute.

Deane looked thoughtfully seaward, and his face hardened as he crumpled the note up in his hand. Then he rose to his feet. "I am going in to see about the trains for you," he said.

He hired a cart from the village, and they stood together on the platform of the nearest railway station, an hour or so later. She laid her arm upon his sleeve.

"Will you stop for a moment, please?" she said. "I am afraid I must have seemed ungracious. After all, I ought to be very grateful to you."

He shook his head. "No!" he answered. "It is always I who must be your debtor. I ought to have been firmer with your brother when I sent him to this man Sinclair to make terms. It was a desperate enterprise, after all, and I ought to have realized the danger of your brother being tempted to use violence. To me he was nothing more than a unit of humanity, and I took him at his word. If he had brought me the paper I wanted, I was quite prepared to ask him no questions whatever, and he would have been a rich man. I can't help feeling that in a sense I am responsible for his present position and yours."

She looked away from him. Her eyes were fixed upon the horizon. She appeared to be steadily thinking the matter out. The wind blew little wisps of fair hair over her face. Her eyes were steadfast, her forehead a little wrinkled. She seemed to be endeavoring to arrive at a conscientious decision.

"No!" she said, after some time, "I cannot see that you are to blame. I am sure that it never entered into your head that my brother might be tempted to use violence."

Deane looked away with a little frown. In his heart he knew very well that he was not so sure! "Well," he said, "we will let that go. At any rate, my responsibility to you remains. Tell me what I can do? How can I help you?"

She shook her head. "I am going back to my work," she said. "I need no help."

"Your work?" he repeated.

She nodded, with a little sigh. "I am a typist," she said. "You know what that means, — genteel starvation, long hours, gray days. Never mind, I am almost used to it."

"You need be a typist no longer unless you choose," he said. "Part of what I promised to your brother belongs to you."

She shook her head. "Don't speak of it!" she exclaimed. "I should feel that it was blood money."

"At least let me hear from you sometimes," he said. "Don't let me lose sight of you altogether while your brother is unable to help you."

She hesitated. Then, lifting her eyes to his, "I don't believe," she said softly, "that you would tell me anything that was not true."

"I don't believe that I should," he answered.

"Then tell me this," she said, "honestly. When you made my brother that offer, when you sent him to deal with this man Sinclair, can you tell me that you had not an idea in your mind that he might be led on to do something rash?"

Deane hesitated. He was not a man of over-strict scruples, but he hated lies. Somehow or other, it seemed to him impossible to look at this girl and tell her anything that was not the truth.

"I am not altogether sure," he answered. "At the back of my head there was just the idea that your brother was desperate, that he would gain what he wanted, somehow or other."

She turned away, and walked a little way down the platform. The train was already in the station. She entered a carriage and sat in the furthest corner. "Thank you," she said. "I am glad that you have told me the truth. Would you mind going away now, please?"

"I am sorry," Deane said simply. "Remember that I only did what ninety-nine men out of a hundred would have done in my place. I wanted that paper, and your brother begged for just such an enterprise."

She held out her hands. "If you please!" she said. "Good-bye!"

Deane turned away. The girl was a little fool, of course. Yet as he turned and watched the smoke of the train disappear, and thought of her in her empty third-class carriage, alone, he was conscious of a sense of acute depression—none the less acute because it was vague. He turned back to the village, walking with heavy steps. It was as though a new trouble had come into his life.

CHAPTER XVII
A NEW DANGER

Deane was shown into what was apparently the morning-room of the Sarsby domicile by an open-mouthed and very country-looking domestic, who regarded him all the time with unaffected curiosity. Mr. Sarsby was sitting in an easy-chair, reading the Times. Directly he recognized his visitor he showed signs of nervousness.

"Ah, Mr. Deane!" he said, rising. "How do you do, Mr. Deane?"

Deane shook hands. His host did not ask him to sit down, nor did he himself resume his seat.

"I looked in," Deane explained, "to know what your niece had decided to do."

"She has decided to go to London at once," Mr. Sarsby answered, — "at once. It is very inconvenient for all of us. I am almost sorry that you ever happened to point out the paragraph, especially as there seems to be no property of any sort to be found."

The door was suddenly opened and Ruby Sinclair entered. There was a frown which was almost a scowl upon her dark, handsome face. Little Mr. Sarsby seemed suddenly to have become a person of no importance.

"Mr. Deane will excuse me," he said hurriedly, yet with a marked attempt at stiffness. "I have to return the Times."

He left the room. Deane looked after him with some surprise.

"What is the matter with your uncle?" he asked the girl.

"He has just heard," she answered, "that a young lady from somewhere or other spent the night out at the tower last night."

Deane looked at her in amazement. "And what business is it of his?" he asked.

"I don't know," brusquely. "As a rule, gentlemen when they're living alone don't have young lady visitors,—not to stay the night, at any rate."

Deane laughed. "The young lady in question," he said, "came to see me on a very important matter. If you heard anything of the storm last night, you would understand that it was scarcely possible for any one to have found her way from the tower to the mainland after the flood-tide was in."

The girl nodded shortly. "It's not my business," she said. "I am glad you came. I wanted to ask you something. Who is this man Rowan who killed my uncle?"

Deane shook his head slowly. "No one knows very much about him," he said. "They were out in South Africa together. It was there, perhaps, that their quarrel, if they had one, started."

"It says in the Times this morning that he has been reprieved. Why?" she asked fiercely. "Why don't they hang him?"

"Because they came to the conclusion," he answered, "that there had been a fight, and that it was not a deliberate murder."

"They ought to have hanged him," she declared. "It was brutal — hideous!"

"You are going to London, are you not?" he asked quietly.

Her eyes flashed. "Yes!" she answered. "I am going. I am afraid it will be too late. All the papers declare that my uncle's possessions were of little value. He has been robbed. I am sure he has been robbed. His letter told me that he would have plenty of money. He would not write and tell me that if he had nothing."

"You will be able to find out," Deane answered, a little coldly.

"I shall find out," the girl declared. "I am going to a good lawyer. He wrote as though he had something in his possession which was worth money. It was for that, I am sure, that this man Rowan tried to kill him. I shall find out all about it when I get there."

"The man Rowan was arrested on the premises," Deane reminded her. "There was no time for him to have taken anything away, and the room was locked up by the police."

"I don't care," she answered. "Oh! Can't you understand what this means to me?" she cried, jumping up from the chair in which she had seated herself a moment or so before. "I am starved for life here, starved for the want of it," she cried. "I was never meant to live in a place like this—a life like this! It isn't fair. Other girls have clothes and jewels, and men to admire them, and go to theatres, and see the world. Why shouldn't I? I will! I am going to London to find out what that man killed my uncle for, and I mean never to come back here again."

The girl was evidently in earnest. Her bosom was heaving, her dark eyes were full of fire. Deane noticed the firm lines of her mouth, the crisp determination of her speech, and he realized a new danger. This girl was not one to be bribed or put off. Every word she had said she had meant. There was a distinct change in her whole appearance since the last time he had seen her. She was at once handsomer and less attractive. The wistfulness of her few sad speeches to him had passed away. The vague discontent seemed suddenly to have become focussed in a passionate anger against this untoward stroke of fate.

"Well," said Deane at length, rising as though about to leave, "I hope you may discover, after all, that your uncle was a man of property."

"Why won't you help me?" she asked suddenly. "You could if you would."

"Could I?" he answered. "I wonder."

"Of course you could," she declared, coming a little nearer to him. "I suppose I seem a very ordinary discontented sort of creature to you, but you haven't lived as many years as I have pushing against the walls of a prison. I think I am one of those persons who would improve a good deal with a little prosperity," she added, with a sudden smile which transformed her face, a smile which was almost brilliant. "Why won't you help me?"

"Do you mean that you would like me to go to London for you, and search through your uncle's effects?" Deane asked quietly. "If you gave me a letter, I suppose I could do that."

"Come with me, then," she begged. "I mean to do everything for myself, but there are many little things I am ignorant about. If you would come with me, I promise you," she added, looking into his eyes, "that you would not find me ungrateful."

"When are you going?" he asked.

"Monday morning," she answered.

Deane walked to the window, and looked out for a moment at the tangled wilderness of cottage flowers, which seemed to have been encouraged to grow there in wild profusion—a brilliant spot of color, as he remembered very well, from the sea line. In a day or so at most, this girl might, if she realized her position, or if she were properly advised, be in a position to bring ruin upon him. An alliance with her was obviously the very best thing that could happen for him. Yet he felt a certain distrust, a certain unexplained reluctance to accepting her overtures. If she discovered her power, she would drive a hard bargain—he knew that well enough. If she did not discover it—

He turned away and faced her suddenly. "Yes!" he said, "I'll help you if I can. We'll go to London together on Monday morning."

A curious look came into her face. She drew him out of the room. "Come," she said, "I won't ask you to stay to tea, because my aunt thinks that you are a most improper person. I'll walk with you back across the marshes. I want you to tell me what you really think, and I want to show you the one letter I received from my uncle...."

She read the letter to him as they walked side by side on the top of the dyke path, which was high enough now from the receding waste of waters. The air was unusually salt. Great masses of seaweed had been brought in and left by the ebbing tide. The wind had freshened since the morning. She walked on in supreme disregard of her disordered hair and skirts.

"You see," she said, "he writes distinctly as one who has, or expects to have, money. Listen! 'I did no particular good out there,'" she read, "'but I have brought something home with me which will mean a fortune of some sort or another. I expect you have had quite enough of your country life, and you won't object to coming and sharing it with me. I am rather a rough sort, and I have a few vices that your respected uncle Sarsby knows all about, but I fancy you will get a better time with me than with that solemn old prig. I'd like to do what I can for you, though we haven't seen much of one another, but your mother was the best sister a man ever had, and for her sake I look upon you as the only relative I've got worth counting.'"

She looked up at him eagerly. "Now tell me," she asked, "would he have written that if he hadn't something—jewels, or estate, or something of that sort, which he knew was going to bring him in money?"

"It doesn't sound so," Deane admitted.

She thrust the letter back into her pocket. "You will help me," she said, her face glowing, her eyes full of anticipation. "We will go through his papers carefully. We will find out, somehow or other, what he meant. Oh! It is good to think that I have only a few more days to eat and to sleep in this ghastly wilderness."

"You may be disappointed," he reminded her.

"Never!" she answered. "My uncle was no fool. What he had I shall discover."

"You may be disappointed," he continued, "in the things which wealth itself brings you. You may find life not so very much more wonderful a thing in the city than here in the wilderness."

"Don't you believe it!" she exclaimed, with a scornful laugh. "I am not that sort. I am not an artist who can sit about here for days and potter about with a paintbox, and look at a sunset or a streak of wild lavender, or the shimmering of the yellow sands, as though it were something so marvelous that life itself stood still while they realized it. I like beautiful places and beautiful things, but I hate the impersonality of it all. I want to feel the touch of lace and furs and fine linen, to eat soft food, to listen to music, to ride when I want to, to sleep when I want to, to have friends who admire me, men friends worth speaking to, different from these yokels round here. I suppose I have got it in my blood," she added, with a little laugh. "The milk-and-water ways of life don't attract me. I want the big things."

"Do you know what the big things are?" he asked.

"When I have found my way where I mean to find it, I shall know," she answered. "Here, one might live till one's hair was gray and one's looks had passed, live — if you call it living — and never once see over the wall. When I have come so that I can see over the wall, then I will tell you, if you are still curious, what the big things of life are for me!"

CHAPTER XVIII
AN EXPENSIVE KEY

It was three o'clock in the morning when Deane softly opened the door of his bedroom in the Hotel Universal, and looked up and down the side corridor. There was no one in sight, no sound of any one passing in the main corridor, a few yards away. For several moments he stood and listened intently. Then he moved a few yards to the left, and stopped opposite another door. He scrutinized the number, — 27. It was the number he sought. He felt in his pocket for the keys which he had collected from various sources. One by one he tried them in the lock. In vain! Not one fitted. He tried the handle of the door softly There was no doubt about it. The door was securely fastened. He recognized at once the failure of his first attempt, and returned to his room. His bed was as yet undisturbed. He had not even changed the tweed travelling suit in which he had journeyed up from Rakney. It was a fool's errand, after all, he thought, on which he had come. Yet somehow or other, after his conversation with Ruby Sinclair, after he had realized how thorough her search would indeed be, how convinced she was that somewhere amongst the effects of the dead man lay the secret of wealth, he had realized more completely than ever before the danger in which he stood. Granted, even, that no suspicion of complicity with Rowan attached to him, his financial ruin would be none the less complete if that paper should ever come into the hands of people who understood its worth. Never had the situation seemed so clear, so dangerous, as that night after he had walked home with the girl and turned his face again toward the sea. Something in the very desolation of the marshes seemed to help thought, perhaps by the absence of any distracting object. There was a sense of breadth about the place. As he walked, with only the murmur of the sea in his ears, he saw things clearly. He saw himself in the prime of life, suddenly flung from the place to which he had climbed, flung down to join all those poor millions of strugglers whose first foot has yet to be planted upon the first rung of the great ladder. He was too old to begin at the beginning. There was no place for him down amongst those on whom failure had already placed her mark. He could not have borne it. To be stripped of his riches, his name, the position of which he was without a doubt proud, to suffer the breaking of his engagement, the downfall of all his ambitions, — the very thought of it was intolerable. And in the deep silence of that night, as he listened to the gurgling of the sea below, and the faint movement of the wind across the level land, he realized, with a sudden pain at his heart, the danger in which he stood. In three days the girl would be there. Scotland Yard would send one of its myrmidons with her. She would have free access to all the dead man's belongings. She would take with her a lawyer. Every scrap of paper the man had possessed, every trifling object, would have its value. The Little Anna Gold-Mine was world famous. There would be no chance of their overlooking a single document bearing such a name.

Before he had reached his strange dwelling-place he had come to a resolution. Early next morning, stopping only to leave a note telling the girl where to find him when she arrived in London, he was off by the early train. By means of a little diplomacy he had succeeded in gaining a room within a few doors of the one in which Sinclair had been killed. Only a few feet of wall separated him from the room in which, somewhere or other, was to be found the paper he coveted. Well, his first attempt had been a failure. He knew quite well that the place was paraded by night watchmen, and that any attempt to gain an entrance into the room by orthodox means would result in prompt discovery. There was nothing to be done until the morrow. He threw himself upon the bed and tried to sleep. Waking with the first gleam of daylight, he took off his clothes, bathed, and made a leisurely toilet. Then he rang for the valet de chambre. The man was a pleasant-faced, loquacious sort of fellow. Deane talked to him for a while, and then made his effort.

"Wasn't it upon this floor," he asked, "that a murder took place lately?"

The valet looked around him for a moment before answering. "Yes, sir!" he replied. "In the very next room. We are not allowed to talk about it more than we can help."

Deane nodded. All the time he was watching the man, wondering how far he dared go. "Look here," he said "you seem an honest fellow. I suppose you'd have no objection to bettering yourself in life?"

"No objection in the slightest, sir," the man answered.

"I am on the staff of a newspaper," Deane said slowly, "and my people are particularly anxious that I should inspect the interior of the room in which that murder was committed. Your people downstairs have absolutely refused to allow me to do anything of the sort. I have taken this room in the hope of being able to get in there. Do you think there is any chance for me?"

"I should say not, sir," the man answered. "The door is locked, and Mr. Hartshorn himself, the manager, has taken the key."

"There isn't such a thing as a duplicate, I suppose?" Deane asked.

"Not that I know of, sir," the man answered.

"You couldn't suggest any means by which I could enter that room, even if it were an affair of say fifty pounds to you?" Deane asked calmly.

The man started. Fifty pounds was a great deal of money. On the other hand, the fifty pounds would take some earning. "I am afraid I can't, sir," he said. "There is no duplicate key that I know of, and in any case I dare not run the risk."

"Fifty pounds is not enough, perhaps," Deane said. "Money is no particular object to me. If you said that you thought you could provide me with the key for a hundred pounds, I would willingly pay it."

"I am afraid not, sir," the man answered, turning as though to leave the room.

"Two hundred pounds!" Deane said.

"It isn't a matter of money, sir," the man declared. "I daren't do it. I should be certain to be found out, and I should be sent away without a character."

"I will take you into my service," Deane said.

The man shook his head. "Thank you, sir," he said. "My character is worth a good deal to me. I think I'll keep out of this, if you don't mind."

Deane called him back imperatively. "Let us understand one another," he said, drawing something from his pocket. "Are you going down to the manager to tell him what I have told you?"

The man hesitated. Deane held out a five-pound note. "There is no reason for you to do so, you know," Deane said, "just as there is no reason why you should not accept this tip."

The valet hesitated, and finally accepted the five-pound note which Deane was holding out.

"I am sure I don't know why I should take it, sir," he said, "but there is no reason, after all, why I should say anything of what you have been talking about, downstairs."

Deane sat in his chair, waiting. There was a knock at the door and a chambermaid entered, to retire at once in confusion. Deane looked at her curiously. Something in her figure and her start had seemed familiar to him. He got up and rang the bell. In a moment or two a waiter appeared. He was obviously a German, dark and sallow. He spoke imperfect English, and there was a gleam of cupidity in his eyes which to Deane seemed hopeful.

"Bring me some tea at once," he ordered, — "nothing to eat."

The man departed, and reappeared in a few minutes.

"Anything else, sir?" he asked, after he had set down the tray.

Deane did not answer him directly. "By the way," he said finally, "wasn't there a murder committed in one of these rooms?"

"It was next door, sir," the man answered.

"The room is locked up?" Deane asked.

"Yes, sir!"

"That is a pity," Deane remarked. "Do you know who has the key? I should very much like just to have a look around."

The waiter shook his head. "The key is downstairs in Mr. Hartshorn's office, sir, and we have no duplicate here. The police who came, they desired that no one should enter the room until they had removed the effects to Scotland Yard."

"So I was told downstairs," Deane remarked. "Do you suppose," he continued, "that it would be possible to get hold of a duplicate key? I should like very much to see the interior of that room—if possible to take a photograph of it for my newspaper. I am willing to pay."

The waiter shook his head reluctantly. "I do not think that there is a duplicate key," he said, with his eyes fixed upon Deane's right hand.

"Perhaps you could make inquiries," Deane suggested smoothly. "I want to get a photograph of the inside of the room for my people, if possible. It would be worth quite a great deal of money."

The man was impressed. "I will go away and see," he said slowly.

"Keep this to yourself," Deane ordered. "I don't want it all over the hotel."

The man made a sign of assent and withdrew. Deane rang for the chambermaid. Once, twice, three times he rang, without response. Then a middle-aged person came shuffling in, very much out of breath. Deane gave her some trivial order.

"By the way," he asked, "are you the chambermaid who waits on this room?"

"No!" she answered, with some hesitation. "The regular chambermaid is down at her breakfast."

Deane nodded. "Will you tell her," he asked, "that I should like to see her as soon as she is up? I want to see about some laundry," he added.

The woman disappeared. Deane was left alone once more. He unpacked some books, and made himself comfortable in an easy-chair. He was not able even to descend to the smoking-room. Mr. Stirling Deane, it was well known, had left town for Scotland. Mr. B. Stocks, who had arrived at the hotel the night before and taken this room, was a person who had particular reasons for not desiring to be seen even in the precincts of the hotel. Deane settled himself down to read—a somewhat difficult task. By the time he had smoked several cigarettes, there was a soft tap at the door and the waiter reappeared.

"I beg your pardon, sir," he said.

"Go ahead," Deane answered.

"I have found a key in the service-room which I think would open Number 27."

Deane nodded. "Very well," he said, "let me have the use of it to-night, and I will give you twenty pounds."

The man moistened his lips with his tongue. Twenty pounds was a wonderful sum! But—!

"There is a good deal of risk about it, sir," the man said slowly, "and I have to divide with the night-porter, who told me where to find this key."

"Very well," Deane answered, "I will give you twenty pounds each,—no more."

The man placed the key silently in his hands, and Deane counted out eight five-pound notes.

"If I were you, sir," he said, "if you want to be alone in the room and be sure of no one seeing you, I should use it between four and five to-morrow morning. Everyone is off duty then except the night-porter."

Deane nodded. "By the way," he said, "do you know anything about the chambermaid on this floor—the young, slim one?"

The waiter shook his head. "She has only just come."

"Do you know her name?" asked Deane.

The man smiled. "It is always the same," he answered,—"always Mary."

"She would not be allowed in 27?" Deane asked. "She would not be likely to be there to clean it out, or anything of that sort?"'

The man shook his head again. "No one is allowed to enter it," he said. "No one has been in but the detectives and lawyers."

Deane dismissed the man and settled down once more to his reading. He found it difficult, however, to concentrate his thoughts. The key was on the chair by his side. It was all he could do to restrain himself from stealing down the corridor and commencing his search.

CHAPTER XIX
THE SEARCH

Deane remembered afterwards, with a painful exactness, every step which he took in his stockinged feet down the dimly-lit corridor. Only one of the electric lights had been left burning, and that one was encased in a shade of red glass, and was set in the wall facing him. A few seconds ago he had heard Big Ben strike four o'clock. For the last two hours he had sat in his room and waited. Time seemed to have stood still. In that two hours he had seen himself stripped of all his possessions, dishonored, friendless. He had seen himself married to Lady Olive, richer and more prosperous than ever, a successful politician, a man on whom the eyes of the world were turned always with respect and approval. Hope and fear had swung in his mind like the movement of a pendulum. All that he needed was that paper! If once he could see it burning into white ashes, or torn into a hundred pieces, he knew that there was nothing in the world strong enough to bar his progress.

Four o'clock at last! At the sound of the hour he had sprung to his feet. Before the echoes of the last stroke had died away he was absolutely committed to his enterprise. For a moment he stood outside the door of his room, which he had left ajar. He looked toward the main corridor and listened intently; there was no sound to be heard. The night watchman—if, indeed, he were making his rounds—was nowhere in that vicinity. In all the great hotel, not a soul seemed to be stirring.

Deane drew one long breath, and without a second's hesitation stole forward until he stood in front of Number 27. Once more he looked around him. The lights from all the transoms in sight had been extinguished. There was only that dimly burning electric light at the end of the corridor, to dissipate the gloom. He fitted the key into the lock and turned it. The door swung open. Deane closed it behind him, turned on the electric light, and gazed around him with fast beating heart. He was there at last! Within this room, if anywhere, was his salvation!

It was, after all, a very ordinary hotel apartment. There was a small single bed, a wardrobe, a toilet table and chest of drawers, a hard, uninviting-looking sofa, and an easy-chair with a stiff back, and armless. Upon the bed were laid out a number of articles of wearing apparel, and upon the floor were two empty portmanteaus. Upon the dressing-table were a number of papers, arranged with some appearance of method. The toilet things were still in their places. Everything was arranged in a stiff and precise condition. It was evident that official hands had been at work.

Deane's rapid glance around lasted barely a few seconds. Then he moved toward the dressing-table and commenced a careful search amongst the papers there. One by one he glanced them through, — a bill for clothes, a restaurant account, half-a-dozen counterfoils of theatre and music-hall tickets, an account for wines and cigars consumed on the steamer Arizona, homeward bound from Cape Town. There was the address of a manicurist, a programme of the Empire. Very soon Deane had come to the end of them. From the first to the last, there was not a single document there of any interest or importance.

He turned away toward the clothes which were laid out upon the bed. One by one he lifted them up and laid them down again, until he came to the gray suit which the man Sinclair had been wearing on the day when he had made his eventful visit to the city. Deane held up the coat, and a little exclamation almost escaped from his lips as he saw where in a certain place the lining showed signs of stitching, as though something had been sewn inside the pocket. He thrust his hand there. There was an opening, but it was empty! He tried the other side, but in vain. Then he began slowly to realize that this search of his was doomed to end in failure. There was nowhere else to look. He glanced at his watch. Although it seemed to him that he had been in the little room for hours, he had indeed been there for barely five minutes.

He moved toward the door, opened it softly, and listened outside in the corridor. There was no sound of anyone stirring, no sign of life or movement anywhere. He returned to the room and renewed his search. One by one he lifted up the different articles of clothing and felt in the pockets. His search was rewarded with the discovery of a single halfpenny in an odd waistcoat pocket. He left the clothes alone then and went through the papers once more, with a similar lack of success. Softly he opened all the drawers, ransacked the wardrobe, searched every inch of the room. When at last he desisted, it was because there was nowhere else to look, nothing else to attempt. He stood up in the middle of the room and drew a little breath. He had found nothing, nothing had transpired to compensate in any way for the risk which he had run. Yet there was one consolation. It was scarcely possible that Ruby Sinclair could be more successful than he. The paper which might make her fortune and ruin him was not here.

Deane turned at last toward the door. There was no need for him to prolong the risk he ran. He would return to his room, and leave the hotel later in the morning.

He took a few cautious steps toward the door. Suddenly he stopped short and held his breath. Very slowly he turned his head, and listened intently. Someone was stirring in the next room. There was a connecting door, hidden by a curtain, and even as he stood there he heard the handle shake as though it were being turned. He leaned forward and turned out the electric light. Standing there in the darkness he distinctly heard a key inserted in the lock of the hidden door. He heard it softly opened and the curtain pushed back. There was someone else in the room, someone else whom he could not see, someone else who also took an interest in the effects of the murdered man!

There was an interval of several seconds—it seemed minutes—it might well have been hours. Then the stealthy footsteps came towards him. A little stiff rustle of draperies proclaimed the sex of the intruder. Without a second's warning, the electric light flashed out all over the room. The girl would have screamed, but Deane, who was prepared, leaned forward, and his hand suddenly closed over her mouth. She looked at him with dilated eyes.

"You!" she exclaimed. "You!"

"Good God!" he answered. "Winifred Rowan!"

Their mutual surprise was something paralyzing. They drew apart and looked at one another as they might have done at ghosts.

"What do you want here?" he asked hoarsely.

Was it his fancy, he wondered, or did her lips curl for a moment in something like mockery?

"I came to repay a debt," she whispered. "I came to find the paper which you are afraid may fall into someone else's hands. I came to search for it, but it is not here."

"And I," Deane answered.

"You have found it, perhaps?" she exclaimed.

He shook his head. "It has gone!"

"Perhaps he never had it," she whispered.

Deane shook his head. He was being led away by the excitement, the tenseness of the moment,—the unexpectedness of the whole situation. "He showed it to me," he answered, "only just before that night."

"Ah!"

The monosyllable seemed to leave her lips dry. She moistened them with her tongue, and moved a little towards him. There was something in her face which he could not recognize. And then, before further speech was possible, they heard something which, coming so unexpectedly against such a background of silence, terrified them both. An electric bell somewhere close at hand was ringing out its sharp summons into the night.

"What is that?" Deane asked quickly.

"Someone is ringing from one of the numbers opposite," she answered. "Get back to your room quickly. They have heard us talking. Someone will be in here to search."

"But you?" he objected.

"I am safe," she answered. "I am on duty on this floor. I have something to do in the next room. Quick!"

He slipped from the door. The little side corridor was as yet empty. For a second or two he listened intently. There were no footsteps as yet audible in the main corridor. In half-a-dozen swift strides he reached the door of his own room, turned the handle, and passed inside. Almost immediately there were footsteps in the corridor outside. The bell of the room opposite was answered. Again silence! The seconds grew into minutes, and the minutes passed away. Then his door was suddenly opened from the outside, softly and silently. Winifred Rowan stood there on the threshold of his room, with the handle of the door still in her hand, and to his fancy there was something ominous in the way she looked at him.

"You need search no more," she said. "I have found the paper."

He held out his hand. "The reward is yours!" he declared.

She drew away from him. "I shall claim it very soon," she said. "Ring your bell at seven o'clock, when I shall be on duty, and I will bring it to you. Hush!"

She glided away and closed the door. Deane drew a long breath. So it was over, then, — over, and he had won!

CHAPTER XX
IN DOUBT

Punctually at seven o'clock next morning Deane rang his bell. Once more the fat old lady entered, with her amiable smile and slow movements.

"Some tea, sir?" she asked.

Deane looked at her for a moment without speaking. "When does the other chambermaid come on duty?" he asked.

"She ought to be on now," was the answer, "but she hasn't come. I've just sent the 'boots' up to her room."

Deane ordered some hot water and lay still for half-an-hour. Then he rang the bell again. The same woman came.

"Would you like your tea, sir?" she asked.

"If you please," he answered.

She was already half-way out of the door before he stopped her.

"You are still on duty, then?" he said.

"The other chambermaid can't be found, sir," she answered. "Her bed hasn't been slept in, and she doesn't seem to be anywhere about the place."

Deane nodded. It was, after all, perhaps the most sensible thing she could do to get clear away! "Send me my tea at eight o'clock," he ordered, "and let me have a bath at once."

"The valet shall come and tell you when it is ready, sir," she answered.

He passed a tip across to the woman, who accepted it. "Tell the waiter when he brings the tea to give me my bill," he said.

In an hour's time Deane had left the hotel. He had seen nothing more of Winifred Rowan, and on the whole he was disposed to applaud her precaution. He drove at once to his rooms, where Grant, his man, was already installed.

"I shall catch the mid-day train to Scotland, Grant," he announced. "Telephone up for seats and sleeping-berths. Also telephone to the office, and tell them to ring up here at once if a young lady should make any inquiries for me. Perhaps they had better send her on here."

He went out and did some shopping. The sun was shining, and a soft west wind blowing. London, which seems to hold its populace longer than any other great city, was gay, almost joyous. He had to elbow his way through crowds as he passed along Piccadilly. The streets and shops were thronged. The sky above was blue. The rare sunshine seemed to make cheerful even this most sombre of cities.

Deane had the feeling of a man who has escaped from a great danger,—who has been able to throw off a heavy weight. This miserable document of Sinclair's was as good as in his possession! After all, Basil Rowan was not suffering in vain. The girl should have every penny that he had promised her brother! Her way in life should be made easy! It was a very small price, indeed, to be free from such torture as he had suffered during the last few weeks. He bought presents a little recklessly—presents for Olive—something, too, for Winifred Rowan, a gold cigarette-case for himself. He ordered a great basket of flowers to take with him to Scotland, and paid a visit to his gunmaker's. Then he returned to his chambers, fully expecting to have some news of Winifred Rowan.

"Any one rung up?" he asked his man.

"No one, sir, of any importance," was the answer.

"Did you ask the office about Miss Rowan?"

"No young lady at all has inquired for you there, sir," Grant answered.

Deane was a little surprised, but after all what did it matter? He travelled up to Scotland with a lighter heart than he had carried for months. Lady Olive, who met him early in the morning at the small wayside station which was nearest to her father's seat, was amazed at his vivacity.

"I expected to find you a pale, worn-out thing," she remarked, as their motor-car climbed the white, stone-bordered road which crossed the heather-covered mountain. "You don't look as though you needed a change at all."

"I've found so swift a tonic, you see," he answered, pressing her hand.

She laughed gayly. This was more the man as he had been before the days of their engagement! "I think it is the smell of the powder," she said. "You men are all like schoolboys for your holidays. Father says that the birds are much too wild, and that it will be all even you can do to hit them."

Deane smiled. "There is nothing in the world," he answered, "which I want to do so much as to lie up there in the heather and close my eyes, and feel the sun and the wind."

"In other words," she said, "you are lazy!"

"Is that laziness?" he asked. "I don't think so."

"Rest, then," she said.

"Ah! That is a very different thing!" he replied. "We all need rest."

"Especially you," she said, "who carry about with you always the memory of some things from which you can never escape."

He looked at her quickly, but it was obvious that her speech was wholly unpremeditated.

"I often wonder," she said calmly, "when I see you in the evenings, how you manage to shake off all your anxieties so easily, for I suppose," she continued, "that success, like everything else, carries always its anxieties."

"Sometimes more than failure," he answered.

"Well," she continued, "it doesn't seem possible to associate the word 'failure' with you. Some day you must tell me the whole story of your life. I can scarcely believe that there has ever been a time when you haven't succeeded in anything you undertook."

He laughed grimly. "You should have been with me in Africa," he said, "after the fighting was over. We expected to go about picking up gold almost on the streets."

"You were too sanguine," she laughed.

"It was hard enough work to live," he answered. "I tried many things, — failures, all of them!"

"Until the Little Anna Gold-Mine," she remarked.

"Until the Little Anna Gold-Mine," he assented, "and that, at first, seemed hopeless enough. The mine had been deserted twice. The natives there had a name for it which means the Grave of Dead Hopes!"

They turned into the avenue, and the house was at once visible, standing on the edge of a lake, large and a little bare. The lawns and gardens were brilliant with color, and the hills on the other side of the water were purple with heather.

"Well, here is all the rest you want," she said. "We haven't a neighbor within six miles, and a most harmless lot of guests."

He drew a long sigh of content. The tragedy, indeed, of the last few weeks seemed to lie far behind in some other world!

CHAPTER XXI
RUBY IS DISAPPOINTED

The solicitor hung up his silk hat, motioned his two visitors to seats, and took his accustomed place in front of his writing-table. "I am afraid," he said, turning toward Mr. Sarsby, but in reality addressing his niece, "that your visit to town has been, in some respects, a disappointment to you, especially," he continued, "bearing in mind the letter which you, my dear young lady, have just shown me. Still, there is no getting away from facts. We have carefully examined every paper and every portion of the personal belongings of the deceased, and I am afraid we must come to the decision that there is nothing in those effects worth taking away."

"It certainly seems not," Mr. Sarsby assented. "I must say that from the first I have discouraged my niece in her expectations. I never knew Sinclair, but everyone spoke of him as being a shiftless and impossible sort of person."

The lawyer nodded. "From the state of his effects," he remarked, "that seems very possible, and yet one cannot help wondering what it was that he had in his mind when he wrote to your niece, — what it was, too, that induced him to take rooms in a hotel like the Universal."

Ruby Sinclair rose slowly to her feet. She came to the table before which the solicitor was seated, and she looked down at him with blazing eyes. "Can't you see, you two," she exclaimed, — "can't you understand that the man has been robbed of something? He would never have written me in that strain if he had not believed that he possessed something which was at any rate worth money, and a great deal of money. He would never, with only twenty pounds in his pocket, have gone to a hotel like the Universal, drunk champagne there, and lived as though his means were unlimited. These things are ridiculous!"

"But, my dear young lady," the lawyer commenced, —

"Can't you see the truth?" she exclaimed. "My uncle was murdered. Why? What was the motive? Robbery! Do you think that it was for the sake of the twenty pounds or so that he had on him, and which were found untouched? The man Rowan was in South Africa with my uncle, — he knew his business. It was no ordinary quarrel, this. I tell you that Rowan robbed my uncle of something — I don't know what — but something which was the backbone of this letter!" she exclaimed, dashing it upon the table, — "something which justified him in staying at the Universal, something which must be found!"

The lawyer nodded. "That point of view," he admitted, "has occurred to me, I must confess. And yet, you must remember that the man Rowan was arrested upon the premises. He had nothing with him which could by any chance have belonged to the dead man."

The girl stamped her foot impatiently. "Have you read the evidence at the trial?" she asked. "It is very clear that this man Rowan was no fool. Whatever he wanted from my uncle, he secured and disposed of before he was arrested. The last thing he would do would be to carry about with him on his person anything which he had taken from my uncle."

"What you suggest may be possible, of course," the lawyer remarked, "but, unfortunately, we have not the slightest indication of it. The man Rowan was not seen to speak to anyone in the hotel, and it is known that he did not leave it after the quarrel until his arrest."

"And you are content to leave it like that?" the girl asked.

The lawyer shrugged his shoulders. "It is not that we are content," he said, a little stiffly, "but there certainly seems to be no cause for any further action."

The girl turned to Mr. Sarsby. "We had better go," she said abruptly. "There is nothing to be gained by staying here."

The solicitor accompanied them to the door. "Miss Sinclair," he said, "I can sympathize with your disappointment, but I do beg of you not to go looking for a mare's nest. It is disappointing, of course, to find that your uncle was practically a pauper, especially after that letter of his, but, on the other hand, men in his position, I am afraid, are proverbially given to exaggeration."

"Thank you," the girl said sharply, "I think that we will not talk about this any more."

Mr. Sarsby and his niece walked slowly up a little side street which led into the Strand. The former, who was sharing to some extent his niece's disappointment, found compensation in the thought of a speedy return to Rakney.

"I am afraid, Ruby," he said, "that you are very much disappointed, and it seems to me that we have wasted our railway fares to London. It can't be helped. We may as well make the best of it and get back at once. I can see no reason why we should not catch the three o'clock train. I shall be able to play my match, then, with Colonel Forsitt to-morrow morning."

"You can go and play your match if you want to," the girl answered. "I am going to stay in London."

"To stay in London?" Mr. Sarsby repeated.

"I mean it," the girl answered. "I don't mean to be robbed. I mean to stay here and find out why this man Rowan quarrelled with my uncle, and what my uncle meant when he wrote to me about a fortune. You go back, if you like," she continued. "Give me five pounds to stay here with, and I'll come back when I've found out the truth."

Mr. Sarsby was aghast. He looked at his niece with wide-open eyes. What had come to her that she should speak of such a sum as five pounds almost carelessly!

"I shall do nothing of the sort," he answered decidedly, "nor shall I allow you to stay up here alone—a most improper proceeding, I should call it,—quite unheard of. We will go back to the hotel, pay our bill, have a little lunch at an A B C shop, and catch the three o'clock train home."

"If you won't let me have the five pounds," she answered, "all right. Good-bye!"

She turned abruptly away, and before his astonished eyes plunged into the stream of traffic, making for the other side of the street. He followed her as soon as he saw a safe opening, and found her on the point of entering a small restaurant.

"My dear Ruby," he exclaimed sharply, "you are mad! How dared you leave me like that?"

She shrugged her shoulders. "I have been mad," she answered, "to live that awful life down at Rakney for these last few years. I've had enough of it, uncle. I am here, and I am going to stay here. If I can't succeed in what I am going to undertake, I shall try and find some work."

Mr. Sarsby gasped. It was a wholly unexpected revolt. "You mean to say that you don't want to come back to Rakney?"

"Never, if I can help it!" the girl answered. "I hate the place. I hate the life. I am tired, sick to death of it all!" she cried passionately, "and I would as soon come up here and live for a week or two, and then throw myself into the Thames, as go on with it any longer. If you won't let me have the five pounds," she continued, "I have enough jewelry with me to fetch about that. The money would only mean a week or two longer."

"But where would you live?" he exclaimed. "What would you do?"

"That is my affair," she answered simply. "First of all, though, I should go to Mr. Deane, and I should ask him to help me. Any man of common sense would agree with me at once in believing that my uncle was robbed."

"But your aunt?" Mr. Sarsby exclaimed weakly.

"My aunt can get on very well without me," the girl declared.

Mr. Sarsby felt that a situation had arisen with which he was unable to cope. The only thing that occurred to him to do was to temporize. "You will have to come back to the hotel," he said, "to get your luggage. We will talk it over on the way there."

"Just as you please," the girl answered carelessly, "only so far as I am concerned, there is nothing to talk over."

Mr. Sarsby hailed a 'bus which deposited them presently within a few yards of the semi-private hotel in Montague Street at which they were staying. It was one of those establishments which, from being a small boarding-house, had blossomed out into a hotel, with all the outward signs of its more prosperous rivals. There was an entrance hall, a reception office, and two long-limbed giants in light blue livery, who spoke every language except their own. The people who frequented it were either Americans, or people from the isolated country places, such as Mr. Sarsby and his niece.

"I am not going to talk anything over until I have had some lunch," the girl declared. "We need not go out. It is only eighteenpence each here. You can afford that, especially as you are probably going to be rid of me forever."

Mr. Sarsby frowned. "We will lunch here if you prefer it," he said. "I am not aware that I have hesitated at anything on the score of expense."

The girl laughed. There was a note in her mirth which was strange to Mr. Sarsby. He relinquished his well-worn silk hat to a boy in buttons, straightened his old-fashioned tie before a passing mirror, and led the girl into the dining-room. The size of the apartment, the number of the waiters, the indefinable sense of being in a great city, which had oppressed him since the train had rolled into the terminus on his arrival, once more had its effect upon him. He felt sure that his niece understood nothing of what she was talking about. He drank bottled beer with his lunch, and soon summoned up courage to reopen the matter.

"It was a very good idea of yours, my dear Ruby," he said, "to lunch here. I am sure that for the money it is a most excellent meal."

She gave vent to a little interjection which might have meant anything. If he had not been so sure that she was unused to such magnificence, he would have believed that it was intended to indicate a certain amount of contempt at her entertainment.

"And now," Mr. Sarsby continued, "let me speak to you seriously."

The suggestion that there had been anything of mirth from which Mr. Sarsby desired to lead the way appealed to the girl's sense of humor. Her lips parted, and the sullen discontent of her face was for a moment lightened.

"Very well," she said, "let us be serious. Go on. Tell me what you have to say."

"What I want to put before you is briefly this," he declared. "You do not understand the impossibility of a young girl barely twenty years old, with your"—he coughed a little—"personal attractions, being left alone in London. Of course, it is difficult for me to explain to you exactly what I mean."

"You needn't," the girl interrupted contemptuously. "Do you think that I am a fool? I know all about those risks which people speak about with bated breath, and I should like you to know that I am quite able to take care of myself. I am not afraid, so I do not know why anyone need be afraid for me."

Mr. Sarsby looked at her and wondered where amongst the wastes and wind-swept places of his lonely home had the girl acquired the knowledge which she alluded to so scornfully,—had she learned, too, he reflected, to carry herself, as she had done since their arrival, with an ease and assurance which he had tried in vain to emulate. He realized at that moment that all further argument would be wasted. Nevertheless, he continued to ease his conscience.

"You may know a good deal," he said, "or think you do,—girls nowadays read and talk of most surprising things,—but London is not a safe place for a young girl, whatever you may say, especially a young girl without enough money to live on."

"I suppose," she said, laughing at him openly, "that Rakney is a safe place. Well, I have tried it for a good many years, and I have had enough. You needn't be afraid," she continued, "that I shall return to Rakney in the guise of a prodigal daughter. If I don't succeed in tracing Richard Sinclair's fortune, I shall find something else to do. If you will give me the five pounds I ask for, it will make things easier. If not, I shall get on without it."

He felt that he was being weak. Even his conscience told him that greater firmness was necessary. And yet he recognized something in the girl's demeanor which assured him absolutely that any protests were hopeless. There was a hidden strength there, shared by neither her aunt nor himself,—something which kept her apart from them,—which made him half believe, in spite of himself, that what she set herself to do she would accomplish.

"At least," he said, "we must know where you are going to live."

"There is no need for you to stay in London," she answered, "while I look about for a room. I know exactly the sort of place I am going to take. I am going out in the Tube to one of the suburbs, where a bedroom is not very expensive, and I shall take my meals out. It will cost me very little to live, and five pounds will go quite a long way.

By the time it is spent, I think that I shall have discovered something. I will not write you for any more money, I promise."

Mr. Sarsby sighed. "I suppose you must have your own way," he said. "I don't know what your aunt will say."

She laughed. They had finished their luncheon and had risen from the table. "Enough about my aunt," she said. "She will have all the anxiety of her preserves upon her mind directly, and I think she will be glad not to be bothered with me. You catch your three o'clock train, and play your golf match to-morrow."

"I suppose I may as well," he said weakly, "although I never can putt after a railway journey."

"Go and try, anyhow," she answered. "We will say good-bye to one another here, if you don't mind. The porter will take care of my luggage until I have taken my room."

"I suppose if I were to stay up with you for a few days," he began, —

"Please, uncle, don't!" she began firmly. "It isn't any use. You have been kind to me in your way, but the life at Rakney is horrible to me. I have made up my mind to have no more of it. You've done your best for me, you can't do more. Good-bye! There is your bag, and you haven't too much time to catch the three o'clock train. Take the first turn to the left from here, and book to King's Cross by the Tube. Good-bye!"

Mr. Sarsby picked up his bag and departed without any further protest. The girl stood upon the steps and watched him, and as she watched, some of the darkness seemed to pass away from her face. He disappeared around the corner. She was alone—free, at any rate! She drew a long breath, and the dull streets and gray sky seemed suddenly to have become like the walls and canopy of a new paradise.

BOOK TWO

CHAPTER I
FREE TO DIE

At about quarter past ten in the morning, a man, still young, but deathly pale, with hollow cheeks and receding eyes, stood on the edge of the pavement outside a great and gloomy-looking building. A nail-studded door had just been opened and closed to let him pass. The attendant, who wore prison livery, leaned forward curiously to look at him as he walked out with uncertain footsteps. The prison doctor stood by his side and called a four-wheel cab.

"You are sure," he said, "that you have somewhere to go to, Rowan?"

"Quite sure, sir," the man answered.

"Keep your courage up, my man," added the doctor. "If your friends can afford it, go down to the South at once. You will find it easier there. There's your cab. You have some money, have you not?"

"Plenty, thank you, doctor," Rowan answered. "You've been kind to me, sir," he added. "Thank you!"

"There wasn't much I could do," the doctor answered, helping him into the cab, "except to get you out of this hole. Make the most of your time now. Good luck to you!"

The cab rolled off. Rowan, after the first few minutes' exhaustion, due to his unaccustomed preparations, leaned forward on the seat, looking out with hungry, wistful eyes upon the world which he had scarcely hoped to see again. Very soon the full flood of London traffic was flowing past him, the streams of men and women jostling one another upon the pavements, the long, tangled thread of moving vehicles, taximeter cabs, hansoms, and wagons. The sun was shining, the faces of the people seemed to him, accustomed to the white, hopeless countenances of the men he had passed in his daily exercises and in the prison infirmary, unusually buoyant and cheerful. It was a glad world, this, into which he had come, a world which he was so soon to leave. It was hard to think he was free only that he might crawl away into some corner where he could die.

The cab stopped at last before a block of offices in a by-street of the city. Rowan reluctantly alighted, and crossing the pavement entered the building. He passed through a swing door to a desk. A small boy poked his head out of an inquiry office.

"Can you tell me if Miss Rowan is employed here?" Rowan asked.

"Yes, but you can't see her," the small boy answered. "She's in with the guv'nor now."

Rowan hesitated. "Perhaps you will kindly tell her, when she is disengaged," he said, "that her brother is here, and would like to speak to her for a moment."

The office-boy withdrew his head, but he seemed uncertain. Rowan seated himself upon a hard bench set against the wall. On a small round table in front of him were pens and paper and a copy of the trade journal. Rowan turned over its pages listlessly for a moment or two, and then set himself down to wait. It was quite half-an-hour before a door in front of him opened, and Winifred Rowan appeared. She looked at her brother in blank astonishment. She was paler than ever, there were dark rings under her dilated eyes. She looked at him as one looks upon some strange monstrosity.

"Basil!" she murmured. "It can't be you! And yet—Basil!"

"It is I," he answered.

"Free?" she cried.

He laughed, a little bitterly. "They have let me out to die," he answered. "The doctor to-day signed a certificate that I have no reasonable chance of living longer than another month, so here I am, free, Winifred, if you like to call it freedom."

She came and sat on the bench by his side. At that moment it was hard to say, from their appearance, which of the two seemed the nearer death.

"When were you released?" she asked.

"Half-an-hour ago," he answered. "I came straight here. I wondered whether you could get a month's vacation, and come with me somewhere south. We have enough money for a little time."

"If they will not let me go," she answered, "I will leave. That is simple enough. We have enough money, Basil. We will go this afternoon."

He shook his head. "First," he said, "I must see — I must see —"

"Whom?" she asked.

"A friend," he answered, "someone who may be inclined to do something for me, — not for myself," he added hastily, — "that, of course, is ridiculous — but it is of you I am thinking, of you after I am gone."

"I shall be all right, Basil," she said. "We have several hundred pounds left, you know."

"It is not enough," he answered firmly. "Winifred, will you go on an errand for me?"

"Where to?" she asked, with a sudden sinking of her heart.

"To a man whose address I will give you, — a rich man, a great man. I think that he will be willing to do something for us. His name is Stirling Deane. I will write his address down for you."

"Mr. Deane!" she repeated. "I have been before to see him, Basil. I went before your reprieve came."

"Of course," he said. "I had forgotten. Well, I want you to go up to him now. I want to see him, but I do not want to go to his offices. Where do you live, Winifred?"

"It is an apartment house for women only," she answered. "I cannot take you there."

"Then we must go to a hotel," he said. "It seems a mockery to buy clothes, but there are one or two things I must have. To-morrow we will go somewhere south."

She glanced at the clock. "I will see whether I can get away now," she said.

She disappeared, and came out again in a few minutes with her hat on. "Come," she said.

He led her to the cab outside. "We will drive to a hotel," he said. "When we have taken some rooms, you shall go and see Mr. Deane. I think that he will come to me if you will tell him that I am free, that I have only three weeks to live, and that I should like to see him."

"Very well," she answered.

They stepped into the cab. "Tell him to drive to one of the large hotels," Rowan said, — "any except the Universal."

She shuddered as she gave the order. She, too, had her memories of the Universal, of which he knew nothing. Slowly they made their way westwards. The girl held his hand in hers.

"It is good to see you again, Basil," she said.

"It is good to be here again," he answered, "to be out in the world, even though it be to die. I suppose the authorities have really been kind to me. It is as much as anyone could expect. And yet, Winifred, I should like you to remember this always. The quarrel between Sinclair and myself was of his seeking — not mine. The blow of which he died was struck purely in self-defence. I could box and he couldn't, or he would have half killed me that night."

"I know," she answered breathlessly. "Don't talk of it."

He went on, as though not hearing her. "He came at me with both hands clenched, and I hit him under the chin. I had to, or he would have killed me if he could. He was a strong man, and he had been drinking until he was half mad. It was not my fault, Winifred."

"Oh, I know that!" she said. "Try and forget it now. It was a wicked, wicked accident."

"Life has been wicked enough for you and me lately," he answered, sighing. "You are worn to a shadow, Winifred. I suppose it is this wretched typing, day by day. We must put an end to it."

She shook her head. "I must earn a living, dear," she said. "But don't bother about me. I shall be all right. See, he has stopped. This must be — yes, it is the Grand Hotel. Will that do?"

He nodded. "Quite well," he answered.

He paid the cabman, and making some excuse at the office about luggage to come, took rooms. Then he put Winifred into a hansom, and wrote down for her Deane's address, which she already knew.

"Bring him back with you if you can," he begged. "Bring him back here. I shall be waiting in the reading-room, just round the corner there to the right."

She hesitated. "You look so faint, Basil," she said. "I am not sure whether I ought to leave you."

"I am going to have some brandy and milk," he answered. "I am going to sit down and have it there in that corner. I shall wait till you come. You will know where to look for me. Hurry, dear, please. I shall know no peace until I have seen Deane."

CHAPTER II
A LAPSE OF MEMORY

Deane sat at his desk, immersed once more in the affairs of his great business. His cheeks were bronzed with the sun and heather-scented wind. His eyes were clear and bright. All traces of the unsettlement of those few nervous weeks seemed to have passed away. One thing only occasionally disturbed him — the non-appearance of Winifred Rowan. Since those few seconds of tremulous excitement when they had stood face to face in the darkened room of the hotel, he had neither seen nor heard from her. He could understand her having left the hotel hurriedly. He could have understood her keeping away for a day or two. But a whole month had passed, and she had taken no steps whatever to communicate with him. He had left exact instructions as to what was to be done should she come to the office while he was in Scotland. He had had the whole of his private letters forwarded, lest by chance a word from her should fail to reach him. There was something a little ominous in this absolute silence, something which troubled him occasionally, which set him thinking, wondering, whether under that still, quiet demeanor there might be qualities of which he had taken no account, — whether indeed she, too, were not a schemer who meant to make the most of this opportunity which chance had thrown in her way.

A clerk entered and stood at his side. "A young lady is here to see you, sir," he announced, — "Miss Rowan."

"Miss Rowan," Deane repeated mechanically.

"Yes, sir!" the clerk answered. "We have instructions outside to let you know if she called at any time."

Deane leaned back in his chair. With a few quick words he dismissed his secretary from the immediate business in hand. "You may show Miss Rowan in," he said.

A moment or two later she entered. Deane watched her with a new curiosity as he rose to his feet. She was as quietly dressed as usual, as pale, and her eyes, except for one upward glance, seemed always to be seeking the carpet. There was something curiously negative about her appearance, — something, it seemed to him, almost wilfully so. The rich brown hair, which had flashed almost to golden in the morning sunlight at Rakney, was drawn up and concealed, as though the owner's sole object was that it might escape attention. Her clothes were not unbecoming, but they were the quietest of their sort. Her eyes, which should have been beautiful, were so perpetually veiled and hidden that their quality was lost. Both physically and in her reticent speech she appealed to him more than ever that morning as a woman whose desire seemed to be to creep through life unnoticed.

"At last!" he remarked, holding out his hand pleasantly. "I have been expecting to see you for some time, Miss Rowan."

"You have been expecting to see me?" she repeated, raising her eyes to his. "How strange!"

"Why strange?" he answered, glancing around the room, and lowering his voice a little. "Don't you remember at our last meeting you promised to bring my tea a few hours later? Since then, I have not even seen you, nor have you sent me a line."

She raised her eyes again and looked at him. They were very beautiful eyes, but he did not understand the somewhat blank expression which shone out of them. "I do not understand you," she said quietly.

Deane would have been irritated, but something in her manner struck him as so strange that his feeling turned to one of bewilderment. "Come," he said, "you are not going to suggest that I have been dreaming, or that you have had one of these fashionable lapses of memory? You remember meeting me in that room in the Universal Hotel?"

Without change of countenance or expression she answered, "I have never been in the Universal Hotel in my life!"

Deane looked at her, his lips a little parted, and as he looked his feeling of bewilderment grew. "My dear young lady," he protested, "do you mean to tell me—"

"You have been mistaking me for someone else, I think," she said calmly. "There are so many people about who are like me. We will not talk of this just now, if you do not mind. I have come to you from my brother."

"Well?" said Deane.

"My brother is free," she went on. "He was released at nine o'clock this morning. The doctor at the prison signed a certificate that he has only a month or so to live. He is free on the understanding that he goes away to some quiet place. He came to me an hour ago. It is at his wish that I am here."

"Go on," Deane rapped out.

"He wishes to see you," she said. "That is all. He does not think that there is any risk about it, under the circumstances. We are staying for the night at the Grand Hotel. To-morrow we shall go down to Devonshire or Cornwall. He will be glad if you will come and see him as soon as possible."

"I will come," Deane said, "but first, Miss Rowan, I must have an understanding with you."

"An understanding with me?" she repeated slowly.

"Naturally," he answered. "I want to know, first of all, whether you are my friend or my enemy, — whether, in short, you mean to play the blackmailer, or whether you mean to return to me that document which you abstracted from amongst Sinclair's effects."

She drew a little sigh. "I am quite sure now, Mr. Deane," she said, "that you are mistaking me for someone else. I do not know what you are talking about."

Deane was silent for several moments. He was feeling nervous and disturbed. There was something uncanny about this quiet, persistent denial, — the still face, the steadfast, beautiful eyes, which seemed yet like unlit fires devoid of sympathy or apprehension.

"I scarcely know," Deane said, "how we are to continue this discussion. For some reason or other, you are sitting there within a few feet of me and denying something which we both know to be the truth. You have a motive, I suppose, but whatever that motive may be, you cannot imperil it by speaking openly here. We are absolutely alone. There is not a soul within hearing. You and I both know, Miss

Rowan, that you hold that paper to obtain which your brother risked his life and met with such misfortune. It would be his wish, I know, that you should give it to me. The terms I offered him for its recovery were surely liberal. If you think otherwise, tell me your price. We are alone. You are not giving yourself away. Tell me your price!"

"I have no price, Mr. Deane," she said, "because I have no paper. I am not a thief, nor have I stolen anything from anybody. All that you say is strange to me. My brother is waiting, and he is very ill. Will you come with me now, or will you follow as soon as you can?"

Deane leaned back in his chair and laughed. It was not altogether a natural laugh, but it was the only relief he could find from his overwrought feelings. "What sort of a game you and I are going to play, Miss Rowan, I cannot imagine," he said. "I have made the first and the obvious move, and you have declared your opening. We must let it go at that, I suppose. When you are disposed to talk common sense, I and my cheque-book will be glad to listen to you. In the meantime, let me beg of you one thing, and that is, keep that paper in some safe place!"

She rose to her feet with a little sigh. "You are mistaking me for someone else, Mr. Deane," she said.

He crossed the room and fetched his hat and gloves from a cupboard. He glanced into a looking-glass for a moment to straighten his tie, and met the girl's eyes fixed upon him. He stood quite still, watching. She was looking at him, at his back, as he stood there. There was expression in her face at last, an expression which puzzled him, which he failed altogether to understand. He stood quite still, with his fingers still upon the sailor knot of his tie. As though she realized the possibilities of the mirror, she suddenly turned around. When he came towards her, the mask, if it was a mask, was there once more.

"If you will come with me," said he, "I should be glad to go and see your brother."

They passed through the offices side by side. Many curious eyes followed them. Deane paused at one or two of the desks to leave a few parting instructions. Then he handed the girl into the electric brougham which was waiting at the door.

"The Grand Hotel," he told the man.

He got in and seated himself by her side. "Miss Rowan," he said, "you are beginning to interest me exceedingly."

"I am sure that you cannot be in earnest," she answered, without turning her head. "I am a most uninteresting person, living a most uninteresting life."

"I think you said that you were a typist," he remarked.

"I am," she answered. "I am employed by Messrs. Rubicon & Moore in St. Mary's Passage. I have been there for three years."

"With occasional holidays," he remarked, with a smile.

She shook her head. "The only holiday I have taken," she answered, "was when I came to see you."

He deliberately leaned forward to look into her face. The memory of that moment when he had held her in his arms, the breaking of the storm, the thrill, the wonderful, unanalyzed excitement which seemed to play about them like the lightning which was soon to flash across the sea and land, came back to him. He looked deliberately into her face, — still as the grave, — at the large eyes, which were listlessly fixed upon the streaming people.

"You are the most amazing person!" he said softly. "Perhaps, as you were never at the Hotel Universal, you were never in Rakney? Perhaps it was not you who came to me with the storm, who tapped at my window, who stood there like the daughter of the storm itself, who — "

"It was I who came to Rakney," she said. "You know that very well, Mr. Deane. Neither have I forgotten it. But I think that you should not remind me just now of that."

Of course she was right, but Deane felt a little unhinged. Her invulnerability was maddening. "Perhaps not," he answered. "Perhaps I have no right to remind you of that night, of the time when you crept in from the storm, crept into my arms."

She turned her head slightly away, as though interested in the passing throng. No flush of color tinged her cheeks. Her straight, firm lips never trembled. He tried to take her hand, — small it was, and encased in old, neatly-mended gloves. She drew it quietly but firmly away. She remained silent.

"Perhaps I have no right," he continued, "to remind you of these things, but neither have you the right to deny our later meeting. You are playing some sort of a game with me," he continued, a little roughly, "and your methods, whatever they may be, include a lie. Therefore, I myself take license."

"If you have quite finished, Mr. Deane," she said, "I should be glad. My visit to you, and all the circumstances connected with it, is one of the things which I wish to forget."

"To relegate to the same place in your memory," he remarked, "as your brief essay in the rôle of a chambermaid."

She leaned out of the window. "Here we are," she remarked. "I am anxious about my brother. Please hurry."

CHAPTER III
A PAINFUL INTERVIEW

Rowan sat still in his corner, and although the hotel could not be called fashionable—perhaps, in these later days, scarcely luxurious—the little ebb and flow of life upon which he looked seemed tinged with a peculiar bitterness. His hollow eyes followed each group of these men and women, so full of vivacity, of happiness, of affairs. The envy in his heart was like a real and passionate thing. It was an envy scarcely founded upon comparisons. For them was life,—for him was none! In front of him always was that ghastly, unchanging verdict: a month—two at the most—thirty days of ill-health, of suffering, of weakness, and after that—what? He caught his breath with a little shudder, and calling a passing waiter, ordered some brandy. He looked around and longed to find someone to speak to, someone to occupy his attention for a single moment, to stop the flow of gruesome fancies which seemed always biting their way into his brain. He had faced death readily enough in those old days, when Deane and he had ridden side by side, and the bullets had whizzed around them like rain, and the dead men lay in heaps. But this was different! The blood ran warm in their veins then, their hearts were strong. He had no strength now to battle with these fancies, no strength to do anything but cower before the slowly coming, grisly shadow of his fate. He looked continually at the door, longing always for the return of his sister and the coming of Deane. Even the prison hospital was better than this.

A girl passed by, young and beautiful, carrying in her arms a little dog. She threw a compassionate glance at Rowan, and he felt the sweat break out upon his forehead. It was too awful, this! He was rising to his feet even as Deane and his sister entered the lounge. He moved toward them with uncertain footsteps.

"We must have a sitting-room," he said. "I cannot face these people. I am beginning to feel a coward."

Deane went to the office, and very soon they found themselves upon the third floor, in an apartment overlooking Northumberland Avenue, gorgeous with plush and gilt mirrors, stiffly arranged chairs, an ornate chiffonnier. Rowan, who had come up in the lift muttering to himself, but obviously anxious for silence from his two companions, threw himself, almost as the door closed, upon the hard couch.

"I am broken!" he cried out. "I am broken!"

Winifred sank on her knees by his side, her arms went round his neck. Deane turned away and walked to the window a little awkwardly. Somehow he felt that it would be taking a mean advantage if he should look into her face, though all the time he was longing to see if her eyes had really softened, if those lips were really trembling a little, lips that were pressed to her brother's forehead.

"Basil," she whispered, "you mustn't! Bear up, please. Mr. Deane is here. He has come with me. Sit up and talk to him."

Rowan pulled himself together. He sat up, and Deane, obeying a gesture from her, crossed the room once more.

"Rowan," he said, "I am very sorry to see you like this."

"It's my first day out," Rowan answered. "It's a little trying, you know, especially when the end is so near. I wanted just a few words with you, Deane. It is good of you to come."

Deane nodded. "I only wish there was something I could do," he said.

"There is nothing," answered Rowan.

The girl turned away. "When you want me, Basil," she said softly, "I shall be in the next room."

"You might have some brandy brought up," he said. "I must talk for a few minutes, and I am not feeling very strong."

"I will ring the bell in the other room," she said, "and order it."

She disappeared through the connecting door. Deane, who had found himself watching her slow, even progress, turned once more to the man who sat by his side.

"I never thought I'd see you again," Rowan commenced. "I did my best, Deane. I made friends with Sinclair all right—he was glad enough to have anyone to drink with—and before long he began to tell me about his claim to the Little Anna Mine."

"Did he believe in it?" asked Deane.

"Absolutely," Rowan answered. "I am quite sure of that. He absolutely believed that directly he put it into the hands of any solicitor, you would have to come to him and buy, even though it cost you half your fortune. He was waiting those few days to see if you came."

Deane nodded. "Tell me how it happened," he said.

"It was like this," Rowan continued, speaking hoarsely, and with difficulty, "that night he wasn't quite so drunk. I pressed him a little too closely about his claim, and where he kept the paper. He was suddenly suspicious and quarrelsome. He tried to turn me out, and when I wanted to soothe him down, he struck me. He was a strong man and I was weak. I think that he meant to murder me. I remember I was half on the floor. My forehead was bleeding already, and he was coming towards me, shrieking with rage. 'I am going to finish you!' he called out. Then I struck, hoping only to stun him, and, as you know, the blow killed him. I forgot for a moment about the paper. I thought only about making my escape. I had bad luck, and I did not succeed. I am afraid it was a bungling sort of job, Deane."

"I am very sorry indeed," Deane said, "that I ever suggested it to you."

"It wasn't your fault," Rowan answered. "Nothing of this sort would have happened if he hadn't come for me. I meant to rob him if I could—I'll admit that—but no more. You see it was useless for me to try and open negotiations. He was too confident altogether. He spoke of a million pounds as his price. Tell me," he went on, "how do things stand now? Who has possession of the paper?"

Deane hesitated for a moment. "I do not know."

Rowan's face fell. He seemed disappointed. "I had an idea," he said slowly, "that you might have made some attempt to recover it.

Everything was left in the room at the hotel for some time. It was easily done."

"I did make an attempt," Deane said slowly. "I have searched the room for that paper, but failed to find it."

"You yourself?" Rowan asked eagerly.

"Yes! I heard that there was a claimant coming for Sinclair's effects, and that they were going to be removed to Scotland Yard. I took a room at the hotel, and I got hold of a key. I went through everything the man had."

"It was in the breast pocket of his gray coat, underneath the lining," Rowan gasped.

"I found the place," Deane answered, "but it was empty."

Rowan wiped the sweat from his forehead. His breathing was becoming difficult. Already the excitement was affecting him. "But it was there on that night!" he exclaimed. "He took off his coat a few minutes before, and I saw him feel it in the lining."

"All I can tell you," Deane answered, "is that the lining of the gray coat was torn, as though something had been abstracted. The paper was not there. It was not anywhere in the room. I ran a risk," he continued, after a moment's pause, "which I dare not think of, even now, but it was in vain. Someone had been before me."

"Was there anyone else upon the scent, then?" Rowan asked.

"Can you think of anyone?" Deane asked.

Rowan looked at him with distended eyes. "You don't mean to insinuate," he began, "that I — that I had given it away?"

"Not wilfully," answered Deane. "Is there anyone at all to whom you spoke of this?"

Rowan shook his head. "Only to my sister," he said, "and she is as silent as the grave."

"Nevertheless," Deane said, "the paper has gone. Someone has it — is holding it now — for a purpose, I suppose. There can but be one purpose. Perhaps," he added, "you had better ask your sister, to be quite sure whether she ever mentioned its existence to anyone."

"We will ask her at once!" Rowan exclaimed. "I will ask her before you. Let me get up. Help me. I will fetch her."

Deane stretched out his hand. "No!" he said. "You must not excite yourself Rowan. I will knock at the door and call your sister."

Rowan lay back, gasping. Deane crossed the room and knocked at the door which led to the inner apartment.

"Miss Rowan," he said.

She opened the door almost immediately. "Yes?"

Deane stood aside. "Your brother," he said, "has a question to ask you!"

CHAPTER IV
A QUESTION

Winifred came slowly into the room. It seemed to Deane, watching her curiously, that she had been steeling herself to defiance. There was no change in her expression, and her lips seemed tighter drawn than ever. She went at once to her brother's side.

"You have been talking too much, Basil," she said. "You know that it is not good for you."

He leaned across to the little table which stood by his side and helped himself to brandy. He was indeed looking terribly ill. The lines under his eyes seemed traced with a coal-black pencil, and his hand shook so that half the brandy was spilled.

"Winifred," he said, "I must ask you a question. You remember that I spoke to you of a document—Sinclair had it. I was trying to deal with him, trying to get it back for Mr. Deane here."

"Yes," she answered calmly, "I remember your speaking of it."

"We have reason to believe," he continued, gasping a little,— "reason to believe that it has been stolen. Mr. Deane wants to know whether at any time you have mentioned its existence to anyone."

She looked at Deane and back at her brother. Her face was unchanged. "No!" she said. "I have mentioned it to no one."

"You see," her brother continued, "it's like this. No one but I knew of that paper. Deane here told me, and I told no one except you. And yet we have evidence, we know that it has been stolen from Sinclair's room since his death. That is why we want you to be quite sure that you did not mention its existence to anyone."

"No mention of it has crossed my lips," she answered. "I have no friends, no confidants. I have spoken to no one about it. Nothing in the world," she continued, "would be more improbable than that I should have done so."

He turned to Deane, who stood by with impassive face. "You hear?" he exclaimed. "You hear? I was quite sure about Winifred. She doesn't go talking about. She's no gossip, are you, Winifred?"

"I hope not," she answered.

"I have no reason, I am sure," Deane said slowly, "to doubt Miss Rowan's discretion."

She raised her eyes for a moment, and met his. The faint satire in his tone was intentionally provocative, but it failed to move her. Her regard of him was entirely impersonal. He looked away with a light shrug of the shoulders.

"Well, Rowan," he said, "it seems there is nothing further to be done. If the paper does turn up," he added, "I shall know how to deal with its holder. In the meantime, about yourself."

Rowan laughed a little hysterically. "About myself," he repeated. "That's a fruitful subject, isn't it?"

"Doctors make mistakes sometimes," Deane said. "Let us hope that they may have made one in your case. Anyhow, there is no reason why you should not be comfortable, and have the best medical advice. Go wherever you think best, and send me your address. I shall not forget that your accident took place when you were engaged upon my affairs."

"You are very good, Deane," Rowan said.

The girl looked up. "Mr. Deane's kindness is quite unnecessary," she said. "We are in no want of money."

"Your sister does not quite understand," Deane said, turning to him. "We have been through too many rough times in Africa together to stand upon ceremony now. You will perhaps be able to explain to her later on."

He took up his hat and turned toward the door. "I shall expect to hear from you," he said, "as soon as you have decided where to go,—either from you, Rowan," he added, shaking hands with him, "or from your sister."

"You are very kind, Deane," Rowan said. "I am sorry I have made such a mess of things."

"It was not your fault," Deane answered. "Good-day, Miss Rowan!"

She looked at him for a moment, but she did not offer to take his outstretched hand. He smiled, and withdrew it at once.

"Good-day, Mr. Deane!" she said.

The door closed behind him. Rowan was watching his sister anxiously. "Winifred," he said, "what is the matter with you? You were scarcely civil to Mr. Deane."

"Oh! I think I was," she answered. "In any case, we don't want to take alms from him, do we?"

"It isn't exactly that," Rowan objected.

"It is."

"He can afford it," Rowan declared. "He is very rich. A thousand pounds to him is like sixpence to us."

"It doesn't alter facts," she rejoined. "I do not like Mr. Deane, Basil. It is through him that this trouble has come upon us. You have taken enough of his money."

"And when I am gone?" he asked. "What about you then?"

"Have I ever failed to make my own way?" she asked quietly. "I shall be safe enough, Basil."

He commenced to cough, and very soon further speech was impossible. He was painfully exhausted. She sat by his side until he went off to sleep. Of his hopeless state there could no longer be any doubt. He was wasted almost to a shadow. Even in sleep his breath came heavily, and a fever seemed upon him. She stole softly from his side, and stood for a few minutes at the window, looking out. Below, the pulse of the great world was beating with the same maddening regularity. The stream of wayfarers swept on, the roar of traffic was as inevitable as the waves of the sea. She stood by the window with small, clenched hands. Behind her, his loud breathing seemed to beat out the time toward Death.

Deane himself was one of those wayfarers, but at least his thoughts, as he was being whirled eastward in his brougham, were fixed upon the tragedy which he had left behind him. He knew very well that it was not a question of months but of days with Basil Rowan. Was it only for that that the girl was waiting? Her whole attitude towards him had about it a certain flavor of mystery which oppressed him. It was like trying to face an enemy hidden in a darkened room, listening for his footstep, not knowing whence the blow might fall. Notwithstanding the warm sunshine, he shivered a little as he descended from the carriage and entered his offices.

CHAPTER V
MUTUAL INFORMATION

The girl was sitting in the middle of a hard horsehair sofa, her elbows upon her knees, her head resting in her hands. She looked across the dreary apartment and out of the ill-cleaned windows, with dull, despairing eyes. This, then, was to be the end of her dreams. She must go back to the life which she felt to be intolerable, or she must throw herself headlong into the maelstrom.

There was one other occupant of the room, and, curiously enough, his attitude appeared to be a somewhat similar one. He was a short, thick-set young man, with brown moustache, flashily dressed, with a red tie, an imitation diamond, and soiled linen to further disfigure an appearance at no time particularly prepossessing. He was standing with his legs a little apart, looking out into the uninspiring street. His hands were thrust deep down into the pockets of his trousers. He had all the appearance of a man who finds the burden of life an unwelcome thing. Presently he began to whistle, not cheerfully, but some doleful air of sentimental import. The girl upon the couch seemed irritated. She herself was in the last stage of dejection, and the sound grew maddening.

"Oh, don't do that, please!" she exclaimed at last.

He turned around in amazement, for the first time realizing that he was not alone. "I beg your pardon," he said.

The girl remembered that he was a stranger to her, but after all, what did it matter? "I asked you to stop whistling," she said.

He answered "Certainly!" and continued to look at her. She returned his gaze with a disapprobation which she scarcely attempted to conceal.

"Sort of habit I get into," he explained, "when I'm in the dumps."

"Does it do you any good?" she asked. "If so, I'll learn how to whistle myself."

"Meaning," he remarked, "that we are companions in—dumpiness?"

She shrugged her shoulders, but did not trouble to reply.

"I wish to God," he exclaimed, "I'd never left Cape Town!"

Then for the first time she looked at him with a gleam of interest, and asked, "Do you come from South Africa?"

He nodded. "I did, and I only wish I were back there. I could always keep my head above water there, but London is a rotten hole. I suppose it's because I don't know the runs," he added meditatively. "Anyhow, it's broke me."

She continued the conversation without feeling the slightest interest in it, but simply because it was an escape—a temporary escape—from her thoughts. "What did you come over for?" she asked.

"A fool's errand!" he answered. "I lent a man some money—a sort of speculation it was—and I came over to see how he was getting on."

"And I suppose he'd lost it," she remarked.

"He's lost himself," answered the man, "which is about as bad. I wish I could lay my hands upon him. I'd get a bit of my own back, one way or another."

"London is a big place," she returned. "People are not easy to find unless you know all about them."

"This man left South Africa only a month or so ago. He gave me an address here where he said I should always hear of him. I've been there nearly every day. He turned up there all right regularly after he first landed. He hasn't been there at all for two months, and they haven't the least idea where he is."

"You don't even know," she asked, "whether the speculation is successful or not?"

He shook his head gloomily. "It don't make much odds, so far as I can see," he said. "If it came off, he's bolted with the profits. If it didn't, he's hiding for fear I shall want my money back again. It's a rotten sort of show, anyway."

"What was his name?" she asked idly.

"His real name," the man answered, "was the same as your own, — that is," he added, "I think I heard old Mrs. Towsley call you Miss Sinclair, didn't I?"

She looked at him steadily for several moments without speaking. He was not a person of quick apprehensions, but even he could not fail to see the change in her face. Her lips were parted, her eyes were suddenly lit with an almost passionate fire. The change in her features was illuminating. She was no longer a tired, depressed-looking young woman of ill-tempered appearance. Her good looks had reasserted themselves. Life seemed to have been breathed into her pulses.

"His real name was Sinclair," she repeated softly. "He came from South Africa. Tell me some more about him?"

"Why?" he asked bluntly.

"Because," she told him, "my name is Ruby Sinclair, and I am here on very much the same errand as you, only with this difference," she added, — "I know where my uncle is. I know what has become of him. There are other things for which I seek."

He came over from the window, and stood on the hearthrug by her side. Some part of her excitement had become communicated to him. "I say," he exclaimed, "this is a rum go, and no mistake! If it's the same man, we may be able to help one another. It's Richard Sinclair I am looking for, called over there Bully Sinclair. He was a man about fifty years old, been in South Africa for the last twenty years, a mine prospector and general adventurer. He'd had his fingers in a good many pies, had Richard."

"What was he over in England for?" she asked.

The young man hesitated. "I don't know that there's any harm in telling you," he said, "only remember its information for information. I'm giving you the whole show away."

"I'll tell you all you want to know," she interrupted. "Go on."

"Well," the young man said, "he came over to lay claim to a gold-mine that he considered he'd been done out of."

"A gold-mine!" the girl repeated breathlessly. "Was it a rich one — very rich, I mean?"

"I should say so," the young man answered. "It was a complicated bit of business—the mine's in other hands, you see—but Sinclair reckoned that he'd got a claim to it, anyway, and he expected either to be squared for a big amount, or to get a syndicate to take the thing up. He came to me dead on his uppers. My name's Hefferom. He and I had been pretty thick at odd times, and though we'd been in a good many deals together, we'd kept friends in a way. He came to me, as I say, in Cape Town, and he told me what the game was. He wanted a matter of two or three hundred pounds to get over to this side, and to start things properly. Well, I thought it out, and though it was about all I was worth in the world, I let him have it. Over he comes. I got a letter from him to say he'd landed, and never another line. I cabled—no answer. Over I came myself, for he'd scarcely left Cape Town before a little affair that I was mixed up in went plumb wrong, and I lost every penny I'd got left. So over here I come, and I've been here a fortnight, and I tell you Sinclair seems to have vanished from the face of the earth. The worst of it is," he continued, "I'm stoney-broke. I've got to leave this place to-day because I can't pay my bill, and I've no idea where to raise a sovereign."

The girl's sense of humor triumphed for a second over her excitement. "There are your diamonds," she reminded him. "I heard you talking about them at dinner the other night. One of them you said was worth a hundred pounds."

"A bluff," he answered readily. "They are false, every one of them. I talked like that to get old mother Towsley to let my account go on a bit, but she wasn't having any. Now, I say, I've told you my story. Tell me why you are so keen on knowing about it."

"Yes," she said, "I will tell you. My name is Ruby Sinclair, and I am the niece of the man whom you have come to England to find."

He made use of an oath for which he forgot even to apologize. "You know where he is!" he exclaimed. "Come, remember it was a fair bargain. Information for information!"

"He is dead!"

The young man staggered back. His first emotion of shocked surprise lasted only a few seconds. Anger and disappointment took its place. "Dead?" he exclaimed. "And my money—what about that?

What he left belongs to me, anyway. It's got to be made up. I can show you his note for it."

"You had better wait," she answered coldly, "Until I have told you everything. I suppose you don't read the papers?"

"Never," he answered. "What good are they to me?"

"They might have been of some use on the present occasion," she answered. "They might at any rate have saved you from wasting a good deal of time. My uncle was murdered in the Hotel Universal by a man named Rowan."

The young man swore again, — fluently, volubly, — swore until he had come to the end of a varied and extensive vocabulary. When he had finished, there was an excited flush in his cheeks and a bright light in his eyes. "By Rowan — Basil Rowan?" he exclaimed. "He was one of us out there when we were prospecting up the Newey Valley. Look here," he continued, "you and I have got to have this out. Murdered, was he? Well, I'm the man that may be able to throw some light upon that. What's happened to Rowan? Had he anything to say?"

"I will tell you all that I know," the girl answered. "My uncle wrote me directly he arrived in England. He told me that he had been fortunate in Africa, that he had come to take possession of a large fortune, and that he would be sending for me in a very short time to live with him, and that, as he had no other relative, I should be rich all my days. I replied, of course, asking whether I could not come at once. He wrote me again to tell me to wait for a day or two, until his affairs were settled. Then I heard no more. I waited. I wrote again. I waited, and wrote again. There was no reply. I found afterwards that my letters had never even been called for at the address where he told me to write. Then one day a stranger who was staying at Rakney told my uncle there to look at the papers. We found the story of his murder. He had been dead some time."

"Rowan was tried, I suppose?" the man asked. "Did he say what his motive was? Has he been hanged?"

"He insisted upon it that it was a quarrel," the girl said. "I do not believe him. He was found guilty and reprieved. I saw in the papers last night that he had been released. I believe that he has only a few days to live."

"And you?" the young man asked.

"I came up," the girl said slowly, "to take possession of my uncle's effects."

"Have you got them?" he asked breathlessly.

"Yes!" the girl answered.

"There were papers?" he demanded.

"Some," she answered, "but none of any importance."

He looked at her suspiciously. She shrugged her shoulders. "Look here," she said, "I am telling you the truth. Look at me, look at my gloves—mended half-a-dozen times. Look at my clothes, just hanging on my back and no more. If there had been a single thing amongst my uncle's papers on which I could have raised even a five-pound note, do you think that I should be sitting here like this, wondering which might be the quickest way out of the world?"

The young man moistened his lips. He was obviously in a state of excitement. "Listen," he said, "among these papers was there a sort of deed on yellow parchment paper, roughly written, with a government stamp in the left-hand corner, a paper which spoke of a gold-mine called the Little Anna Gold-Mine?"

She shook her head decidedly. "There was nothing of the sort."

Then the young man swore again, and this time he seemed to surpass himself. "Your uncle was robbed!" he exclaimed,—"robbed of that paper! I tell you," he added, "he was murdered for it, and for no other reason!"

"How do you know?" the girl cried.

"Why, it's as simple as A B C," he explained. "He had the paper in his possession when he came to England. The mine has been claimed by a great syndicate who are working it now. He came to see them, to make terms. The next thing we hear is that he is murdered and the paper is gone. They thought that no one else knew of it. Young lady," he exclaimed, "you may thank your stars, as I do, that you and me have come together. We'll have justice, and we'll have that fortune yet!"

CHAPTER VI
AN OPPORTUNE ARRIVAL

With his feet to the sea, and his head pillowed by many cushions, Rowan lay in a long invalid chair at the edge of the little strip of shingle which separated the tower of Rakney from the sea. Every limb was at rest, every nerve seemed lulled into quiescence. The sun and wind had left their traces upon his hollow cheeks. It seemed, indeed, as though Death had lifted her hand from his forehead. It was only when one looked closer that one realized his terrible weakness, realized how slender, indeed, the thread was by which he held on to life. There was scarcely a breath of wind stirring. The sun was high in the heavens, and the whole country seemed lulled into a state of almost unnatural repose. The distant trees were motionless, as though, indeed, they were simply painted things against that background of deep blue sky. The smoke from the little cluster of cottages crept upwards, straight as a ruled line. The cattle in the fields seemed all asleep, exhausted by the unexpected heat. The sea was like a lake, unruffled, almost unrippled.

The man dozed, and Winifred sat by his side, with her eyes fixed steadily and yet absently upon the distant horizon. A week, at most, the doctor had given him, and after that — what? She looked backwards to the window, — the window through which she had entered on that wild night earlier in the year. She looked away again uneasily. She was afraid of such moments as these. It was to escape from them that she had protested so vehemently against their accepting Deane's offer of his cottage.

At low tide, a rough, pebbly road led from the village to the cottage, as well as the dyke footpath higher up. Along this came two people, a man and a woman, mere specks at first in the distance, but rapidly becoming more and more evident. They walked fast, and they looked always anxiously toward the tower, which stood out at the end of the road against the background of the sky, — a curious, almost uncanny, sort of building.

"If they see us coming," said Ruby Sinclair, "they will certainly try to prevent our seeing him. Our only chance is to come upon them unexpectedly. They can watch the dyke path from the front, but few people ever come by this road. It winds about so, and it is generally thick with sea mud."

The man nodded. He too was keeping his gaze fixed in a strained manner upon their goal. "Now that we are so near," he said, "so near to him, we will make him speak. We will not be driven away. He cannot escape from us there."

There was a curious air of determination about these two, a certain grimness which seemed common to both of them, as they hurried along the rough, stone-strewn road. They had reached the last hundred yards now, and their course was perfectly straight. They walked single file along the little stretch of marshland which served as a footpath.

"He is in front, lying on a chair," she whispered. "They won't be able to get him in now before we are there."

The road terminated suddenly upon the beach. The man and the girl scrambled up a little shingly mound. When at last Winifred heard the sounds of their approach, they were already between her and the house. Any attempt at escape was useless. She came a few steps toward them.

"Who are you, please, and what do you want?" she asked quickly.

Hefferom stretched out a hand toward the prone figure of Rowan, who was lying there still with closed eyes. "We want a few words with your brother," he said. "We shall not keep him long, but it is very important. We have come a long way to see him."

"It is impossible," she said firmly. "He is very ill indeed. The doctor allows him to see no one. I don't know how you found your way here, but you must please return at once."

"I have come a long way," Hefferom said slowly.

"I am sorry," she answered, "but can't you see that it makes no difference? If you were to ask him questions, he is not well enough to answer you—scarcely to understand. Any sudden shock at all—even a recognition—might kill him."

Hefferom hesitated no longer. He pushed Winifred away, and motioned to Ruby to follow him. At that moment Rowan opened his eyes and turned his head. Hefferom walked towards him and leaned over his chair.

"You remember me, Rowan?" he said. "My name is Hefferom, Steve Hefferom. We were up the Newey Valley together, camped out, you know, at Prince's Gorge, for more than a month,—you and I and Deane, and a lot of us."

"I remember," Rowan faltered, trying to raise himself. "Yes, I remember!"

He had a fit of coughing. Winifred passed her arms around him and held him up. "If you stay," she whispered to Hefferom, "you will kill him. He ought not to speak ever a sentence."

"It isn't much we want him to say, miss," Hefferom answered doggedly, "but there's a question he's got to answer. If he is as near death as you say, it can't make much difference what happens, and it means more than death to me and to this young lady."

Rowan had recovered sufficiently to drink from a glass which Winifred had handed to him. He turned once more toward Hefferom. "That is all finished," he said painfully,—"those days. I am ill,—too ill to talk, too ill to think, too ill to live! Please go."

Hefferom bent over him. "Rowan," he said, "you and I were never enemies, even if we didn't exactly hit it off together. Listen to me for a moment. Sinclair borrowed my last three hundred pounds in Cape Town to come over here and lay claim to the Little Anna Gold-Mine. He had the government deed with him. I have seen it. I followed him over to claim my share, and I found him dead, killed, and the paper gone. I am not asking you to give away your game, whatever it was, but we want the paper. This is Sinclair's niece with me, and I am his partner. We inherit his claim to the Little Anna Gold-Mine, and we want that document."

"The document was not amongst Sinclair's effects when they were examined after his death," Rowan said. "I did not take it. I do not know what has become of it. That is the truth. Leave me alone now. I cannot talk any more."

His head dropped back upon his pillow. He was white to the lips. Winifred hurried to his side. Once more she turned upon the two.

"Are you satisfied?" she cried. "You have nearly killed him—for nothing. I know very well that no document of any sort such as you describe has been found. If Mr. Sinclair ever had it, it was probably stolen from him."

"Stolen, yes!" Hefferom said,—"stolen right enough! That is what we are here about. This young lady is his niece, and I'm his partner. What was left behind belongs to us, and, so far as I know, the only thing worth having was that document. We want it, and, by God," he wound up, "we've got to have it!"

"Do you imagine," the girl asked, without change of countenance, "that you will find it here?"

"I will tell you what I do imagine," Hefferom answered. "Men don't commit murder for nothing. Your brother tried to steal that paper, or rather he did steal it. The game's up now. He's no opportunity to make use of it, and it belongs to us. It belongs to us and we've come for it. There, now you know the truth. We've come for it, and we've come to stop until we get it."

Rowan raised himself a little in his seat. "Hefferom," he said, "it's no use talking like that. I haven't got it. I'll be frank, frank as you have been. I know no more than you do who has got it. I quarrelled with Sinclair, and he got suspicious. We fought in his room, and the result you know, but I was arrested before I left the hotel. Everyone knows that. The paper—I never had it—I never even saw it. Where it is now God only knows. I don't."

Rowan fell back in his chair, coughing violently. For several moments he was incapable of speech. Winifred knelt by his side. When he had finished coughing, she held a wineglass to his lips and made him sip its contents. He lay back now as though completely exhausted. She turned to face these unwelcome visitors.

"You see," she cried, pointing to him, "a little more of this and you will kill him. Go away, both of you. He has nothing to tell you."

Hefferom laughed a little brutally. "Come," he said, "this game won't do. We are here for the truth, not to be put off with these fairy-tales. It is the truth we want, and the truth we'll have, or I'll wring it out of him even if it kills him."

Rowan's eyes were closed, and he showed no sign of having heard. Winifred stood up boldly before him. "You are fools!" she said. "He has told you all he knows. If Sinclair ever had the deed you speak of, he parted with it to someone else, not to my brother."

"Someone else!" Hefferom repeated. "Do you take us for fools? If he parted with that deed, he parted with it for a fortune. Where's the money? Show us the deed or the money, and we are satisfied. Show us neither, and we'll not leave this place until he has spoken."

A step upon the shingle behind suddenly diverted their attention. The eyes of every one of them were fixed upon the tall figure who was walking swiftly up the slope. They had been so engrossed that they had not even heard the sound of the motor-car which was standing there, splashed with mud, and with its engine still panting. With his glasses in his hand, and his long gray coat thrown open, Stirling Deane strode up to them.

"Come," he said, "it seems to me that I have arrived opportunely. What does this mean? Who are these people? Miss Sinclair, is this man your companion? What does he mean by speaking in such a tone to a dying man?"

No one answered him. Hefferom stood as though turned to stone, but his eyes never left Deane's.

CHAPTER VII
HEFFEROM IS OPTIMISTIC

Ruby Sinclair leaned forward and touched her companion's back as they flew through the village of Rakney. "Look," said she. "You see that cottage we are just passing? That is where I have lived for the last four years."

Hefferom followed her outstretched finger. He saw the little grove of bare trees, and the marshland stretching out beyond to the bare sea. "Winter and summer?" he asked.

"Winter and summer."

He nodded. "About time you went fortune-hunting!" he said.

No other word passed between them until they reached the railway station. They descended from the car, and watched it almost immediately swing round and disappear.

"So this is the end of our little excursion to Rakney," Ruby remarked.

"Yes!" Hefferom answered. "Aren't you satisfied?"

"Why should I be?" she asked. "What have we gained?"

Hefferom drew a long breath. "Ah, I forgot!" he said. "You don't understand."

He drew her into the refreshment room. She declined to drink, but she sat in a corner while he disposed of several whiskies and sodas. At first he would say nothing, and she waited. Presently he began.

"You think," he said, "that I was a coward, because when Deane bundled us off in his car and told the man to drive us to the nearest railway station, I did not protest. You think that I should have made a scene there? It wasn't worth while. Deane's coming gave the whole game away. Don't you really understand?"

"Not a word," she answered.

"Listen, then. Stirling Deane is the man who is supposed to be the owner of the Little Anna Gold-Mine, which was really your Uncle Sinclair's."

She looked at him with gleaming eyes. "Say that again," she said. "I don't quite understand."

"The deed which is missing from your Uncle Sinclair's effects," Hefferom said slowly, "is the title-deed to the Little Anna Gold-Mine. That mine was illegally taken possession of by Stirling Deane. He sold it to the company, of which he is now president, at an enormous price. He is the man with whom your Uncle Sinclair came to England to treat. Sinclair was murdered. By whom? By Rowan. Who was at the back of Rowan? Whose tool was he? We know! Chance this afternoon made everything clear to us. Can't you see that Rowan killed your uncle and stole that deed to save Stirling Deane from ruin, — at his bidding, as his accomplice?"

"It takes my breath away," the girl murmured. "Now I think of it, of course, it is Deane's cottage they are in. He was there himself only a few weeks ago. It was through him that we heard of my uncle's murder."

"The whole thing's as simple as A B C," Hefferom declared. "Can't you see that Deane has given himself into our hands? Of course Rowan stole the deed! Of course Deane has it! He will have to pay for our silence! By God, he will have to pay!"

The girl looked up from her seat on the leathern couch, looked at her companion long and critically. "Do you think we can hold our own against a man like Stirling Deane?"

"It depends upon the cards, and they are in our hands. We must go back to London. We must wait till he is at his office. Then I will see him. You can leave the thing in my hands now. I shall know how to approach him. He cannot deny his friendship with the Rowans. They are occupying, even at this moment, his own cottage. Very likely I shall be able to discover other things connecting him with them. The newspapers you showed me spoke of great influence which was brought to bear on the granting of the reprieve. We may find that Stirling Deane was at the back of that. Anyhow, he is connected closely enough with them. I am here, ready to swear that when Sinclair left

Africa he left with the original title-deed of the Little Anna Gold-Mine in his pocket. I think that the friendship between his murderer and Stirling Deane, who sold that mine for close upon a million pounds, is a thing that will need a little explanation."

"And in the meantime," said the girl bitterly, "we are starving."

"Not quite," he answered. "We have thirty-eight shillings. That will take us back to London, and find us rooms somewhere for the night. We must scrape along somehow until I can get to Deane's offices."

"You are not forgetting," the girl remarked, "that the thirty-eight shillings you are speaking of is my property?"

"We are partners," Hefferom declared. "You shall carry the purse if you will, but there is no object in it."

"You seem to do most of the spending," she reminded him. "If you think that we can afford it," she added, glancing at his empty glasses, "I should like a cup of tea."

He ordered it at once, and sat down by her side. "Look here," he said, "I don't see what you want to be so blooming stand-off for. Times are a bit rough with us just now, but, you mark my word, we shall pull through all right. This man Deane is in the hollow of our hands. He has been Rowan's accomplice. No one who knows the facts could possibly doubt it. A word from us would ruin him."

The girl sighed. She had drawn a little away from the man. "Do you believe, then," she asked, "that Mr. Deane has the deed?"

"Either that, or it is destroyed," answered Hefferom. "But don't bother about that. Whether the deed is still existing or not, we know enough to make it worth his while to buy us, even though it costs him half his fortune."

"In the meantime," the girl said, "please get the tickets. The train will be in, in a few minutes."

"Come with me," he said suspiciously. "Remember, we're partners."

"Oh! we are partners right enough," she answered, rising and following him out of the place. "You needn't be afraid that I am going to let you go. Just now you are all that stands between me and a return to Rakney."

On the way up to town he began to build castles. He was optimistic, sanguine in the extreme. The girl listened almost stolidly. Her companion had begun to depress her. He was badly dressed, his linen was soiled, his imitation jewelry was hideous. He sat opposite her in the train, and there were things in his face from which she shrank. She was more than thankful that they were not alone.

"Are you tired, or what?" he asked at last, a little sullenly. "Surely I made it all plain enough? You don't doubt that there's money in this for us?"

"There should be," she admitted slowly. "And yet—"

"And yet what?"

"I have seen Mr. Deane before," she said hesitatingly. "I have talked with him once or twice. Somehow or other, when I think that it may come to be a struggle between you and him—"

He interrupted her with a brazen laugh. "You think I won't be able to stand up against him! Well, you shall see. There's a good deal in holding the cards, you know."

"You haven't the deed," she reminded him.

"I don't want it," he answered. "I am not afraid of Stirling Deane. I have known him a good many years, and he knows me. We are up against one another now, and you may fancy his chances; but I tell you my back's against the wall, and his isn't. He's there fighting in the open. I've got him, I tell you,—got him!"

She half closed her eyes. This was not the way in which she had hoped to come into her fortune. In her heart, she could not believe a word he said. Deane was a strong man; Hefferom, she was already beginning to discover, was nothing but a bully and a craven. If it came to a duel between the two, she found it easier to believe that Hefferom would be worsted.

At King's Cross Station they separated. Hefferom, a little sulkily, accepted his dismissal, and parted with half of the money which he had.

"You can go where you choose," she said. "You can come back to Mrs. Towsley's, if you like, but I tell you frankly that except while we are on business I think it better that we should stay apart."

"I can't see why," he muttered.

"For one thing," she said, "we might be taken for adventurers. I do not know much about the law, but it seems to me you won't be very far out of its clutches when your negotiations with Mr. Deane begin."

"I can take care of myself," he answered gruffly. "Can I see you back to the old lady's, anyhow?"

"No!" she answered. "I would rather go alone."

"Come and have one drink in the refreshment room, just to wish ourselves luck," he begged.

She went in with him and drank a cup of coffee. He had two liqueurs, and would have had more, but she dragged him sharply away.

"Remember," she said, "that I have nothing more I can raise money on. These few shillings are all we have. If Mr. Deane does not return for several days, we must leave."

"Deane will come back," he said, with a defiant laugh. "I let him have things his own way to-day, but he knows just where he is. Mark my words, he will be at the office to-morrow morning, and he will be there expecting to see me."

CHAPTER VIII
A BOLD MOVE

Hefferom was over sanguine. It was three days before he was able to see Stirling Deane. During that three days he had lived on a few shillings, spent mostly in drinks. He swaggered into Deane's office, an untidy, dissolute-looking creature. His efforts to seem at his ease were almost ludicrous.

"A bit different, this, to the Newey Valley," he remarked, as he sat down without waiting for an invitation. "Things have gone pretty well with you, eh, Deane? Slap-up offices you've got, and the chink of money everywhere. It reminds me of what I've come about."

"You have come for money, have you?" Deane asked.

"Well, I don't know about that. I don't know how you look at it, but it seems to me that there's a bit owing, a bit which might come my way. I should tell you, perhaps, that I am representing Miss Sinclair as well as myself."

"Richard Sinclair's niece?" Deane asked.

"Exactly. She is heiress to anything the old man had, and I was partner with him in the Little Anna Gold-Mine."

"In what?" asked Deane.

"In the Little Anna Gold-Mine," Hefferom repeated distinctly.

Deane leaned back in his chair. "I must ask you to explain yourself," he said. "The Little Anna Gold-Mine belongs to the syndicate of which I am a director."

"That's all very well for a bluff," answered Hefferom, "but you got rid of Sinclair a little too easily."

"Got rid of him?"

"Oh! I'm not thinking of this last time," Hefferom interrupted, with a hard laugh. "I am thinking of the time he put you on to the mine, and you took possession of it."

"It was perfectly legal," Deane remarked.

"Perhaps so, — perhaps it wasn't," Hefferom answered. "Anyway, I know very well, and so, probably, do you, that Sinclair left South Africa six months ago, with the government title-deed of the Little Anna Gold-Mine in his pocket. I advanced him the money to come, and he made me his partner."

"These are amazing statements of yours," Deane said. "May I ask where is this wonderful deed?"

"You may ask," Hefferom answered, "but not me. Better go to Rowan. He knows, though he keeps his lips tight shut. He knows, and so do you! Never mind about that. You don't want a lawsuit, — no more do we."

"Who are 'we'?" Deane asked.

"Miss Sinclair and myself," Hefferom answered. "We are partners in this. I have come to you as a reasonable man. Sinclair landed in this country with the title-deeds of the mine which you have always considered yours, in his pocket. To-day he is murdered, and his papers have disappeared. He was murdered by Rowan, whom you are now befriending. There's a story there for the newspapers, — there's something more than a story, Deane."

"Do I understand," Deane asked calmly, —

"You can understand what you please," Hefferom said. "I want my money back, and I want big interest. And then there's the girl. She should be standing at this moment in your shoes. Half of the Little Anna Gold-Mine is hers by right. It is for you to say what it would be worth your while to put down to close this business."

"Now," Deane remarked suavely, "you are talking common sense. But what I should like to know is, where is this wonderful title-deed?"

"Oh, d—n you, it's in the fire, I suppose!" Hefferom cried. "You and he know. Rowan's your man, and he's the sort to die game. But he didn't kill Sinclair for nothing. I wouldn't mind betting that that deed has been burnt to ashes, but even then, I know a little too much, eh?"

Deane shrugged his shoulders. "You know a great deal too much," he said. "I am to understand, then, finally, that you want me to buy your silence?"

"Put it that way if you choose," Hefferom answered, "only I warn you that I haven't come here on a child's game. This is a big business,—a big business for me and for the girl. She must have her share, and I mine."

"And the amount?"

"One hundred thousand pounds. Remember that it has to be divided."

"In other words," remarked Deane, "I am to buy your silence as to these matters upon which you have spoken, for the sum of one hundred thousand pounds?"

"It is too little," Hefferom declared. "The mine is worth ten times as much—the mine and your position."

"If I give you this sum," Deane asked, "do I understand that it closes the whole affair? You must remember that I do not admit having even seen this deed you spoke of. Supposing it turns up in somebody else's hands?"

Hefferom laughed ironically. "We'll guarantee you against that," he declared.

"That's easy to say," Deane objected, "but I don't see how. Come, I will be perfectly truthful. I haven't got that deed. If it should be still in existence, and be used against me after I have paid you this sum of money, I should be in somewhat an unfortunate position."

"There isn't the slightest fear of it," Hefferom said. "Besides—"

"Besides what?" Deane asked, looking up from his desk.

"It isn't as though the deed were a certainty," he said slowly. "Of course, the law is a little complicated. There would be witnesses on both sides, and the case might go anyhow."

"It would depend a little, I think," Deane said quietly, "on which side you gave evidence for. I think you could upset that deed if you chose."

"Perhaps I could," Hefferom said gruffly.

"Will you do it," Deane asked, "if it should ever be set into action against me? Remember that even though I know you will not believe me, the fact remains that although I have defended Rowan, I am not in possession of that deed."

Hefferom leaned across from his chair. "Listen, Deane," he said. "I am not here to bluff about that wonderful document. Perhaps it isn't worth the paper it's written on. Anyhow, here's my word for it. I'll see if ever an action is brought against you on the strength of that deed, that you blow it all sky high in five minutes."

"Is the deed a forgery?" Deane asked.

Hefferom did not answer.

"Or is it only the date?" Deane continued.

Still Hefferom was silent. Then, "There is no necessity," he said, after a pause, "of putting these things into plain words. You have only to find the money, and your anxieties are over."

Deane touched a bell by his side. "Yours, I am afraid," he answered, "are only just beginning!"

The curtains behind were suddenly thrown aside. A tall, spare-looking man stepped out. Deane turned towards him.

"Inspector," he said, "I give this man in charge for a barefaced attempt at blackmailing me. You have heard all that has been said. I don't think that there is anything for me to add."

He rang the bell by his side a second time. A moment later a policeman entered from the outer office. Hefferom, who had sprung to his feet, was glaring at them both, white with passion.

"So this is your game, Deane!" he exclaimed. "By the Lord, you shall pay for it! You to dare to use the law against me, — you, who sent Rowan like a paid assassin to murder Sinclair!"

"A gross calumny," Deane answered calmly. "I had no interest in Sinclair's life or death."

"It's a d—d lie!" cried Hefferom. "If you are going to do any arresting, inspector, arrest that man!" he cried, pointing with his fat white forefinger to where Deane stood, debonair and well-dressed as usual, and with a little bunch of violets in his buttonhole. "I tell you that he paid the man Rowan to kill Bully Sinclair in the Universal Hotel. I tell you I can prove it. I can prove this — that Sinclair left South

Africa six months ago, with the deeds of the Little Anna Gold-Mine, which this man dared to sell as being his own at close upon a million pounds less than six months ago. I can tell you more! —"

They led him from the room, still shouting. At the door he turned back. "It's a bold game this, Deane," he cried, "but by heavens I'll cry quits with you before long! You think you have a case against me. I am only certain of one thing, and that is that you have driven a nail into your own coffin. If I could only get at you, you — you blackguard!"

His eyes were bloodshot. He strained and struggled to free himself from the grasp of the two men.

"I'd kill you where you stand!" he cried. "Do you think that I can be muzzled? Do you think that the truth won't come to light? People shall know it even if I never leave off telling it till my last breath comes."

Deane listened to him with immovable face. They got him outside at last. He heard him being dragged down the corridor, protesting all the time. Then he resumed his seat. "It's a bold game to play," he said to himself thoughtfully, "and yet, if they really haven't the deed, there was nothing else to be done!"

CHAPTER IX
LORD NUNNELEY IS FRANK

"I asked you to lunch at the club, Deane," said Lord Nunneley, "because I thought that we could talk here without being interrupted. If you came to Cavendish Square, Olive would walk you right away from the table, and if I asked to have a chat with you alone, there would be a perfect avalanche of questions to face."

Deane looked up a little curiously. For the first time he realized that this was not simply a casual invitation. His prospective father-in-law had really something to say to him.

"There was some matter which you wished to discuss, then?" Deane asked. "I need scarcely say that I am quite at your service."

Lord Nunneley passed his cigarette-case across the table. They were nearing the end of a very excellent luncheon. "Well," he said, "there were a few things I wanted to say to you. You see, Deane, the city is no longer a mythical place to us idlers. We meet people whose life is centred in money-making, every day. I have friends, friends beside yourself, who come from Lombard Street, and one hears things, gossip, I mean, and stray talk."

Deane seemed suddenly to recede into himself. His host noticed the change, and blamed himself for his want of tact. Nevertheless, as he had begun, so he went on.

"You see, Deane," he continued, "Olive is my only daughter, and it makes one more than ordinarily cautious. This blackmailing case of yours has set people talking a bit. Of course, I think you were right. It was a brave and sportsmanlike thing to do. The man is committed for trial, and I only hope he'll get penal servitude. All the same, there are a lot of people, you know, Deane, who don't take quite the same view of it."

"Naturally," Deane assented. "One can scarcely occupy such a position as mine without having enemies. There are wheels within wheels in the financial world, you know, Lord Nunneley, just as there are in the social world. There are a dozen men who covet my post, and as many hundreds of hangers-on and parasites who would be glad to see me out of it."

"Quite so," returned Lord Nunneley. "Of course, this man Hefferom's attitude was distinctly belligerent, and his solicitors evidently knew what they were talking about when they reserved his defence. Tell me, when Sinclair came to you first had he really any papers at all which were likely to cause you embarrassment?"

"He had an original claim to the Little Anna Gold-Mine," Deane admitted, "but it had lapsed before I took possession. It was not worth the paper it was written on."

"Still, he had got that document?" Lord Nunneley asked.

"Without a doubt," Deane answered.

"You have no idea, I suppose, what became of it?" Lord Nunneley asked.

"Not the slightest," replied Deane. "I only know that it was not found among his effects."

"Would it have been of any interest to you to secure it?" Lord Nunneley continued.

"I would have given a few hundred — perhaps a few thousand — pounds for it," Deane answered, "partly as a curiosity, partly in order to save any possible trouble."

"Of course," Lord Nunneley said, leaning back in his chair and sipping his coffee, "the world is full of people who love to gossip, and you cannot gossip unless you invent ill about someone. Somehow or other, it never amuses people to talk good of their friends; conversation only becomes interesting when one can associate evil with them. There are things being said in connection with this Hefferom affair, Deane, which are not altogether pleasant."

"Go on," said Deane.

"For instance," his host continued, "I was told last night that Hefferom's tale was in substance true, — he did advance this man Sinclair money to come to England and assert his right to the Little

Anna Gold-Mine. Sinclair was murdered with this deed in his possession, and it is freely whispered that you have befriended Rowan—his murderer. The paper has disappeared. We know that. Still, there is a further rumor that it may turn up at his trial. In that case, wouldn't you be rather badly hit?"

Deane shrugged his shoulders. "The exact facts are these," he said. "Sinclair's claim to the Little Anna Gold-Mine is worth very little. Nevertheless, he knew that any action he might take against me in the present state of our money market here would be somewhat disastrous. It would upset our credit and bring down our prices. Therefore, his idea, without a doubt, was to come to England and make a bargain with me. He didn't expect the mine. What he wanted was blood money. He came, and, perhaps unwisely, I would have nothing to do with him. Rowan was known to both of us out there. He came to see me a few days afterwards, and I commissioned him to buy this deed, if he could. He went to look for Sinclair, they drank together, an old quarrel was revived, and they fought. The end of that you know. Where the document has gone to, I can't imagine, but I can assure you that it was never meant to be the basis of a serious claim, merely the foundation stone of a perfect system of blackmailing. If I had listened for five minutes to Hefferom I should have been in his power all my life. I should have lost my self-respect. Very soon I should have lost my nerve. I couldn't do it. I preferred to face him in a court of justice. He came to blackmail me, and he deserved to be punished. If he can prove that it is I who am the ill-doer, I will take my punishment. I can say no more."

"You talk," Lord Nunneley said, looking at him kindly, "as I would have my own son talk. And yet, Deane, this whole affair is distressing to me. I tell you frankly that it has upset all the pleasure with which I consented to your engagement. I cannot bear that anyone associated with Olive should ever find himself in such a position. This case, of course, may go all in your favor, or it may not. If it does not, well, you know very well that it would be the beginning of very unpleasant things."

"Does Olive know of this little luncheon party of ours, Lord Nunneley?" Deane asked.

"She does not," Lord Nunneley asserted. "Olive is, above all things, staunch. She is, I believe, too, sincerely attached to you. I am speaking entirely for myself. I am speaking, too, as the father of an only daughter, whose engagement to you was, after all, a little experimental. I should like to see my daughter released from that engagement, Deane."

Deane smoked steadily for several minutes. Finally, "This is a little hard on me, isn't it, sir? I have only done what you yourself would have done—refused to have underhand dealings with men who made dishonorable propositions to me."

"It is hard on you, Deane," Lord Nunneley declared. "It is very hard indeed. But remember, I never wanted Olive to marry anyone in the city. I know you, and I like you. If you came to me with your hands clean and plenty of money, I should not hesitate for a second, for I believe that Olive likes you. But I hate scandal, I hate gossip, I hate notoriety! This blackmailing case of yours is going to result in all three. I'd like to go home and lay the case before Olive, and have your permission to say that if it seems good to her mother and myself, the engagement between you two is broken."

Deane leaned back in his chair. It seemed to him that he had so little time to give to thoughts outside the immediate trend of the day's work. It was proposed that his engagement with Olive should be broken. What did it mean to him, this engagement? How far into his life had she come? What place did she hold in his heart? His thoughts travelled backwards. He remembered his almost meteor-like accession to wealth and influence. He remembered how all doors had flown open to him. He remembered and realized exactly where he stood. He thought of Lady Olive. He remembered the first day when he had decided that she was the woman who would look well at the head of his table, who would be a pleasant companion for him, and would insure his having friends, when he gave up his struggling, amongst, the class of people with whom he desired to associate. It was in that way that he had looked at it from the first. Was it the same now? He had touched her hands. He had even kissed her lips. She had come into his arms and allowed him to embrace her, without any obvious reluctance. Only a few weeks ago she had kissed him voluntarily, absolutely of her own will. During their fortnight in Scotland she had shown herself more feminine than he had ever believed her. She had insisted upon taking him for walks by herself. She had taken his arm, encouraged him to make love to her, had deserted the bridge table in the evenings to sit in dark corners with him, had allowed him to hold her hand, even to snatch a few kisses. If she did not care for him, at least she was very near it. And as for him,—he was fond of her, without a doubt. Somewhere in the background of his apprehension there was some shadowy idea of a greater thing than this, a love more thrilling, more passionate, more mysterious,—music in the veins, which no Lady Olive in the world had ever created. But there was about these thoughts something absolutely unreal, fantastic. They had never taken to themselves shape, never become associated with any human being. They were nothing to trust to, he told himself,— nothing. He looked out of the rain-swept window of the club. Curiously enough, he had a sudden vision of Winifred Rowan's quiet, set face. The memory of one passionate moment seemed suddenly to creep along his heartstrings like the wind over the strings of a harp. Such folly, he thought, frowning! Such absolute folly!

"Lord Nunneley," he said at last, "I am only anxious to do what Lady Olive wishes. If you will go home and tell her exactly what you have told me, I should like you to add that it is only her happiness that I wish, and that if she desires to release me, I shall accept her decision without a murmur."

Lord Nunneley played with his coffee-spoon nervously. "I knew you'd say something like that, Deane," he said. "Of course, it will not be easy. I believe that my daughter is really fond of you, and our influence over her, both her mother's and mine, is somewhat limited. You wouldn't feel inclined, I suppose, to come over to our side, to realize that under the circumstances an alliance between you and her could scarcely be a satisfactory thing,—in short, to encourage her to bring it to an end?"

"In other words," Deane said, "you propose that instead of suffering myself to be jilted by Lady Olive, I should offer myself as a victim?"

"It's asking a good deal, I know," Lord Nunneley said, "and, of course, it all depends upon how you feel about it. But I tell you frankly, I can't help thinking—you must realize a little that this blackmailing case, even if it turns out well, is bound to put a different complexion upon things."

"You must convince Lady Olive of that," Deane said. "I am ready to accept my dismissal, but you must forgive me if I decline to do anything to facilitate it. On the contrary, I shall insist upon seeing Lady Olive before she absolutely decides. I shall not plead with her—you need not be afraid of that—but I shall want to be quite sure that there has been no misunderstanding of any sort."

"There is no time like the present," Lord Nunneley said. "Drive home with me, and we will interview my daughter at once."

She heard all that her father had to say, listened to him gravely and attentively. Then she turned to Deane. "And you?" she asked. "What do you say to it all?"

"My dear Olive," said Deane, "it amounts to this. I am to be the hero or victim, as the case may be, of a cause célèbre. I cannot come out of it with any considerable credit; I may come out to find myself under very grave suspicion. I admit that appearances are against me. There will even be people who will whisper that I sent Rowan from my office as an assassin to Sinclair, and that the deed he brought with him from South Africa is in my safe, or at the back of my fire. No one has ever been free from calumny. I certainly am going to have my share of it. It may—it very likely will—lessen my prestige. You will find some of your friends who will talk of the 'Deane Blackmailing Affair,' and who will never be quite sure whether I was prosecutor or defendant. You will find all your life my name looked upon with a certain amount of suspicion, because, in a case of this sort, prosecutor and defendant, and even the witnesses, are all classed together by that somewhat vague portion of the public which your friends represent. I admit all this. I also admit that it would be an act of perfect justice if you should tell me to kiss your hands and go."

She pointed to the door. "Father," she said, "will you leave us for a moment? There is something which I have to say to Stirling."

CHAPTER X
A BROKEN ENGAGEMENT

Even after the door had closed upon Lord Nunneley, and Deane was alone with his fiancée, words did not seem to come easily to either of them. Lady Olive was sitting back in the corner of a low couch. Deane was standing upon the hearthrug, his hands behind him, his face a little wrinkled with perplexity.

"I suppose," he said thoughtfully, "you would like me, Olive, to explain exactly how this claim came about?"

"On the contrary," she answered, "I do not wish you to do anything of the sort."

He looked at her in some surprise. Her voice had prepared him for a change of some sort, but he was nevertheless puzzled. There was a slight flush of color in her cheeks, and her eyes were softer than usual.

"Stirling," she said, "come and sit down here by my side."

He obeyed at once. She turned and faced him.

"I am puzzled, Stirling," she said. "I want to ask you a question. You have been lunching with my father?"

"Yes!" Deane answered. "At his club."

"I know that he feels very strongly about this matter," she said. "Tell me, did the suggestion that our engagement should be broken off come from him?"

"Certainly."

"And you?" she said. "Tell me exactly what you felt, what it meant to you? I don't want you to fence with words, please," she went on. "Tell me this honestly. Was it anything of a relief to you?"

"Assuredly not," he answered wonderingly.

"Think again," she begged. "You answer quickly, but is that because you are very, very sure, or because you are taking it for granted? You see you are one of those men, Stirling," she went on earnestly, "whose disposition does not allow them to look back. We are engaged, I was your deliberate choice, and after that, so far as you are concerned, the matter was ended. The possibility that you had made a mistake would never occur to you, simply because you would regard the matter as inevitable. Tell me, if it were not inevitable, if you were not engaged to me at this moment, Stirling, would you ask me again?"

Her words amazed him. He had never given her credit for such insight, such perceptions. It seemed, indeed, as though she had realized something of which he himself was not yet conscious, and yet something which might very well exist.

"How long have you had this idea, Olive?" he asked gravely.

"All the time," she answered. "At first, of course, it seemed all right, but up in Scotland, and since then, I have wondered whether you have not looked upon me as something quite outside your life, — a necessary and desirable adjunct, perhaps, to your household and growing prosperity. Don't think that I am complaining," she continued, "but in all our recent communications the personal note has not been very strongly marked, has it? I can see exactly, too, how my father's suggestion has moved you. You don't feel, do you, as though the sun had ceased to shine, or the world to move, because there is a chance that you may lose me?"

Deane was not often so doubtful of himself. In a sense he knew that she was right. And yet, her very apprehension of these things, the new earnestness with which she was looking at him, the thought that he was very near indeed to losing her, seemed to stimulate his interest, — made him feel, indeed, that it would not be a light thing to give her up.

"Olive," he said, "I wish I could make you know exactly how I feel. If I have been a little slow and reticent of speech, believe me, it is not that I have not cared. On the other hand, there is some truth in what you have said — I mean that I do honestly believe that I have taken things a little too much for granted, that knowing there was no other woman in my life, knowing how desirable you were, and how really fond of you I was, I think I was content to let the rest come, as I certainly did feel that it would come."

"I think I understand," she said slowly. "Now tell me exactly what you think of my father's request?"

"I think that it is reasonable," Deane answered. "It is more reasonable, even, than your father knows of. I think that I have been a little too successful, perhaps, during these later years of my life. I have grown to underestimate the possibilities of trouble."

"This is really serious, then?"

He nodded. "I am afraid," he said, "that I have been a little over-bold. I ought to have kicked that man Hefferom out of my office half-a-dozen times, until he came to reason, and then bought him off for good for a thousand pounds. But you see I didn't. All my life I have hated compromises. I knew that he was a blackguard, and I dealt with him as a blackguard, and I have left him with the cards in his hands."

"Then I suppose my father was right," she said, sighing.

"I suppose he was," Deane answered.

She held out her hand. "Very well, Stirling," she said, "let it be so. Our engagement is broken, and I will see that the proper steps are taken to announce it. But I want you to understand this from me, that if you had cared, if I could have seen any signs whatever of your caring, no word of my father's, nor anything that could have happened to you in the city or elsewhere, any disgrace or any loss of money, could have separated us."

He took a step towards her. "Olive!" he exclaimed.

"No!" she said, a little sharply, and rang the bell.

He turned and walked out. In the hall he passed Lord Nunneley. "We have arranged it according to your wish, sir," he said, "your daughter and I."

Lord Nunneley looked at him curiously. Deane had the look of a man who has been hard hit.

"I am sorry, Deane. I hope you understand there's nothing personal in it."

"I understand!" said Deane, briefly.

CHAPTER XI
BITTER WORDS

From the pit of the world—from the Law Courts, hot and crowded, where the atmosphere was heavy with strife,—the modern battleground, where the fighting was at least as dramatic over the souls of men as on those other fields, reddened with their blood, Deane escaped to find himself, after a few hours' journey, in this strangest of churchyards upon the bare hillside. The church itself, squat, square-towered, and tumbling into decay, stood out like a watch-tower upon the cliff. The churchyard, bordered by low gray stone walls, seemed to contain little more than a dozen or so of graves, and from one of these Deane turned away, and with Winifred by his side commenced the long descent to the level of the sea. The half-a-dozen who had attended the ceremony out of curiosity had already melted away. The parson, with his book under his arm, had gone into the vestry, but neither custom nor age had failed to rob those few sentences of their wonderful, threatening pathos. Even Deane was a little moved. The girl who walked by his side carried still with her that impenetrable mask, but there was something more like real sadness in the steady gaze of her unseeing eyes.

The air was filled with sunshine, the singing of larks, and the calling of the white-winged seagulls wheeling about their heads. Below, the sea had receded to its furthest limits. The creeks were dry. The shore was piled with masses of fragrant seaweed. The grass-grown dykes which led down to the tower stood high and dry, like ribbons across the land. Little sandy spits were visible, far out from the shore, and only the white-topped posts marked the way of the tidal river out beyond the island of seagulls and sand.

Deane, after his anxious days and his tearing ride from town in the great motor, felt the peace of all these things, showed it in his face, felt it in his heart. The last few days had taught him a good deal. Never had he been so weary of his place in the great world as he was that afternoon. Even that little ceremony in the wind-swept churchyard, the coffin lowered into the grave, the heaping of earth, the simple words spoken by the bareheaded vicar,—even that little ceremony had left its impression. After all, how small the difference between Death and Life,—ignominy and greatness! His own reputation had many times during the last few days trembled in the balance. What was the value of that, even,—of all his wealth,—compared to the great primeval facts of life?

His thoughts suddenly turned to the girl by his side. He looked at her pityingly,—looked at her, too, with curiosity. She had accepted his coming almost as a matter of course. All the time, though he had known well that she was suffering, she had been wordless, as though her grief were something so great that no outward sign of it could be anything else but pitifully inadequate. In her quiet, graceful walk, the very reserve, the negativeness, so to speak, of her coloring, her speech, her looks, she still represented to him an insoluble enigma. Was it possible, now that her brother had gone, that she would speak? In any case, the silence between them could not continue much longer, for already they were down on the marshes, and, as though by common consent, had turned seaward, towards where the lonely gray tower stood out on its little sandy eminence.

"Tell me, Miss Rowan," he said, "what are your plans now?"

"My plans?" she repeated, without turning her head.

"Yes!" he went on. "I know that your brother's death is a blow to you, but remember that it was inevitable. It was a thing which was bound to come, and in many ways it was kinder and better that it should happen like this. You could not have chosen for him a more peaceful ending, a more peaceful resting-place. For anyone with even the faintest beliefs in the future life could anything be more beautiful than to rest there, with the eternal lullaby of the sea in his ears, free from encroachment, save the encroachment of nature herself?"

She turned to look at him, and the calm scrutiny of her level gray eyes somehow disturbed him. "It is easy for you to talk like that," she said. "You are still young and strong, and if the pendulum of fate swings against you one day, it pays you back the next. You are selfish because you cannot help it. You cannot even realize the hideousness of death! You cannot realize it because it comes to other people, and not to you!"

"You are a little unfair, Miss Rowan," Deane answered. "You must remember that your brother was a doomed man."

"Yes, but why?" she cried. "He was younger than you. There were no worse things in his life. Always he was battling with failure and disappointment. And this is the end,—to sit opposite a doctor, and be told you may live a month, three months, a measure of time. Oh! it's easy to think about it for other people! Think of yourself going about with the knowledge in your heart that as the days passed one by one they brought you nearer to the end, that every morning when your eyes opened, instead of the joy of life would come once more that terrible fear."

"Your brother was not a coward, Miss Rowan," Deane said.

"A coward! You mean that he did not show his sufferings!" she exclaimed. "That does not mean that he did not suffer. Oh! I have heard him in the night when he thought that he was alone, I have heard his agony. And that is the end!"

She turned and faced the little stone church on the hill, the rudely enclosed churchyard, in the far corner of which was still visible the bare heap of mould.

"He felt it coming, he felt the strength pass from him day by day,—he, who had never known what it was to live, who had never known the days of riches or success or power. There he lies,—God knows for what purpose, to what end!"

Deane walked for a little way in silence. It seemed to him that the girl's bitterness was scarcely reasonable. Yet he realized that at such a time reason loses its power.

"His last days, at least, were as comfortable as possible."

"Comfortable!" she exclaimed scornfully. "He lived in hell!"

"You are not blaming me, by any chance?" Deane asked quietly.

She turned upon him, and the mask seemed suddenly raised. There blazed into her eyes a great fire. There trembled in the notes of her voice a wonderful passion. Her form seemed to dilate. They were walking now upon the top of the dyke, and she seemed to have been suddenly transformed into something vengeful, some grim representation of Fate.

"Blame you!" she cried. "I tell you that I hate all you smug, successful, phrase-making men, who succeeded where he failed. What are you that he was not? He was brave, he worked hard, he was honest, courageous, he was all that a man should be. If you were ever these things you at least were not more, and to you comes wealth and easy days, honor, a long, peaceful future. London — the world — is full of you, grubbing your way through life, thinking what magnificent creatures you are, opening your pockets to help with your alms those who have fallen, those who, if there was justice upon the earth, should be in your places!"

"This is unreasonable," Deane declared coldly.

"Unreasonable! Who said it was anything else?" she cried. "What reason is there in life, in death, in success or failure? Can you tell me the laws by which life is ruled, can you find them anywhere, at the base of any man's success or another's failure? Reasonable, indeed! One man swims and another drowns. Who can tell why? One man grows rich, another starves, and as often as not it is the clever man who starves and the fool who grows rich. There is no reason in those things. There is no reason in my hate for you and all those who have lived easy lives, and who go on living them while he — lies there!"

She turned back once more and pointed with outstretched hand towards the little church. The wind blew her skirts about her, — disturbed for once the trim, uncompromising arrangement of her hair. The color had come into her cheeks at last. Deane wondered why he had never before thought her beautiful!

"I am sorry you are feeling like this," he said. "I did what I could for your brother."

"Be silent!" she interrupted fiercely. "You did what you could! To insure your own safety you sent him on a desperate, unworthy mission — to worm his way into the confidence of a drunkard, to steal for you, to be your jackal. What did you care what the consequences might be! What did you care, so long as your own reputation and wealth were saved! He was to be one other — my poor Basil — one other of those to be crushed beneath the great wheels!"

"It is not fair," replied Deane, "to make such statements. Your brother knew his risks, and he took them."

"Knew his risks!" she repeated. "You mean that because you were on your feet when he was on the ground, you would make use of him like any other lump of mud you would spurn with your foot if you had not found a use for it. He did your bidding, poor fool, but where he failed, I succeeded. You have to deal with me now, and I think that it is my turn to make terms!"

Deane looked at her curiously. "At last," he said, "you are going to admit your possession of that little document?"

"At last," she admitted, "I am going to tell you that I have it!"

"And to name your price?" he asked.

There was a queer little sound in her throat, like an unnatural laugh. "My price! Yes, that is another matter!"

CHAPTER XII
A STRANGE BETROTHAL

Southward, through the country lanes whose hedges were still wreathed with late honeysuckle, on to the great mainroad, Deane's car was driven through the night,—always southward, till the lights of the great city flared before them up into the sky. Deane himself, for hour after hour, had sat back in his corner, buried in thought. His companion was even more invisible, but as the end of the journey drew near he roused himself with an effort, turned on the electric light which hung down from the roof of the car, lit a cigarette, and, bending forward, looked into the half-hidden face of the girl who was reclining by his side.

"My dear fiancée," he said, "we are nearing London. Won't you rouse yourself and give me your further orders?"

She sat up, with a little yawn. "Let down the windows, please," she said. "We will have some fresh air in for a few minutes."

He obeyed her at once. The sweet midnight air through which they were rushing was like a douche of cold water upon her face.

"How far are we from London?" she asked.

"Less than twenty miles. Unless we are stopped, we shall certainly be there in half-an-hour."

"Why did you disturb me?" she asked.

"To know your wishes."

"You had better leave me at one of the small hotels in the west end," she said. "I daresay you can think of one at which you are known. In the morning, please come and see me and bring some money. I shall want to engage a companion and a maid, and to buy some clothes."

Deane looked at her curiously. Her manner was perfectly natural. "Anything else?" he asked calmly.

"I don't think so," she answered.

"You mentioned the fact, I believe," he continued, "that you were—that you had done me the honor—that you were, in fact, my fiancée."

"Well?" she murmured.

"Under those circumstances," he continued, "don't you think—"

His hand rested for a moment upon hers. She drew it at once away. "No, I think not!" she answered.

"I have not had much experience," he went on, "in being engaged, but it seemed to me that there were certain privileges which belonged to that state."

"You are perfectly well aware," she answered, "that ours is not an engagement of that sort. You know something about the world in which the men marry for position and the women for money, don't you? You can look upon our engagement as being of that order. I marry you because it is the only way I can make you pay your debt. I have given you notice from the first. I mean to gain everything I can, and to give nothing."

"Nothing?" he repeated.

"As little as possible," she answered. "As a matter of fact, you are singularly indifferent to me. You simply represent the things I desire, the things which are owing to me, the things which were owing to—to him. I marry you to acquire them. You marry me because you must."

"Well," he said, "ours promises to be a novel matrimonial experience."

"Not at all," she answered.

"You have been reading too many novels," he declared. "People really don't marry in this sort of way at all. There is always a pretence of sentiment about it. If not, for very shame's sake, they try to cultivate it."

"Then we," she answered, "will remain exceptions."

"Do you dislike me?" he asked.

"Personally I have not thought about you," she answered. "Apart from that, I hate you. You represent the victor, and all that I have loved upon this earth have been the vanquished. Willingly I would not give you so much as the touch of my fingers. If I thought that my presence was a pleasure to you, I would shrink back into myself. If I thought that any happiness could come to you from our association, even now I would throw myself from the car and end it."

"Our prospects of matrimonial bliss," he remarked, "appear to me to be distinctly above the average."

"I do not expect," she answered, "to find any pleasure that may come to me in later life, at your hands."

"I shall certainly not allow you to flirt."

"I know the law," she answered. "I know what I may do and what I may not do. I shall not transgress it. I want your money, I want your position, I want your power. These things I will share with you. For the rest, you cannot keep too far away to please me."

He leaned towards her, heedless of the fact that she was shrinking away. There was something a little pitiful in the blue-gray eyes which tried so hard to hold him at a distance. "Well," said he, "it will be an interesting experiment, at any rate. Personally, I think that you are a brave woman. I wonder that you did not take the money without me."

"What good would that have been to me?" she answered. "I have no name, no friends. Can't you imagine the sort of people who would have come hanging on to my skirts, if I had made my début on the scene as a widow or a spinster with a large fortune, unattached, looking for companions? No! I need your name, Mr. Stirling Deane."

"I am not at all sure," he answered grimly, "that you will find that much of an asset."

"You must see to it that I do find it an asset, and a valuable one," she answered. "You are relieved now from any fear of that deed being produced. There is no shadow of evidence to connect you with the man Sinclair, or with my brother's transaction with him. If your lawyers are clever and you are brave, you must win your case with honor, and Hefferom will be sent to prison. He deserves it, in any case."

Deane nodded. "I shall win my case all right," he said. "For me there never was any danger except in the production of that document, concerning which you have been so mysterious."

"It was mine," she answered. "I ran all the risk to get it. I ran risks the memory of which will haunt me all my days. I have lost Basil. All that I can do is to exact the utmost price that you can pay for that little paper."

"It isn't worth it, you know," said Deane. "I believe, even now, that I should win my case, anyhow."

She smiled—a curious little contraction of the corners of her lips. Her eyes mocked him. "Perhaps," she said, "but it is a different thing since Sinclair's murder. Its production to-day would ruin you inevitably, whether it were held a legal document or not."

"We all make mistakes," he said, looking out of the window.

"But too often others pay for them!" she murmured, turning away.

Presently he gave some instructions to the chauffeur. The pace of the car slackened as they reached the outskirts of London and turned westward.

"Well," he remarked, "the world is full of surprises for us. I little thought, when I came down to Rakney, that it was to find a bride!"

She shivered a little at his words, but made no reply.

"Forgive me," he said, "if I do not seem very coherent about it all. As a matter of fact, you see, I was not expecting to take up obligations of this sort again so quickly."

"If you do not mind," she said coldly, "we will not discuss it."

"I may at least be permitted to ask," he continued, "when it is your intention to—marry me?"

"In about two months' time," she answered.

"You would like our engagement announced?" he asked.

She hesitated for a few seconds. "In a fortnight's time," she declared.

"In the meantime," he inquired, "I shall have the pleasure of being received by you?"

"Certainly," she answered. "I shall expect to lunch and dine with you occasionally, to be taken to the theatres, and for short expeditions into the country — Ranelagh and Hurlingham, for instance."

"Delightful!"

The car stopped at one of the smallest and most famous of semi-private hotels, in the neighborhood of Bond Street. Deane assisted his companion to alight.

"If you will come in for a moment," he said, "I will arrange things for you here. They know me very well."

She followed him into the hotel and waited while he interviewed the manager. Then he took his leave of her, bowing over her reluctantly offered hand, and smiling into her face as though honestly anxious to penetrate behind its absolute imperturbability.

"I hope you will find the little suite comfortable," he said. "You must go to bed soon, and try and rest. They will do everything that is possible for you, I am sure, until you have your own maid and things. Good-night!"

She raised her eyes for a moment to his, but there was more indignation than gratitude in the glance she threw upon him. "I am very much obliged to you. Good-night!"

Deane drove back to his rooms. As yet he could scarcely realize the situation. Had anyone ever been confronted with a position so unique? The mystery of the girl's impenetrability was solved at last!

CHAPTER XIII
DESPERATION

The curtain had fallen upon the first act of this little drama in Deane's life. Hefferom was committed for trial. Deane had walked into the court a few minutes late, as though the whole affair was one which interested him only indirectly. He had gone into the witness box without hesitation, and his story had been so perfectly rational and straightforward that people began to wonder whether, indeed, any defence was possible. Cross-examination only amused him. Hefferom, who went into court expecting to be released, was committed at once to the Old Bailey, and to everyone's surprise, his own included, was refused bail.

Deane left the court a few minutes after the case was closed, and paused for a moment to light a cigarette on the steps. On the edge of the pavement there was a woman who watched with steady and scrutinizing interest every person who left the entrance of the Law Courts. When Deane came out she advanced towards him. "Is Hefferom free?" she asked.

Deane looked at her, and recognized at once Ruby Sinclair.

"No!" he answered. "He is committed for trial."

"You—"

She leaned forward as though about to strike him. Deane neither shrank back nor showed any sign of interest in her words.

"What is Hefferom to you?" he asked quickly.

"He is no blackmailer, at any rate!" she answered fiercely.

"The Court has ventured to think otherwise," Deane declared.

She was almost at his side now. Suddenly his eyes caught the sight of something glittering, something half drawn from the pocket of her dress. Her wrist was caught in a clasp of iron.

"Young lady," he said sternly, "are you mad?"

"If I am, it is your fault," she answered.

"Nonsense!" he declared. "You see that policeman there? He is watching us now. Let go the revolver and be off. I don't want to give you into custody—my life is worth something for others as well as myself—and I shall certainly do it unless you obey me."

She gave a little sob, and her fingers relaxed their hold upon the revolver, which Deane transferred into his own pocket. She glided away into the crowd. Deane stepped into his brougham, giving the man the address of the hotel where Winifred Rowan was staying. He leaned back in the seat, looking at the little weapon in his hands. Somehow, the fact of his escape, instead of bringing any exultation with it, seemed to depress him strangely. Deane had never called himself or believed himself to be a religious man, yet there was certainly one principle which had always been part of his creed,— to live and let live. He was not a greedy capitalist. He could look upon money without any desire to absorb it. Yet lately he seemed to have been forced into tortuous paths. From the moment when he had attempted to make use of Rowan as a tool, everything had gone against him. Rowan himself lay dead in that windy churchyard, and the words which had been spoken over Rowan's grave were still fresh in his memory. He had lost Lady Olive, of whom, in a way, he had been fond. And at her own bidding he was engaged to this strange, impenetrable girl, a situation which he could not wholly realize, and yet which he felt to be surrounded with danger and humiliation. Then there was this other,—Ruby Sinclair,—who had come to London expecting to find a fortune, and had found nothing but her uncle's dead body. She, too, looked upon him as a hungry schemer, the indirect cause of her uncle's death, a robber, if not a murderer! He looked at the little revolver, opened it carelessly, and laughed as he stared into the empty breech. It was unloaded, a brand-new toy which had never been discharged. He threw it into the opposite seat with a little gesture of contempt. All its tragedy seemed to have passed away. She had bought it to frighten him with. There had, after all, been no serious purpose in her mind. She too, perhaps, had hoped to play the part of extortioner.

What was his offence, he asked himself, as his brougham glided along the Embankment. Simply this: there had been a claim presented for his mine, which was, without doubt, a fraud, which few people would ever have believed in, and which, in a court of law, would have stood but little chance of success. What a fool he had been not to defy Sinclair, to go to his directors and tell them the truth, to resist stoutly any claim the man might bring! Since his first compromise with Rowan, everything had gone wrong. It was unworthy for a man in his position to have allowed Rowan even to play the ambassador, apart from anything else. He saw very clearly in those few minutes where the mistake of his life had been. What he could not see was whither he was tending.

Winifred was waiting for him in the hall of the small hotel in Dover Street. For three days, at her own request, he had not seen her. Nothing, however, had prepared him for the transformation which he now saw. She was faultlessly dressed in a gown of the latest design, and a picture hat which even he recognized as being something quite apart from the usual efforts of even the Bond Street shopkeepers. In every detail she seemed to express the wholly self-satisfied, half-insolent perfection of the woman who knows that she may and does command the best of everything. And with this change in her dress seemed to have come a similar change in her deportment. Her aloofness was still evident enough, but she carried herself with confidence, and with a sort of languid, graceful ease.

"You are nearly ten minutes late," she said quietly. "Where are you taking me to lunch?"

"Wherever you like," he answered. "What about Prince's?"

She took a gold purse and a tiny black spaniel from the neatly dressed maid who stood by her side, and lifting her skirts in her other hand, passed through the door which he was holding open. The lace of her petticoat, the slenderness of her arched instep, the delicate narrowness of her patent shoes, were revelations to him. He gave an order to his chauffeur, and sat down by her side.

"You appear," he said, "to possess a gift for assimilation!"

"My sex is like that," she said. "I have had a good many years to wait, to store up knowledge in. Besides," she continued, a little mockingly, "you yourself are supposed to be something exceptional in the way of grooming, aren't you? There is no need for other people to find our engagement surprising."

Looking at her critically, "I think," he said, "that there is no fear of that."

"You flatter me," she murmured.

"Not at all," he answered. "People might wonder, perhaps, how it is possible to fall in love with anyone whose expression so much resembles that of those statues in there," pointing to a gallery which they were passing. "You have no other fault. There is none, at least, to be found in your appearance. You certainly do look, however, a little inclined to be faultily faultless."

She laughed, — a laugh, however, which brought no color into her cheeks or light into her eyes. "I am a statue," she said, "into which life has not yet been breathed. You see you have been a little remiss up till now. You have never attempted to make love to me!"

"Do you mean to say —" he asked, leaning towards her, —

She gently pushed back his hand, saying: "Please don't be ridiculous. Of course, you must know that overtures of that sort, under the circumstances, are impossible."

"For always?" he asked.

"Certainly!"

"Perhaps you will draw up a little code of conditions," he remarked. "I feel a little in the dark sometimes as to what is expected of me."

"You will easily pick it up as we go along," she replied. "Is this Prince's? I wonder if I shall succeed in behaving as though I had lunched here every day of my life!"

CHAPTER XIV
AN AFTERNOON'S SHOPPING

Deane found a singular interest, an interest which amounted almost to fascination, in watching the demeanor and general deportment of his companion. Her adaptability was little short of marvellous. She smiled at the right moment at the obsequious maître d'hôtel, and exhibited just the proper amount of interest in the luncheon which Deane ordered. The restaurant was somewhat crowded, but there was no one who attracted more notice than Deane and the girl who sat opposite him,—slim, and elegantly dressed,—looking around her with a certain partly veiled interest, which was all the time in piquant contrast to the languor of her eyes and manner. She was by no means a silent companion, although her conversation consisted for the most part of questions. She had an unerring gift for discovering the most noteworthy of the little crowd by whom they were surrounded, and she was continually asking questions about them, with a persistence which clearly indicated an interest scarcely suggested by her general deportment.

"I wonder," Deane said, toward the end of their meal, "whether social preëminence is amongst your carefully veiled ambitions."

"I am not at all sure," she answered. "Of course, one develops according to circumstances. In the office of Messrs. Rubicon & Moore I naturally cared nothing for the world which I could only read about in the columns of Modern Society. As one comes into touch with things, one appreciates. It is always interesting to know people."

"I am afraid," Deane said, with covert satire, "that my friends are scarcely what you would call fashionable."

"Your friends?" she remarked, looking up at him. "But that doesn't matter, does it? I shall make my own friends later on."

Deane looked across the table. She was patting the head of her little spaniel, and watching, with a self-possession which amounted almost to insolence, the exodus of a party from the neighboring table.

"Young lady," he said, "what sort of a life did you lead before you went to Messrs. Rubicon & Moore's? I always understood that your people were very poor, and only respectably connected."

"You understood the truth," she answered, with composure.

"Will you tell me, then," he asked, "how you learned to wear your clothes? — how you picked up all the little tricks of social life?"

The very faintest of smiles parted her lips, a smile that wrinkled at the corners of her eyes, and suddenly altered her appearance so that Deane was forced to recognize the charm which even to himself he had denied.

"My dear Mr. Deane," she said, "it is the natural heritage of a woman to assimilate quickly, especially," she added, after a moment's pause, "amongst surroundings for which she has had a great desire. Many a time when I was typing price-lists in that wretched little office, in a black alpaca gown, with my hat hanging up opposite me, — a black straw with faded flowers, which had cost me three or four shillings, with darned stockings and patched boots, — many a time I have left off typing for a few minutes, and thought and wondered what this must be like. I suppose I have what you would call a natural aptitude for it. It is because I have thought of it, pondered over it, desired it."

Deane looked at her wonderingly. "Well," he said, "let me congratulate you. You play the game to perfection. If I were in a position to make terms —"

"You are not," she interrupted shortly. "Please to pay the bill. I am going to take you shopping."

They left the brougham at the corner of Bond Street. Winifred had signified her desire to walk for a little time. Deane found himself becoming thoroughly interested — not, as he told himself, in his companion herself, but in his study of her. The women they passed she subjected, nearly every one of them, to a close and comprehensive scrutiny. At the men she scarcely glanced. She found, perhaps, her greatest interest in the shop windows. She led him across the road to the establishment of a great jeweller.

"You have not given me an engagement ring," she said, a little abruptly. "We will go in and choose one."

He followed her obediently into the shop, and stood by her side while she described minutely the sort of ring she required. Her manner inspired instant respect. She knew exactly what she wanted, and what she wanted was the rarest and most beautiful stones, set in the newest fashion. She showed very little enthusiasm—hesitated, even—over the ring which was produced at last, after a little hesitation, and shown almost with reverence. It had been made for a queen, but something had gone wrong—a matter of politics—and they had not dared to part with it. Even Deane stared when the man at his elbow whispered the price, but Winifred never moved a muscle.

"I think it will do," she said, turning to him. "It is very nearly what I wanted. And I want a few pins—emeralds and diamonds I prefer."

The shopman was already producing a tray from the window. She spoke of pearls, and examined those that were shown her with the air of a connoisseur.

"I shall want a rope of pearls very soon," she told the man, "but not just yet. Perhaps you will let Mr. Deane know when you have enough of the ones the color and size I like."

"It will give us very great pleasure, madam, to collect them," the man said, bowing.

Deane produced his cheque-book—fortunately, he was well known—and wrote a cheque for over two thousand pounds in exchange for the receipt which the man handed to him. Winifred calmly withdrew her glove and slipped on the ring. The other things she asked them to send. When she left the shop, it seemed to Deane that there was a little more color in her cheeks and a deeper light in her eyes.

"Jewelry interests you?" he remarked, as they stood for a moment on the pavement.

"Yes!" she answered. "Of course it does. Everything of this sort interests me. Haven't I longed all my days to feel the touch of pearls upon my bare neck, to have something like this upon my finger that I could look at and worship, not only for itself but for the things it represents? Come and buy me some flowers. My sitting-room is a wilderness. Afterwards, I am going into the milliner's beyond."

Deane followed her obediently into the florist's opposite. She chose a great bowl of pink roses and some white lilac.

"How many of the roses, madam?" the shopman asked her.

She looked at him with faintly upraised eyebrows. "Oh! send them as they are," she answered carelessly.

"There are four dozen, madam," the man remarked, bowing.

She nodded indifferently. The fact that they were a shilling each did not appear to interest her.

"Is that all the lilacs you have?" she asked, as they were leaving the shop.

"All we have at present, madam," the man answered.

"Please get some more," she said, "if you can. These hotel sitting-rooms," she added, turning to Deane, "seem to have a sort of odor of their own. One can only get rid of it by having flowers everywhere. Now I am going in here," she said, stopping at a tiny milliner's. "You must wait for me—I know you are dying to smoke a cigarette—but you had better give me your pocket-book."

"I am afraid," Deane answered imperturbably, "that its contents will be of little use to you, for I have only twenty pounds with me. If you will take these"—he handed her the notes—"I will take a taximeter and cash a cheque. I shall only be a few minutes."

She nodded, and disappeared into the shop. When she came out again Deane had returned from his little expedition, and was talking to some men whom he knew. They glanced at Winifred a little curiously as they raised their hats and passed on.

"We can perhaps continue our shopping," Deane said, "more comfortably now."

She ignored the faint note of satire in his tone. "One needs so many things," she murmured. "The woman inside is just making out my bill. I think I shall want another thirty pounds."

"I am afraid," he said, "that you have not been able to find what you wanted. The amount seems trivial."

"Well," she said, "there was a lace dressing-gown about which I could not quite make up my mind. Perhaps, after all, I had better have it."

She turned back into the shop, and he followed her. The lace dressing-gown was still lying upon a chair, and in a few moments Deane found it being held up before him by a vivacious little Frenchwoman, who was endeavoring to convince him that in it Madame would look a dream. It was very filmy, very dainty, wonderfully expensive. Deane heard the price without moving a muscle.

"I think you had better have it," he said. "I am sure," he went on, looking into her eyes, "that you will look charming in it."

For the first time he seemed to score. She bent over some lace handkerchiefs, as though anxious to avoid his gaze. "Very well," she said, "I think that will be all now. Please pay, and let us go."

Once more they were in the streets.

"I want a dressing-bag," she said, a little abruptly.

"By all means," he answered. "We had better go back to the jeweller's. Do you prefer mother-of-pearl fittings, or gold?"

"I am not sure," she answered. "I should like to look at some."

They were twenty minutes or so making a selection. Deane wrote another cheque, and stuffed another receipt into his pocket. He had made a few suggestions himself, which had increased the cost considerably.

"Where to now?" he asked.

"I want some gloves," she said. "Perhaps you would rather go back to your office now. I must not take up your whole afternoon."

"I am entirely at your service," he assured her. "Believe me, I find shopping quite an interesting novelty."

"You mean," she said, "that you like to watch the effect upon me. You think I don't understand. It is quite easy. Tell me how I seem to you?"

"You seem very much to the manner born," he answered, "but you seem also, if I may say so, as though you were getting rid of the pent-up desires of years. For instance," he added, as they strolled along the south side of the street, "there is a certain almost fierceness — I won't say barbarism — in the way you absorb the things you desire. I am not complaining," he added quickly. "As a matter of fact, I am rather inclined to welcome any note of humanity. So long as we are engaged," he added, looking at her sideways, "one would just as soon feel that one were engaged to a living person as an automaton."

She kept her eyes averted, but he saw the faint spot of color burning in her cheeks.

"This is where I think I shall get the gloves I want," she said.

"I will come in with you, if I may," he answered.

Her purchases here showed a little more restraint. Nevertheless, everything she chose was the best of its sort. When she came out, her appetite seemed somehow whetted. She walked along the street almost listlessly.

"Do you know that it is nearly half-past four?" he said. "You had better let me give you some tea."

She nodded indifferently. "Thank you. That would be very nice."

"Will you come to my rooms," he asked, "or shall we go into the Carlton and hear the music?"

She looked at him quickly, and then back into a shop window. "To the Carlton, if you please," she said coldly.

They walked to the corner of the street and stood waiting while the brougham came round to them. She turned toward a florist's and looked into the window.

"You would like some more flowers?" he asked.

She led him into the shop without a word. There was a cluster of red roses over which she bent and selected one. "I should like this, please," she said.

"One only, madam?" the shopman asked.

"One only," she answered composedly. "I will pin it in here if you will cut the stalk a little," she added, removing a brooch from the bosom of her gown. "Will you pay for this, please?" she added, turning to Deane.

He was taken aback for a moment. "You are sure that there is nothing else?" he asked.

"Nothing," she answered.

They left the shop and he handed her into the brougham. Deane was suddenly conscious that his pulse was beating a little faster, even though her fingers had lain in his absolutely unresponsive. He was wondering what sort of a whim it was which had led her to desire that one flower.

CHAPTER XV
A FRIEND

A man in the city, who was an old friend of Lord Nunneley, stopped the latter as he was on the point of entering his club.

"By the bye, Nunneley," he said, "did I understand—I think I saw it in the papers—that the marriage between your daughter and Stirling Deane was off?"

"The engagement has been broken off," answered Lord Nunneley, a little stiffly. "Why?"

"That's all right," said the man. "The only thing was that as I was one of the people you came to, to ask about Deane, I felt that if it was still on I ought to tell you that things aren't supposed to be just the same as they were."

"Do you mean about Deane?" asked Lord Nunneley.

His friend nodded. "There are some very curious rumors going about," he said. "You remember, of course, his charging a man named Hefferom—a South African—with an attempt at blackmail the other day? The man was committed for trial, and there was not much came out in the evidence before the magistrates. Since then, however, people have been talking. They say that Hefferom had actual knowledge of documents proving that Deane's title to the Little Anna Gold-Mine was a false one, and that the mine in reality belonged to Hefferom himself and a partner."

"That sounds like a very curious story," Lord Nunneley remarked. "If it is true, why doesn't Hefferom produce his document and have done with it?"

"Because it has been stolen," the other answered. "There are all sorts of stories going about, too, concerning the theft. The point remains, however, that there is a strong feeling that the document in question does exist, and that it may turn up. If so, of course, it would ruin Deane. I see that the shares of his corporation have had a most tremendous drop, so it seems as though there might be something in it. Buy a special edition this afternoon, and you'll know more about it."

Lord Nunneley nodded. "Thank you," he said, "I will do so."

Lord Nunneley walked slowly along Pall Mall. After all, there was no need to buy a paper. On the placards which the boys were displaying as he neared Trafalgar Square were great headlines, —

EXTRAORDINARY DROP OF SHARES IN THE GOLD-MINES ASSOCIATION. PANIC IN THE CITY.

Lord Nunneley bought a paper, and stood for a few minutes reading it. Then he called a taxicab, and gave the man the address of Deane's offices. He was well known there, and Deane's confidential man at once came forward.

"Mr. Deane will see you, of course, my lord," he said. "He is really disengaged now, but we are obliged to deny him to everybody because of these interviewers. Will you come with me, my lord?"

Lord Nunneley found himself ushered into Deane's private room. Deane was dictating rapidly to his secretary. As usual he was calm, self-possessed, carefully groomed and dressed. There was nothing about his appearance in any way to suggest a panic. He heard his visitor's name, however, with surprise.

"Nunneley!" he exclaimed, rising to his feet.

Lord Nunneley nodded, and held out his hand. "I was in the city and thought I'd look you up, Deane," he said. "Can I have a word or two with you?"

"Certainly," Deane answered. "Give us five minutes, Ellison, — or stay away until I ring," he added to his secretary.

Lord Nunneley accepted an easy-chair and also a cigarette, but he seemed in no great hurry to explain his business. "I was very sorry, Deane," he said at last, "to see the papers this evening. I hope the trouble isn't very serious."

"Do you hold any of our shares?" Deane asked.

"If I did," said the other, coloring a little, "I should not have come here."

Deane accepted the reproof. "I beg your pardon."

"I daresay," continued Lord Nunneley, "my coming seems to you, under the circumstances, a little superfluous. However, what I wanted to say is this. You see Olive is our only child, and that made us very anxious about anything to do with her. I am sure that you yourself must feel now, when you are under so much anxiety, that it is better not to have the added responsibility of your engagement upon your shoulders."

"I have never questioned your wisdom in breaking it off," Deane said quietly. "Under the circumstances, I agree with you that it is a very good thing."

"That's all right," Lord Nunneley continued, a little hastily. "Of course, neither you nor Olive are children, and you are not the sort to wear your hearts upon your sleeve. In short," he added, somewhat abruptly, "you'll both get over it. There's no doubt about that. I didn't come to revert to this matter at all. I simply wanted to say that though our relations are changed, I still do feel a considerable amount of friendship for you, Deane, and I wanted to come and just tell you I was sorry. And look here," he went on, a little awkwardly, "I've between seven and eight thousand pounds for which I am looking for an investment, and if the money's any use to you, Deane, why say the word, and I'll write you a cheque on the spot."

Deane looked at his visitor for a moment in an astonishment which triumphed over the natural impassivity of his expression. Then a little flush rose in his cheeks. He got to his feet and held out his hand.

"Nunneley," he said, "this is awfully good of you. I shall not forget it. Believe that. If we wanted money, or if I did personally, I'd accept your offer like a shot."

"Too much of a drop in the bucket, I suppose," Lord Nunneley remarked. "It isn't much, I know."

"It isn't that," Deane interrupted. "The situation is simply that our shares have had a big drop because of certain rumors about our title to the Little Anna Gold-Mine. If those rumors were confirmed, five or six hundred thousand pounds wouldn't help us. If they are not confirmed, and if they die a natural death, as I imagine they must, our shares will recover themselves and we shall not need money."

"You don't believe in the existence of any such document, then?" Lord Nunneley asked.

"I do not believe that it will be produced," Deane answered, "and if it were produced," he went on, "I do not believe in its validity. I would not say as much, even, as this to the reporters, but the document about which people have been talking is simply an original claim to the Little Anna Gold-Mine, which was deserted by the very man who put me on to it, and in whose name the claim stands. You see, therefore, that any attempt to establish a legal claim is more or less a swindle."

Lord Nunneley rose to his feet. "You are really not so very much alarmed, then?"

Deane shook his head. "This drop in shares, after all," he said, "does not affect us particularly, except for the time. It simply means that the market declares that we are a few hundred thousand pounds poorer to-day than we were yesterday. Whether the market is right or not remains to be proved."

"Well, I am glad to have seen you, at any rate, Deane, and remember, if there is anything I can do—"

"You have already," Deane said, "done a great deal, Lord Nunneley. I shall not forget your visit or your offer."

"That's all right," Lord Nunneley declared. "Olive did not know I was coming, but I'm sure if she had known she would have sent her love. Don't bother to ring. I can find my way out."

The visit of his projected father-in-law seemed to Deane like a pleasant little oasis in the middle of a long, dreary day. These rumors of which Lord Nunneley had heard seemed to have come into existence during the last few hours. There had been some large failures lately, and investors were all nervous. The country was short of money. In ordinary times, an attack upon the stability of such a corporation as his would have been impossible. To-day, nothing seemed impossible. In his heart, Deane knew or felt that the situation was safe. Yet the very fact that these rumors had sprung into being seemed to denote the line of defence which Hefferom's lawyers were prepared to offer in the coming trial. He would be accused everywhere—if not in words, in suggestion—of complicity in the murder of Sinclair. The existence of that document would be believed in. It would be said openly, perhaps, that he was responsible himself for its suppression. It was not the fact that on paper he was nearly a quarter of a million poorer than he had been a week ago that troubled him. It was the reflection that bold though his words had been, it was within the power of the man who lay awaiting his trial practically to ruin him. The question of the whereabouts of the document might be, in a few weeks, the most discussed matter in London.

Deane, acting upon a sudden impulse, left his office by the back entrance and drove to the small hotel where Winifred was staying. Miss Rowan was at home, he was told, and after a few minutes' delay he was shown into her sitting-room.

"Miss Rowan will be with you in a moment," her maid announced, coming through from the bedroom. "She is with her dressmaker at present."

Deane nodded, and took up the newspaper mechanically from the table. The room seemed to him almost faint with the perfume of flowers. He glanced around carelessly, and suddenly found his attention riveted upon her writing-table. In a little silver vase, standing by itself, was the red rose which he had bought for her two days since!

CHAPTER XVI
PASSION

She came to him in a few moments, dressed in a fascinating negligée gown,—came to him with a rustle of silk and a faint expression of surprise upon her upraised eyebrows.

"I did not expect you until this evening," she remarked.

He nodded. "I took the liberty of coming here to ask you a question."

She smiled as she sat down upon the sofa. "Oh, the paper is quite safe."

"How did you know what I came for?" he asked, a little startled.

"My dear friend," she said, shrugging her shoulders, "as I have decided that it is to my interests to link my future with yours, you cannot wonder that I have found such details as those"—she pointed to an evening paper which he noticed now lying upon her writing-table—"interesting. I have been trying to understand how matters stand. Tell me if I am right! It seems to me that so long as that document remains an imagined thing, so long as it is not produced or sworn to definitely, you are safe."

"The corporation is safe," answered Deane, "and in a measure, I suppose, I am. On the other hand, I shall be accused, naturally, of suppressing it, and probably of complicity in Sinclair's murder. There is Hefferom, you see, prepared to swear that Sinclair came to London with that paper in his possession. Sinclair is known to have come to my office. He has certainly been murdered. The paper cannot be found, and the corporation remains in possession of the mine. People will certainly put these things together."

She nodded. "It will be very bad indeed," she said slowly, "for your reputation."

"It will, I am afraid," said Deane, "considerably lessen my social value as your husband."

"It seems to me," she replied, "that money is so powerful. I daresay you will be able to live it down."

"With your help," Deane remarked sarcastically, "it seems to me very possible. By the bye," he continued, "with reference to that document, you must forgive me if I feel some slight uneasiness at times as to its safety."

"You need have none," she answered. "It is in safe keeping."

"It is your own interests as well as mine you are guarding," he reminded her.

"I am perfectly aware of it," she answered. "Since you are here, may I offer you some tea?"

"Thanks," he said, "I think not. By the bye, do you care to go to the Opera to-night? I have two stalls, and Melba is singing."

A sudden light flashed over her face. It was as though the mask had been raised for a moment. Perhaps by contrast her tone seemed colder than ever as she answered him. "I should like to very much. Will you call for me?"

"At half-past seven," he answered. "We will have a little dinner somewhere first."

"You are sure," she asked, "that you do not mind being seen out?"

"It is all to my advantage," he answered. "The men who are most talked about should never shrink from publicity. The people who have been told to-day that I am a bankrupt, a swindler, and a murderer, and that my ruin is only a matter of minutes, will hesitate if they see me with you in the stalls of the Opera to-night."

"Nero fiddled," she reminded him.

"Nero was a hysterical person," he answered. "My tendencies are towards the other extreme. Until half-past seven, then."

"Until half-past seven," she repeated.

He bowed and left her without even shaking hands. She stood quite still for a moment, looking at the door which he had closed behind him. Then she crossed the room slowly, and lifted the vase with its solitary rose to her lips. A second later it lay dashed to pieces upon the floor, the flaming color was in her cheeks, her fists were clenched.

"I hate him!" she declared to herself. "I hate him now more than ever!"

Winifred talked more than usual at the short dinner which they had at a famous café close to the Opera House. Deane, a little weary with the strain of the day, was at first irresponsive, but gradually he forgot himself in the interest of playing his new part. She was wearing a dress of black velvet, a rope of pearls which had been sent for her inspection only that afternoon, and pearl earrings, concerning which she gravely asked his opinion. There was something a little un-English-looking about her to-night,—about the small, delicate head with the masses of brown hair, the pale complexion, the deep eyes with their hidden depths, the pearls which fell so gracefully over her black gown. Many people knew him by sight, and pointed him out to others,—the man whom everyone was talking about, the man who was supposed to be shivering on the brink of social and financial ruin, whose very freedom from justice might be a matter of hours,—sitting there with a girl who was unknown to all of them, yet without a doubt one of his own world! Some of them wondered that she should care to be seen about with him at such a time. These, however, were mostly the men. The women, who saw him as usual, well-groomed, good-looking, debonair, only admired him the more for his courage.

They had driven the few yards together to the Opera House in silence. Nevertheless, Deane fancied that his companion seemed to-night a little more accessible. He was amazed to find how great an interest he was beginning to take in her moods, amazed to find himself taking every opportunity to touch her fingers, to speak covertly of the destined ending of their engagement. He fancied sometimes that her fingers rested more softly in his, that the chill aloofness of her demeanor had been more than once on the point of being raised. And yet, after all, it might only be fancy, he thought, as he followed her and the attendant along the corridor into their places. He was a fool to trouble himself about it. She was very likely what she had always seemed,—a bloodless, indifferent creature, with a greed for jewels and fine clothes sprung up in her,—a fungus growth, the evil result of her long years of servitude. Yet that night his convictions as to her coldness received something of a shock. It was the first night they had been to the Opera together, and he had imagined that she would sit as she had sat through so many theatres,—slightly bored, slightly nonchalant, interested only to know who the people might be by whom they were surrounded, and in the play itself if by chance it was well acted and satisfactory. To-night, he realized that there were things which could move her, even if he himself had not the power. He saw her eyes flash with the glory of the music, and he saw them turn marvellously soft and tender as the white-robed Iseult sang to them with sobs in her throat, sobs which seemed to make that melody only more intense and sweeter. She seemed to respond to every note of the music. More than once he saw her quiver with excitement. By accident her fingers touched his and rested there. He felt a thrill which amazed him. For the moment he, too, forgot that wretched maze of affairs in which he was plunged. The great passionate love-story throbbed, too, in his heart and veins. The figures on the stage were for a moment dim. They existed only as types. In those few seconds he realized, for the first time in his life, the real meaning of this wonderful emotion with which the very air around them seemed charged, and almost at the moment of realization there came to him fiercely, insistently, the great question,—did she share it, did she understand, was it possible that such a passion could be born of itself, without response or encouragement? He leaned forward, and tried to see into her face. A great stillness reigned in the half-darkened Opera House, a stillness except for the wonderful music which still flowed from those divine lips. He leaned forward until he could see her face, and his heart throbbed with the wonder of it! All the passion, all the intense mystery of a strenuous love were there in her glowing eyes, her half-parted lips! It was only a momentary glimpse he had. Then, as though conscious of his observation, she raised her fan. Their eyes had never met. He was left, after all, with the problem unsolved!

Deane came down to earth again as the curtain fell. His companion drew a long, soft breath, and leaned back in her seat.

"Don't you want to go out and smoke or something?" she asked calmly. "I do not feel like talking at all. The music is wonderful!"

He left her without a word. Only as he reached the end of his row and turned to walk up the sloping aisle, he glanced back once more. She had not moved. Her eyes were closed. She seemed, indeed, like a person exhausted with the strain of listening. He made his way out to the refreshment room, humming softly to himself. It was a mask, after all, which she wore! He understood suddenly the relief which had come to him. He understood that this engagement, which had seemed to him like a piece of half-contemptible bathos, had suddenly become the first and most desirable thing in his life!

CHAPTER XVII
A DESPAIRING CALL

The great lawyer whom the telephone message from Deane had summoned sat in a comfortable easy-chair adjoining Deane's writing-table. His manner was serious, but not discouraging.

"You see, Deane," he said, "after all, it depends very much upon this alleged document. The whole case practically hinges upon it. If the defendants are unable to procure it, or a copy of it, or witnesses who can swear to it, I do not think that they can do us much harm, especially if we take the course which I have already suggested to our counsel. As yet we have received no intimation that the other side have the slightest trace of the document in question. If, on the other hand, it should come into their possession, they are bound to notify us. May I ask, Mr. Deane, what you believe the probabilities are as regards this matter?"

"It isn't a matter of probability," Deane answered. "To the best of my belief, there is no such document in existence."

"In that case," the lawyer continued, "I think that you need have no further anxiety about the case. Of course, there is no chance of a long sentence for the defendant. You understand that?"

"Perfectly," Deane answered. "I don't wish it. I should not have prosecuted him at all, but it seemed the only way to stop what might have grown into a serious annoyance."

"I am sorry," the lawyer said, "that the whole thing seems to have been taken so seriously by the Press and the public. I see your shares have dropped to a ridiculous amount."

"A chance for someone to make money," Deane remarked. "I am much obliged to you for coming up, Hardaway."

The lawyer nodded and took his departure. Deane sat for some time in a brown study. Fundamentally he had all the direct impulses and propensities of a truthful man. The course of action into which he was at present driven was distasteful—almost repugnant to him. Yet, after all, he was only fighting Hefferom with his own weapons. The man was a blackmailer,—nothing more or less. Yet the fact did not seem to Deane to make his hands the cleaner. And there was the girl! The memory of her face haunted him, her desperate plight had been only too apparent. If that document of Sinclair's was worth the paper it was written on, it was he who was the supplanter, the thief, morally responsible for her grievous plight! He moved in his chair uneasily. It was almost a relief when the telephone bell at his elbow rang.

"Is that Mr. Deane?" a woman's voice asked.

"Yes!" he answered.

"Mr. Stirling Deane?"

"Yes,—what is it?" he asked quickly.

There was a moment's silence. The terrified voice, which had still seemed somehow familiar to him, was silent. He could hear from the room to which the instrument was connected, the musical chiming of a Swiss clock—the call of a bird—and then silence. His hand was upon the receiver to ring up the Exchange when suddenly a cry of terror, a cry of shrill, agonized terror, rang in his ear.

"Stirling! Mr. Deane! Stirling! Come—"

There was an abrupt cessation of that frantic cry. The last word was muffled, as though something had been dashed against the speaker's mouth. There was the sound of the falling of a chair or heavy piece of furniture. Then silence!—silence ominous, heavy, maddening!...

Deane rang up the Exchange. The young lady who answered him was a little annoyed at his vehemence.

"I want you to tell me to whom I have been speaking!" he exclaimed. "Where was I rung up from a few moments ago?"

"No idea," the young lady answered tartly. "Didn't they give their name?"

"I want to know where the call was from," Deane said. "Please tell me quickly."

"We don't take any note of local calls," the young lady answered. "Ring off, please!"

"Stop!" Deane cried. "Listen, please! This is important! I am Mr. Deane — Mr. Stirling Deane — of the Incorporated Gold-Mines Association. I have just been rung up by a woman in distress — some one who appealed for help. She was dragged away from the telephone before she could tell me where she was speaking from. You must try and find out the number for me. You must do it! It may be a matter of life or death!"

There was an instant's silence — a buzzing noise — then a man's voice. "Sorry, sir," he said, "our operator cannot remember the exact number that was speaking to you. It was a house in Red Lion Square, though. She is sure of that."

"How many subscribers have you there?" Deane asked swiftly.

"Twenty-four or five, sir," the man answered. "Sorry we can't help you further."

Deane left the office in such a hurry that a whole crop of fresh rumors were started. He drove as swiftly as his electric brougham could take him to the corner of Red Lion Square. All the time with a telephone directory on his knee, he was copying out addresses. He entered Red Lion Square on foot, with the paper in his hand. There were twenty-eight addresses. He had no idea where to begin.

Seven or eight were the addresses of business firms. He struck these out. Then he tried the others. One after the other he interviewed all sorts of people unsuccessfully. He was received everywhere with suspicion. Most of the houses were converted flats or cheap lodging-houses. Half-dressed women leered at him over the banisters; shabby men of all ages were slavishly anxious to earn a tip. Gradually he was forced to realize that his was a mad, almost hopeless search. People stood at their doors and watched him, jeering. Women hung out of the windows, shouting coarse invitations or derisive comments upon his perseverance. His nerves were all on edge, his blood was hot with anger. Somewhere within a few hundred, perhaps a few yards of him, this girl was in the hands of persons who meant ill to her. The terror in her voice was no ordinary fear. She was face to face with the worst that could happen.

He reached the last house on his list. It was on the further side of the square, and one of the most respectable in appearance. Contrary to what was apparently the usual custom, the front door was closed, and most of the blinds drawn. There was no sign of life about the place when he rang the bell. Yet after scarcely a moment's delay the door was thrown open, and a neatly dressed parlor-maid answered his summons.

Deane adopted new tactics. He drew a sovereign from his waistcoat pocket, and held it between his fingers. "You are on the telephone, I believe," he said, "number 0198. Someone rang me up from here about an hour or so ago. I recognized the voice, but the message was indistinct. Will you tell Miss Rowan that I am here?"

The girl shook her head. "There is no one of that name living here, sir," she answered.

"A rather pale young lady, tall and slim, who has just arrived," Deane persisted. "I am anxious to find her quickly. Can't you help me?"

He pulled out a handful of gold, and the girl looked at it with covetous eyes. She sighed as she once more shook her head.

"There is no one here of that name, sir," she said, — "no young lady at all, in fact."

"You are quite sure?" Deane asked, with a sinking heart.

"Quite, sir," the girl answered confidently.

She made a movement as though to close the door. It is possible that Deane would have taken the hint and departed, but for that last searching look which he threw at her. He thrust his boot against the door, and resumed his place on the inner side of the threshold. From there he looked at her once more. He was right. There were traces of powder on her cheeks, and her eyebrows were certainly not natural. Underneath her trim black skirt he had caught a glimpse of brown open-worked stockings, and tan shoes with a large bow and high heels. Instinctively he felt that no ordinary servant would have been allowed to go about like this.

"I should like to see your mistress before I go," Deane said firmly. "Please go and tell her. I will not detain her more than a few moments."

"She's not in," the girl answered, with a distinct change of manner. "Please don't stay about here or I shall get into trouble."

"I am sorry," Deane answered, "but if she is not in, I am going to wait for her."

He was in the hall now, — a miserable, untidy place with a broken-down mirror and hat-rack as sole furniture, and covered with a much soiled oilcloth. The stairs were right ahead of him, and Deane looked up. He looked into a woman's face as she leaned over the well of the banisters, looking down. Almost immediately she drew away and came down.

Deane rose up to meet her. She was dressed in black, was very pale, with large earrings, — pretty in a way, and certainly not of formidable appearance.

"You wished to see me?" she asked, a little hesitatingly, as she reached the bottom stair. "I thought I heard you tell my servant that you wished to speak to her mistress."

"You are right, madam," Deane answered. "I do wish to speak to you."

"And what is it that you wish?" the lady asked.

"An act of kindness," Deane answered, "for which I am willing to pay — to pay heavily. I am in search of a young lady who rang me up only an hour or so ago from this locality, — I believe from this house. I am offering a reward of two hundred pounds for any one who may help me in my search."

He raised his voice. He meant the servant, or the person who was posing as a servant, to hear him. He was unable to observe her closely, but he noticed that she moved a little nearer, and appeared to be listening intently.

"I am afraid that you have come to the wrong house," the lady answered gently. "This is not a very nice neighborhood, I know, but we are quite respectable people here, and we are not upon the telephone at all."

"Not on the telephone at all?" Deane repeated. "But I have your name and number from the telephone company, — number 0198 — Mrs. Garvice!"

"Mrs. Garvice has left," the lady declared. "I have taken the house, but the telephone was of no use to me, so I have had it taken away."

"May I see the place where the instrument was?" Deane asked. "I have a particular reason for asking."

"Certainly not!" the lady answered, a little sharply. "Open the door, Hilda. We have nothing else to say to you, sir."

The maid obeyed, and Deane reluctantly took up his hat. He was already upon the threshold when he suddenly stopped. A remarkable change came over him. He stepped quickly back. The woman had gone as pale as death. From one of the rooms upstairs came the shrill, unmistakable summons of a telephone bell, and mingling with it the chiming of a cuckoo clock.

"Shut the door," Deane ordered sternly. "Madam," he said, turning towards the lady of the house, "it is still within your power to earn that two hundred pounds!"

The woman looked at him curiously. "Two hundred pounds," she said, "is a great deal of money. One does not carry about sums like that."

Deane thrust his hand into his pocket, and drew out a little roll of notes. "I have twelve ten-pound notes here," he said, "and I can write a cheque for the balance. You know what I want. If you turn me away, I shall be back with a search warrant in less than half-an-hour."

She held out her hand for the notes. "Follow me," she said. "You understand that I am simply a lodging-house keeper. I cannot be responsible for my tenants or their actions."

"I understand that," Deane answered eagerly. "Quick! Lead the way upstairs."

CHAPTER XVIII
WINIFRED IS TRAPPED

Deane followed his guide up two flights of stairs, — on the landing of the third she paused.

"I do not usually interfere with the comings and goings of my lodgers," she said. "They pay for their rooms. That is all I ask. You see the door opposite you?"

"Yes!" Deane answered quickly.

"That room is tenanted by a young woman who called herself Montague, but received letters under the name of Sinclair. She had a visitor this afternoon who might be the young person of whom you are in search. You had better go in and see."

Deane was across the landing in a moment. He tapped sharply upon the door. There was no answer. He tried the handle. The door was locked!

"Open the door," he cried out, shaking it vigorously.

There was no answer. To Deane the silence was ominous. He turned to the woman who stood silently by his side, with a fierce little exclamation. "Where is the telephone?" he demanded.

"Inside there," she answered. "It used to be my sitting-room."

"The door is locked!" he exclaimed.

"I do not understand it," she admitted.

"Have you another key?"

"No!"

He flung himself at the door, tearing it half from its hinges. Another assault, and with a tearing of splinters it fell inside. Deane stepped over it into the room, and a low cry of anger broke from his lips. The woman at his side fled shrieking downstairs. On the floor lay Winifred Rowan, her limbs bound with cords, a gag in her mouth, her clothing all dishevelled, her eyes shining with an almost painful intensity from her ashen gray face. Deane fell on his knees by her side.

"Winifred!" he exclaimed. "My God!"

He snatched his knife from his pocket, removed the gag from her mouth, and cut all her bonds. Her hands tried nervously to rearrange her dress over her bosom. He tore off his own coat and threw it over her.

"Are you badly hurt?" he asked anxiously.

"I am not hurt much," she answered weakly, "but—"

"But what?" he demanded.

She commenced to cry softly but insistently. Black fear rose up to torture him. "But what?" he repeated, with sinking heart.

"It has gone!" she murmured, crossing her hands upon her bosom.

"What has gone?" he asked. "Quick!"

"The deed!" she whispered. "Don't look at me like that. I couldn't help it. It was a trap, of course, to get me here, and I was a fool. The letter was from you, but I ought to have known that it was a forgery. I was taken unawares. She was like a madwoman. She would have torn the clothes from my body. I struggled. I called out. It was no use. She has taken it away."

"But you are not hurt?" he exclaimed anxiously.

"I—no!" she answered, a little vacantly. "But it is gone! I was not fit to be trusted with it. I ought to have given it up to you."

She was very pale, and he was afraid of her fainting. He summoned the landlady once more. She was waiting on the stairs close by.

"Something very serious has happened here," he said, sternly. "This young lady has been assaulted and robbed."

"I'm sure I'm very sorry," the woman declared. "You can't blame any of us, though. I never heard a sound, no more did Hilda, and I can't prevent my lodgers having visitors."

"We won't discuss it," Deane said sharply. "But if this is Miss Montague's room,—"

"It isn't," the woman interrupted. "It's my sitting-room. Miss Montague has only an attic, and she came to me and said that she couldn't receive a visitor there, and asked me to lend her my room for a few minutes."

Deane nodded. "The other rooms on this floor are unoccupied, of course," he said. "Oh! it's quite easy to understand. I don't need to ask you any more questions. I don't want any more explanations. If you want to keep this out of the police court, you will do exactly as I tell you."

"Yes!" she exclaimed eagerly. "I will do anything."

"Send your servant for a cab," Deane said, "and arrange this young lady's dress so that I can take her home."

"I will fetch her a bodice of my own," declared the woman, hurrying off.

Winifred had risen to her feet, and was sitting in an easy-chair. She was leaning forward, with her face half buried in her hands. Deane turned towards her.

"Winifred —"

She avoided his gaze. "Don't!" she begged. "Please don't talk to me. I can't bear it."

"But I may say —" he began.

"No!" she interrupted, almost fiercely. "Please say nothing. I mean it. I cannot bear to talk! I cannot bear to be talked to!"

A little throb of anger darkened his face. She had not even common gratitude for her rescue! She had but one thought, one regret, — the loss of that future of luxury to attain which she had bound herself to him. A curious anger burned in his blood, — a pain which he could not analyze shook his heart. Then there came the sound of voices on the stairs, feminine voices raised in anger! The door was burst open. Ruby stood there upon the threshold, looking in upon them, her lips curved in an ugly smile of triumph, her eyes ablaze. Behind her stood the landlady, a black bodice in her hand, her forehead wrinkled in a deprecating frown.

"So you've found her, have you?" Ruby exclaimed, her face turned towards Deane, her finger outstretched to where Winifred sat shrinking back in her chair. "Thieves, both of you! Thieves! Thieves!"

Deane pointed to Winifred's torn clothing. "And that?" he asked.

"It was restitution," the girl declared fiercely. "The deed was mine! Your millions are mine! She stole it for you—her brother was a murderer for you! How do you think the story will look in the newspapers, eh? Inciting to murder and theft! Isn't that a crime? Swindlers, both of you!" she cried passionately. "You'd have kept me a beggar, eh," she cried to Winifred, "while you clad your poor body in silks and laces, covered yourself with jewels and made him marry you? And I was to starve!—to starve or worse! Well, we'll see! We'll see!"

"Young lady," Deane said calmly, "you are being led away by your imagination. You have taken a paper away from Miss Rowan which you seem to think is going to turn out a sort of El Dorado. It isn't worth the paper it's written on."

"It's a lie!" the girl shrieked. "I've taken it to the lawyers. It is genuine—they all say so."

Deane almost lifted Winifred from her chair. "That remains to be seen," he declared.

"In any case, it was stolen!" she cried. "That young woman there has got to say how it came into her possession, and what she meant by going around with it sewn into her bodice! Oh, you needn't try to dupe me!" she cried. "I want my money—God knows how I want it! And I mean to make her suffer, too!" she added, pointing to Winifred. "She's a thief! She's lived in luxury while I've starved;—she's worn the clothes of a princess while I've gone in rags! But she shall pay! My God, she shall pay!"

Deane, with Winifred by his side, had reached the door. "I am afraid," he said turning to the girl, who was still regarding them with breathless anger, "that you have let your imagination run away with you a good deal. A dose of the law courts will do you no harm. If you care for a word of warning from me, you can have it: don't build your hopes too much upon that paper!"

"We shall see!" she cried fiercely. "You can't frighten me! If the paper is of no value, why did she steal it, why did she carry it sewn in her clothes? If you—"

She hesitated for a moment. Her eyes rested upon Deane, her expression softened. "If you want to make terms—" she began.

He turned away. "Come, Winifred," he said.

In the cab they scarcely spoke. She had the air of a person utterly exhausted, — indifferent to anything that might happen.

"Tell me," he asked, soon after they started, "what made you go to that house?"

"The letter from you," she answered. "I was a fool, of course, but I went. It doesn't matter, does it?"

"I suppose not," he answered.

The despair in her face nerved him to further speech. "I am afraid," he said, "that you are worrying about that deed — or rather the loss of it. I am sorry that I came too late, but it couldn't be helped. You did all that you could! I am sure of that."

"Of course!" she interposed impatiently. "And I have failed! That is the end of it!"

He looked out of the window, looked with stern, unseeing eyes upon the passing people. The sun had ceased to shine, his heart was heavy as lead. He seemed suddenly to realize the reason of her dejection. She believed in the deed. She believed that he was indeed a pauper. It was for the wreck of her hopes that she was lamenting. The rest went for nothing. He was a poor man — no longer of any interest to her! His manner unconsciously stiffened as the thought came rushing home to him. He drew away from her, and he remained silent until the cab stopped in front of her hotel. She stepped out quickly, and almost ran across the pavement.

"To-morrow," she said, holding out her hand as though to prevent his following.

He bowed and turned away. Her deshabille was without doubt an embarrassment Already he was beginning to find excuses for her. Nevertheless, he watched the slim, swaying figure, as the doors closed upon her, with something of apprehension. Was it ominous that she should pass away without a backward glance? Was she indeed nothing but an adventuress, deprived of her prey?...

He paid the cab and walked slowly back to his rooms. His solicitor had already rung up. Two of his directors were waiting to see him, a reporter buttonholed him upon the pavement. From all of which things Deane knew that Ruby Sinclair had lost no time, that the first note of battle had been sounded!

CHAPTER XIX
MISS SINCLAIR'S OFFER

Miss Rowan had left two hours ago, and had taken all her luggage and paid her bill. Apparently she had no idea of returning, — at any rate, she had not reserved any rooms. The hall-porter of the little hotel looked at Deane with some curiosity as he answered his rapid questions. The manageress came rustling out of her office and beamed on Deane, who had once stayed there for several weeks. She confirmed the information which he had already received, and supplemented it with a few further details.

"Miss Rowan paid her bill?" Deane asked.

"Certainly, sir," the manageress answered. "Miss Rowan was exceedingly particular about paying her accounts the moment they were presented."

"And she left no message?" Deane asked.

"None at all, sir," was the answer.

He noticed the gleam of curiosity in her eyes, and promptly altered his tactics. "Thank you very much," he said, turning away. "I quite understood that Miss Rowan was not leaving until this afternoon. My mistake, I daresay. By the bye, have you any instructions with regard to letters?"

"None," the manageress replied. "If any come, we shall keep them until we hear from her."

Deane turned away and reëntered his brougham. "I shall find a note at my rooms, I daresay," he remarked. "Good morning, Mrs. Merrygold."

His words were prophetic. He called at his rooms on his way to the club for lunch, and found a note there addressed to him in Winifred's handwriting:

Wednesday morning.

> You will understand, of course, that this is the end. The jewels which you gave me I have returned to-day by registered post. One ring I have kept. It is, I think, the least valuable of any, but I did not wish to part with it. If you insist, however, it is always at your disposal.
>
> I am going back where I belong—to the world which I should never have quitted. Everything has been a great mistake. Please understand that you are absolutely and entirely free in every way. I only trust that I may live long enough to atone in some measure for my folly.
>
> Winifred Rowan.

Deane read this letter over a dozen times. One thing alone seemed clear. She had deserted him. She had not even waited for the final issue. She had fled from the sinking ship with a haste almost indecent. She had made no terms, suggested no compromise. Deane, when he thought the whole matter over, was still puzzled. Such precipitancy was not logical. If his hand was no longer strong enough to open the gates of the promised land, it could at least have lifted her up from the miseries of her past life. He found himself, after a study of her few lines, curiously depressed. She had gone—willingly—apparently without regret except for her wasted opportunities. He felt an emptiness in his life which he failed to understand. There had been nothing of the sort when Lady Olive had held out her hand and bidden him farewell. Was he getting sentimental? He set his teeth. Absurd! It was an episode happily concluded! Outside there was thunder in the air—a storm for him to face!...

His solicitor did not beat about the bush. "In the face of that document, Mr. Deane," he said, "the Treasury do not propose to proceed with the prosecution of Hefferom. Its existence, of course, throws altogether a different light upon the whole situation, whatever may be its exact legal worth. Hefferom was simply engaged upon a task of compromise. He had something solid behind him. There is not a shadow of evidence against him."

"Very well," said Deane, "let Hefferom go. I confess that when I sent to Scotland Yard I never anticipated that this particular document would ever come into evidence."

"You knew of its existence?" the lawyer asked.

"Sinclair himself showed it to me," Deane answered calmly. "So far as Sinclair himself was concerned the affair was a swindle, for it was he who recommended me to jump the claim—said he thought that there was some stuff there, but he had no money to work it. I let him off a hundred pounds he owed me, and took his advice. But that is ancient history. The mine is my property all right—or rather it was."

Mr. Hardaway listened with a grave face. "Deane," he said, "I hope and believe that you may be speaking the truth, but the original deed is in the hands of unscrupulous people. We had a notification this afternoon that a suit is about to be commenced against your corporation."

"The sooner the better," Deane answered. "We'll know where we are, at any rate. I claim that by the statute laws of the country that claim was forfeit. If it was not, then the inducing me to sink capital and work the claim was a damnable conspiracy."

"Your corporation fight with you, of course?" the lawyer asked.

"Of course," Deane answered. "What else could they do? We fight to the end!"

That night, shares in the Incorporated Gold-Mines Association stood at 90. At closing time the following day they stood at 74. A few lines in the paper had done it. An action had been started by Hefferom, and the legatees of the estate of the late Richard Sinclair, claiming as their property the Little Anna Gold-Mine. The thing had been talked about for some time, but now that it had actually occurred, people seemed none the less staggered. The city believed in Stirling Deane—it had believed in him so implicitly that in its heart it had never placed any faith in this cloud of rumors. Yet there it was now in black and white. It was no longer possible to speak of compromise. The matter was to be fought out in the open courts, and failure could spell nothing but ruin to one of the richest corporations in London. Deane's photograph was in all the papers—also the menu of a famous dinner which he gave to his directors. He sent a cheque for five thousand pounds to a hospital, and was reported to be going on the turf. The lawsuit he treated everywhere as a joke. He was careful always to wear the usual bunch of violets in his buttonhole, and to affect something of the dandy in his attire. His personal demeanor kept his shares at least ten points higher than they would otherwise have been.

But Deane, nevertheless, was in hell! He was badgered by his directors, worried by his lawyers, and underneath it all, and apart from his financial responsibilities, he was suffering from a sense of personal loss, a wound whose pain left him but little peace. He never stopped to admit to himself exactly what his suffering was. He sat for hours lost in thought, and his thoughts were always of that pale lady of his dreams who had stolen so abruptly from his arms, the girl who had played for a few weeks so strange a part in his life. He tried to find what had become of her, but in vain; she seemed to have completely vanished. He puzzled over her behavior until the lines in his face grew set and hard. Was she indeed ingrate—ready to abandon her strange bargain at the first whisper of disaster? Or had she some other reason? He had accepted her terms because of the power which she held—what if, at the loss of that power, she had taken it for granted that their bargain was cancelled, and had hurried away to avoid the shame of dismissal from him! It was just what she would do—perhaps just what she had done!

Deane was careful, during these days of probation, to attend at his office regularly, and to shrink from none of his customary duties. One afternoon his clerk brought him in a card.

"A young lady to see you, sir!" he announced.

Deane's heart gave a jump, the blood rushed through his veins, he was scarcely able to read the card which he had taken into his fingers with well-affected carelessness. Then the pain came, the black disappointment which seemed to turn his heart into a stone. It was not she! He found it hard to take any interest in this caller, and yet he felt that her coming was significant.

Miss Ruby Sinclair.

"You can show the young lady in, Gray," Deane ordered.

When she arrived, Deane scarcely knew her. She was expensively dressed from head to foot. She carried herself with an assurance which was almost overdone. The fashion of her dress and hat were certainly not chosen with a view to being overlooked. She was very modern— she reminded him exactly of a young lady in a musical comedy with whom he had once had a slight acquaintance. He would scarcely have been surprised had he found, when she lifted her veil, that her eyebrows were blackened.

"You didn't expect to see me, of course," she said, holding his hand for a moment, and looking at him steadfastly. "May I sit down?"

"Of course," he answered.

She chose the easy-chair, and crossed her legs with a good deal of rustle and a considerable display of black silk stocking.

She looked at him curiously. "Are you still angry with me?" she asked.

"Well, I don't usually bear malice," he answered, "but I can scarcely forgive your method of dealing with Miss Rowan!"

"Or its results?" she asked, with a little laugh. "Well, I came out on the top, anyhow, and you must remember, Mr. Deane, that I was desperate,—you don't know how desperate," she continued, after a moment's pause. "I hadn't a shilling left in the world!—not a shilling!—not a friend! And somewhere in London there was wealth that belonged to me!"

"That," Deane remarked dryly, "is a matter which is as yet undecided."

"Well, I judge by facts," she answered with a little laugh. "Lawyers don't usually throw money away, do they? They're willing to advance me all I want on the security of the Little Anna Gold-Mine."

Deane smiled upon her genially. "My mine," he remarked.

"No!" she declared,—"the property of the legatees of Richard Sinclair!"

Deane shook his head. "My dear young lady," he said, "you were more in your element when you walked bareheaded upon the sands of Rakney, and saved me from a wetting, than in your present pose."

"And you," she declared, "were nicer to me, a great deal, for those few days."

"Naturally," he answered, smiling. "How can I be particularly amiable to a young lady who is trying to ruin me?"

She looked at him earnestly. In her fashionable attire she presented, indeed, a very different appearance from the eager, brown-skinned girl, with the shapely limbs and delightful carriage, whom he had first seen at Rakney. Yet he fancied that she was trying to reawaken his earlier impressions of her,—innocent of vanity as he was, he could not misunderstand her appealing gaze!

"I do not want to ruin you," she declared. "I do not want to do anything of the sort. Isn't there enough for both of us? Why should we fight?"

He sighed. "How can we compromise?" he asked. "The mine does not belong to me any longer. I sold it years ago to the Incorporated Gold-Mines Association."

"You could not sell what didn't belong to you," she objected.

"They paid me the money for it, at any rate," he answered.

"If I win," she asked, "who will lose the money?"

"The Incorporated Gold-Mines Association," he answered, "but they would have a claim upon me. I suppose, eventually, that I should."

She held out her hand—no longer brown and stained with seaweed, but delicately gloved, perfumed, elegant. "Let us be friends," she said. "I am sorry I was rough to your little ally! I couldn't help it. She was in my way. I chose the only means. We needn't consider her,—you and I are different sort of people. We know what we want. I am not only a money grubber. I want the rest of life, the whole thing,—the music, the poetry, the passion! Remember my wretched, starved existence! Do you wonder that I am on fire to pass on to the other things. It isn't the money—your money or any one else's! I want life! I want the wine and the spices! I want the dregs! Can't you understand? You must!—you must!"

Her passionate eyes sought his, her body swayed towards him. Deane looked downwards upon his blotter. In the outer office he could hear the clicking of typewriters, the subdued murmur of voices. Through the half-opened window came floating in the everlasting chorus,—the falling footsteps upon the pavement, the jingling of hansom bells, the far-off roar of the heavier traffic. All these things seemed to him curiously unreal. He was conscious only of the intensity of the moment, the pleading of her eyes, the warm breath upon his cheeks. He heard the rustling of her skirts. He felt that she was rising from her chair. Then he braced himself for his effort.

"My dear young lady," he said,—"if you really want to compromise—for a moderate amount—I will send for my lawyer. We cannot arrange this thing by ourselves."

She rose to her feet, but for a moment she was speechless. When he looked at her face, he found it almost unrecognizable. She dropped her veil quickly, but from behind it the flash of her eyes was in itself a threat.

"I am sorry," he said lamely. "I hope you understand."

She turned to the door, and passed out without a word.

CHAPTER XX
THROUGH THE MILL

Deane stood at last on the other side of those long, dragging months of unspeakable weariness. Day after day, in the close atmosphere of the Courts, week after week of what seemed to him unnecessary repetitions and delays, — so the great machine of the law moved on its slow and stately way, and the case of Sinclair v. The Incorporated Gold-Mines Association crept on toward the end. One thing at least Deane had gained. His examination and cross-examination — and he was in the witness box altogether for nearly two days — failed to reveal a single weak joint in the armor of his truthfulness. His story was consistent and honorable throughout. He was able to prove the payment to Sinclair, to prove Sinclair's suggestion that he should have a try at the mine. At the end of the case, one thing remained certain, and that was that morally speaking the mine was Deane's when he had sold it to the Corporation. Yet behind it all there were those title-deeds, with which Sinclair had never parted, and which now formed the backbone of this present suit. The more sensational part of the case, too, concerning which there had been endless rumors, collapsed immediately.

"Is it not true that Sinclair paid you a visit at your offices a few days before his murder?" counsel asked.

"Certainly!" Deane answered.

"Will you tell us what transpired at that interview?"

"Well, it scarcely amounted to an interview," Deane answered composedly. "The man was drunk, and I found him offensive. He brandished the document at me on which the present case is founded, and I suspected him of an attempt at blackmail. I had him thrown out."

"Yet a few days afterwards you commissioned Rowan—the man who murdered Sinclair—to obtain that document from him," counsel said, amidst some sensation.

"Scarcely that," Deane answered. "Rowan, who had been a friend of mine in South Africa, and was a man of an altogether different stamp than Sinclair, called upon me a few days later. I told him the circumstances."

"You incited him to procure that document from Sinclair," counsel declared.

"I cannot admit that," Deane answered. "I told him that I had declined to be blackmailed by Sinclair, but that after all I would prefer to pay a reasonable sum of money for the document in question. Rowan had been on more friendly terms with Sinclair than any of us, and I thought that he might induce him to listen to reason."

"If the document was valueless, why should you bother about it?"

"I'm afraid that you don't know much about the mining world," Deane replied amiably. "Any prejudicial report, however malicious, however false, affects the market, and one must always consider one's stockholders."

"Very well, then," counsel said, "we come to this. You deputed Rowan to see what he could do with Sinclair. Do you realize your responsibility in this matter? You are aware of what happened?"

"Certainly," Deane answered. "I shall never cease to regret it. Sinclair was mad drunk and the two men quarrelled. The blow which killed him was struck in self-defence."

"The law did not take that view."

"I stood by Rowan when he died," Deane said, with a sudden note of solemnity in his tone. "He told me the truth then, and the truth is what I have told you."

"Nevertheless, he stole the document," counsel continued. "It was discovered afterwards in the possession of Miss Rowan."

"So I have heard," Deane answered calmly. "It was a pity that she did not hand it over to me."

"You would have destroyed it, I suppose?"

"Most certainly!" Deane answered. "The mine belonged to me. Sinclair had declared before witnesses that there were no papers, that the claim had not been worked for the requisite time; and, therefore, by the mining laws of the country my purchase was good."

The case lasted well over the Christmas recess. During the holidays, Deane spent a good part of his time seeking for some trace of Winifred Rowan. He went himself to her old employers, but they were able to tell him nothing. They could only show him the testimonial which they had written at her request, and which she had taken away with her a few days after her departure from the hotel. There was no one who seemed able to help him in the least. Very regretfully, he called in the services of a private detective, who, however, was equally unsuccessful. The holidays passed, the case was reopened, and Deane was once more immersed in the struggle....

It was over at last. The strain remained, — the great judge who had heard it declined to pronounce judgment immediately on the conclusion of the pleadings. It might be three days or it might be even a week before his decision was known. Deane turned away from the court with a strong and instinctive desire for solitude. The suspense long drawn out through the weeks and through the months, had become unbearable. He felt himself no longer able calmly to discuss the pros and the cons of the case with his fellow directors and friends. He was sick to heart of it all. He escaped from one or two passers-by, and a reporter or so who tried to buttonhole him, and ignoring his brougham, around which several others were waiting, he sprang into a hansom and drove to the garage where he kept his touring car. A few brief orders, a pencilled note to his servant, and Deane, leaving the garage by the other entrance, took the Tube to its terminus, walked out into the country, and was caught up within an hour by the car, in which his servant was sitting on the front seat by the side of the chauffeur.

The evening passed swiftly into night as they thundered up the great north road into the darkness. Deane, wrapped in his thick coat and rugs, leaned back in his seat, with both windows down, feeling an inexpressible relief in the sharp sting of the night air, the flakes of snow and little clouds of rain blown every now and then through the open windows. He was free at last from the hateful environment of the last few months. No longer was there anyone to point him out as the man who had sold for a million pounds a mine which had never belonged to him. Save for the two motionless figures in front, he was alone. There was no one to ask him wearisome questions, no one to offer him sympathy or wish him good-fortune. On they sped through the night, till the villages were like dead haunts, without a light in the windows, and only an occasional lamp-post to mark the place where men slumbered. They passed through a town, which was like a city of the dead, and on again to the wilder country, where the rabbits rushed, terrified, before the streaming lights of the car, and the wind alone, of all Nature's voices, seemed left to remind him that this was not a world of ghosts through which he rushed.

Presently he saw the man at the wheel swerve a little in his seat, and he lifted the speaking-tube to his lips. "Can we get through to Rakney, Murray," he asked him, "or shall we stop at King's Lynn?"

"We can get through, sir," the man replied, "if we can rest for half-an-hour somewhere."

They knocked up an inn-keeper in King's Lynn, and the two men ate and drank. Deane himself drank a long whiskey and soda, and lit a cigar. Then they rushed onward into the darkness, already lightening a little in the east. Dawn was breaking as they climbed their last hill and ran down toward the marshlands. A red light loomed over the gray, sullen sea. The marshes themselves seemed heavy and undistinguishable—patches of land and dark creeks of salt-water running into one another. Out in the bay the foam-topped breakers came rolling sullenly in. When at last they turned through the gate, and went slowly up the rough road—marked out with white stakes— which led up to the tower, the dawn had actually come, the night was a thing of the past, although its shadow seemed to hang low over the gray land. The sea had been lately over the rough road, and progress was difficult. At last, though, they reached the little bank of shingle on which the tower was built, and Deane, with a little sigh of relief, stepped wearily down. While his servant unlocked the front door and busied himself arranging a bed and lighting a fire, Deane walked down to the edge of the sea, whose white-topped waves were dragging back the shingle as they fell and broke, with a dull, grinding noise. Never, it seemed to him, had the beauty of loneliness appealed to him more strongly than at this hour of dawn. The birds were silent, the wind had fallen, there was no sound whatever from the sleeping land. Only the eternal breaking of the waves continued—a sound which was more like the background for stillness, grim and mysterious, inevitable as existence itself. Far away now seemed that crowded court, with its eager faces, its rapt issues,—far away seemed the importance of wealth, the great question whether he should remain amongst the millionaires—the world buyers, or take his place amongst the poor men of the earth. What did it matter, after all, this kingship of the cities, with their lack of perspective, their crowded hours, their strange, artificial atmosphere? The value of these things was, grotesque, for a moment,—distorted. He had been wise to come here, he told himself, as a breath of the morning wind stole, faint and fresh, across the salt sea. Perhaps he would be wiser still if he defied fortune and stayed here always.

His servant summoned him, and he went reluctantly indoors. He ate some biscuits and drank some milk. Then, as the real dawn broke over the sea, a fiery red, and with many suggestions of troubled weather in its angry glow, he opened the window and threw himself upon the little iron bedstead with its lavender-scented sheets.

CHAPTER XXI
ALL AS IT SHOULD BE

There was one person in London who knew Deane's whereabouts, and from him there came no word. To Deane himself there seemed something unreal about the long hours which he spent in solitude, wandering along the sea front, following the sands left by the receding tide—himself a lonely figure on the great gray plain. A storm of rain once blew in from the sea, but mostly the day was still and colorless. To Deane, after the long hours in the crowded courts, his directors' meetings, his self-imposed mask of ease and confidence, the relief of this absolute solitude was immeasurable. It was just the season of the year when nature and those who minister to her seem alike to sleep. It was too early for any thought of spring; the storms of autumn lay behind. A certain quietness seemed to hang over the land, as though, indeed, sea and resisting sands were exhausted with the long struggle of the winter.

Towards afternoon came some few moments of flickering sunlight. Deane sat on a wooden bar on the top of one of the dykes, and above his head a lark was singing, a little timidly, a little doubtful, even, of his lonely music, but still lending a note of real life to the still, gray world over which he hovered. Deane looked at the queer stone tower on its bank of shingle, and blessed the chance which had led him to purchase it. He looked inland to the little red-tiled village, to the deserted quay, from which all the fishing-boats had been dragged high and dry along the straight line of raised dyke which formed the footpath between him and the village. As he looked, he became conscious that someone had started out from the village along the dyke top. Far away at the other end he could see a slowly approaching figure. His heart gave a little beat. Was it a messenger at last, coming to bring him his fate? He looked up again to where the lark was singing. It seemed, after all, so small a thing! Nearer and nearer the figure came, near enough, at last, for Deane to be able to distinguish something of its outline. Then he rose to his feet with a quick indrawn breath—a little cry of surprise to which there was no one to listen. For this was no messenger from the village coming. It was a girl in a long gray cloak, and a hat which she carried in her hand, as though the fresh salt air of the marshes was something also to her. Deane saw the neatly arranged brown hair blown into confusion about her face. Against the empty background he recognized the poise of her head, the firm but delicate walk, the slender, swaying figure. He knew who it was that came, and it seemed to him that from that moment he knew, too, other things! His sense of proportions was suddenly shifted,—enlarged, perhaps,—altered certainly. He understood things which before had been mysteries to him. He understood, as though in some moment of inspiration, that riches or poverty, life, even, or death, are the incidents of life before its greatest truths. Nothing that he could think of seemed able to hold his thoughts. His heart was beating to music, the lark was singing to him a song of her own—singing in weak, tremulous notes a song of life and love and passion! He rose to his feet and went to meet her. She stopped short and faltered for a moment. He hurried on.

"Winifred!" he exclaimed.

She held out her hands. Her eyebrows were upraised, her mouth was quivering, her eyes were seeking his with a sort of plaintive earnestness. "It is true, then!" she exclaimed. "You are really here!"

"I am really here," he answered, "and it is really you! Nothing else seems to matter very much,—and yet, I would like to know why you alone, of all the world, should have discovered my hiding place."

She laughed, and seemed quite unconscious of the fact that he was still holding her hands. "I have been ill," she said. "I came down here to rest. Last night I heard in the village that you had arrived, that you were here alone. I knew then," she continued softly, "what had happened. I felt that I must come, if it was only for a few moments."

"It was very nice of you," he said.

Then they stood side by side in a silence charged with a sort of impotent passion. Why had she troubled to come, he wondered, now that the bubble of his wealth was burst,—she, who had held him to her cold-blooded compact, who had bound him to her by as sordid a bargain as ever the mind of woman could have conceived.

"I am glad to see you," he said, "and yet I don't know why. You did not hesitate to leave me without word of you, as soon as you saw the breakers ahead."

She drew a little away, looking at him as though she had only half understood. "When I lost the bond by which I held you," she said, "I could scarcely expect you to continue to pay. I have thought it all over since, until I think that I have drunk in all the shame which a woman could feel. It was a hateful, miserable thing, but then my life has been a hateful, miserable thing ever since I was a child, and I did long, yes, I did long," she added fervently, "for something a little different."

"You disappeared, then," he said slowly, "because you imagined, naturally enough, that so soon as you had lost your hold upon me, I should be only too glad to free myself from our engagement?"

"Of course," she answered, the color slowly staining her cheeks. "There was no doubt whatever about that. Only since then I have understood how great a mistake I made. If things had turned out differently," she continued, "I should never have dared to come to you, to tell you this and to ask for your forgiveness. But as it is," she added, "you cannot misunderstand me any longer, can you?"

"I suppose not," he admitted.

"I wanted to come and tell you that I was sorry," she continued softly, "and I wanted, too, to remind you that you are still young, and that the loss of a fortune is not the most terrible thing in the world. I heard yesterday that you were out upon Salthouse Neck, close to the quicksands. You know it is never safe there, with these winter tides. Life is not a thing to be trifled with. It may seem terrible to you just now to have lost your great fortune, to be once more a poor man. These things, after all, don't count for much against the gift of life. I know it sounds like humbug to hear me talk like this, but they were gossiping about you in the village. One man was saying that he shouldn't be at all surprised to hear that you had disappeared, and to find — to find —" she added, with a little shiver, "your body come up the creek with the next tide. You wouldn't do anything like that, would you?"

"Not a ghost of a chance of it," he answered cheerily. "Besides, I am not quite a pauper yet."

"You have lost the case, haven't you?" she asked quickly. "They seemed to think so in the village, and I heard that Mr. Sarsby said his niece had come into a million pounds."

"Up till last night, at any rate," answered Deane, "nothing was decided. The judge reserved his decision."

"Then why," she asked wonderingly, "did you come down here?"

He drew her a little closer to him, and looked into her eyes. "I think, dear," he said, "that it was Providence which sent me."

They walked along the sands, and for them the sun shone still, and the song of the lark was only the faint echo of a still more wonderful music. And then, as they turned back, they saw along the dyke a boy riding a bicycle, a boy with a leather satchel around his waist, and the rim of whose bicycle was red. He pressed her arm.

"Courage, dear," he said. "This is the Mercury who brings us the knowledge of our fate. In a few moments you will know whether you are to become the wife of a millionaire or a working man."

"If you would only believe," she murmured, "how little it matters!"

"I do believe," he answered. "I came down here, for one reason, to escape the shock of hearing the news before others. Now that it comes, I simply do not mind. There are greater things in the world than the Little Anna Gold-Mine!"

He took the telegram from the boy, and opened it with firm fingers. He read it out aloud without a tremor:

> Counsel met in judge's private room by appointment to-day. Have compromised with plaintiffs twenty thousand pounds.

Deane threw a coin to the boy, who remounted his bicycle and rode away. Then, turning to Winifred, "You see," he said, "you have brought me luck."

"I only pray," she murmured, as they turned together toward the tower, "that I may bring you happiness!"

Deane met Mrs. Hefferom a few months afterwards, and was struck at once by her altered expression. They came face to face at the corner of a street, and both involuntarily stopped.

"I hope," said Deane, politely, "that you are making good use of my money."

"And I hope," she answered, laughing, "that you are making more fortunes from my mine."

"I am doing fairly well, thank you," Deane admitted, "but you know that I have a wife to keep now."

"And I a husband," she answered. "I am trying to reform Stephen Hefferom."

"I hope that you are succeeding?"

"On the whole, yes!" she declared, smiling. "We live at Streatham, and he goes in to the city every day. He has bought a share in a business. We are not millionaires yet, but one never can tell."

"At any rate," he remarked pleasantly, "to judge by your appearance I should say that you find it better than Rakney."

"Don't mention the place, or any one in it," she said, with a shiver. "Thank Heaven, I shall never have to go back to it! Stephen is really doing very well, and half the money is still settled upon me. You have no idea," she continued, "how domesticity has agreed with him. He has scarcely a vice left."

"It has made a lot of difference to me," returned Deane. "Can't you recognize my subdued appearance?"

"I never saw you looking so well," she answered frankly. "Now I must hurry off. I am going to call for my husband and take him to lunch."

"And I am going to fetch my wife for the same reason," Deane answered, smiling. "The best of luck to you both!"

They parted in the crowd, swept away by the flood, the endless tide of passing humanity, and with a smile upon his lips Deane went to his appointment.

THE END